D1562166

SEE YOU ON VENUS

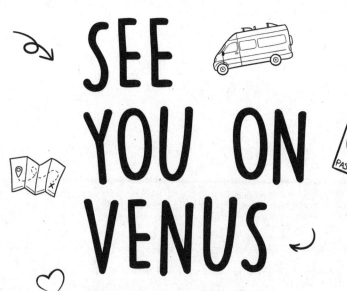

SEE
YOU ON
VENUS

VICTORIA VINUESA

DELACORTE PRESS

Text copyright © 2024 by Victoria Vinuesa
Cover art copyright © 2023 by Pitt Street Productions

Visit us on the web! GetUnderlined.com

Educators and librarians, for a variety of teaching tools, visit us at RHTeachersLibrarians.com

Library of Congress Cataloging-in-Publication Data is available upon request.
ISBN 978-0-593-70513-1 (trade pbk.) — ISBN 978-0-593-70514-8 (lib. bdg.) — ISBN 978-0-593-70515-5 (ebook)

The text of this book is set in 11-point Maxime Pro.
Interior design by Cathy Bobak

Printed in the United States of America
10 9 8 7 6 5 4 3 2 1
First Edition

To my one and only love
One day, I'll see you on Venus

MIA

I was born with an expiration date far too close for comfort. My guess is that's why my mother walked out on me two days after my birth. And since dying before knowing if I guessed right is not an option I'm willing to consider, I have no choice but to ask her myself—even if that means crossing the Atlantic and becoming a runaway.

As soon as I hear the high-heel clicks of Katelynn, my foster mother, receding down the hallway and the squeak of the front door as it opens and shuts, I run to my bedroom and look under my bed. Yup, it's still there, my vintage suitcase, the one I bought at a yard sale a year ago. The sewn flags that conceal its worn green leather speak to me of stunning destinations I can't even pronounce, places I'll never be able to visit. I put the suitcase on the bed, and after ransacking my side of the closet, I pack up all of my stuff: two pairs of pants, three T-shirts, my lucky cardigan, and two sweaters; some underwear, my three diaries, my coloring pens, and my most cherished possession—my camera. I grab the pink wool scarf that hangs on the back of my door like a

Christmas ornament and rub the soft fur against my cheek, and although I know that spring is already here and I'll never use the scarf again, I just can't bring myself to leave it behind, all alone.

As I take it down from the door a shadow darts across the room. Spinning around, I find my own startled reflection staring back at me from the window. I shriek, then burst out laughing. I'm new at being a prospective runaway, and it shows.

I like to think that my heart *chose* to be different, to be one of a kind, and that this is why I was born with no less than three heart defects. Not that it mattered to me, because I had a plan: in exactly one year and two days, on my eighteenth birthday, I would set off to Spain to find my mother. Noah, a friend of mine from photography class, was coming with me. Well, that plan is no longer an option. This time I was in the hospital for two weeks. The doctors informed me that the surgery could not be delayed any longer, but I don't agree. I'll never agree. They don't seem to understand it, but then again, I've given up trying to justify myself.

I'm just not afraid of dying. That comes with being born with a very short shelf life. But I *am* afraid of operations, of getting my heart pried open without having someone who cares about my broken heart in the first place. Sorry, but you can count me out.

The Rothwells never let me travel much, let alone to another continent, which means the moment I board that plane to Spain on Sunday, I'm officially a runaway, the kind that ends up in a missing person report. That leaves me with just two days to find someone willing and able to go with me. My heart begins to pound against my ribs. And although the doctors said the new pills were for emergencies only, I quickly pop one. No way I'm going to risk another relapse, not now.

Shutting my suitcase, I make a mental note of documents to take on my trip. My forged parental travel consent, *check*. Birth certificate, *check*. Fake passport, *check*. My real passport—whoops, almost forgot that. I climb onto my chair, then onto my tiny desk, praying it doesn't collapse under me. Reaching up, I run my hand over the top of my closet. My friend Noah, who was supposed to join me on the trip, hid my passport up here so that my foster family couldn't take it away. Up on tiptoe, I reach even farther and feel around—nothing, apart from some enormous dust balls.

I kneel and make a pile of my senior homeschooling books, which I won't be needing anymore. Then I carefully climb onto those and reach up all the way to the far end of the closet top. As the passport's rough surface finally grazes my fingertips, the front door squeaks open and slams shut. *Uh-oh*. I snatch the passport, then do the whole thing in reverse: books, desk, chair, floor.

Noisy footsteps are racing down the hallway, but I can't make out whom they belong to. I throw the suitcase on the floor. The bedroom door swings open just as I nudge it under the bed with my foot.

"Mia, Mia, you will not believe what happened at school," Becca yells as she barges into the room like a gust of wind. Becca is my younger foster sister and my roommate. She also happens to be my favorite person in the world.

I let out a gasp. "Becca, you scared the life out of me."

Becca flings her backpack to the floor, shuts the door with her heel, and rushes up to me. "I skipped remedial class. I just had to tell you about this. Remember that girl who called me a moron in third grade? Well, today she bombed an English test. And—" She stops short, staring aghast at the passport in my hand, then looks up at me with her small, pleading eyes. "You're leaving?"

"We talked about this," I say in the most soothing tone I can muster. "Remember?"

She shakes her head, and her misty eyes tell me that no, she doesn't remember. Becca was born with a cognitive impairment, and some things simply escape her. I guess that's why we share this room in a family that isn't ours. Her folks decided to get rid of her when her problem became too noticeable. She was five.

I take her soft, freckled face into my hands and give her a smile. That always calms her down. "I'm going to photograph the northern lights, remember?" I whisper. "And it's our secret; you can't tell anybody, ever." I cross my fingers, raise them to my lips, and nod: our secret sign, the one I learned at St. Jerome's, the group home I grew up in.

Becca grins, looking so excited it hurts me to lie to her, but I learned years ago that some things are safe only if they remain unspoken. Besides, how can I tell her that I'm never coming back? I guess it doesn't matter much since Becca's attention is already focused on the street out front.

"Look," she says, peering through the window. "It's the guy from the football team. The one who killed Noah."

Her words send a sob through me that I just manage to stifle.

"Becca, don't say that." I frown. It's not so much Noah's death that saddens me as the suffering of those who will never forget him. "It was an accident." I stand next to her and see the boy leaving the house across the street. "I can't even imagine what he must feel like." Actually, I can, because I've thought about it countless times since it happened. How is he going to live with it?

His name is Kyle, and although he was Noah's best friend, we never met. My foster parents never let me leave the house, unless it's for a doctor's visit, Sunday church, my photography class, or the occasional morning walk. Josh, the guy who lives in that house, was also in the car that day. They say he's in pretty bad shape.

I watch Kyle just standing there, in our narrow street, motionless, gazing off into space, as if time had stopped for him alone, and try to imagine what he and Josh have been talking about, what might have happened between them.

"What's he doing?" Becca asks, tugging at my sleeve. "Why's he standing there?"

It's hard to be sure from this distance, but it looks to me like he's on the verge of tears. He looks off to the right, toward town, then to the left, toward the woods. Slowly, as if in a daze, he turns left and begins to walk, limping slightly, his eyes looking straight ahead, his backpack slung over his shoulder.

"Where's he going, Mia? What's he up to? What's his deal?"

Before I can come up with a convincing reply to her questions, a bus pulls into our street, drives past our house, and stops right in front of Kyle. We lose sight of him for an instant, and when the bus pulls out again, the sidewalk is empty.

Becca gives me a puzzled look.

"Did he just get on the bus? Mia, why's he taking that line? It only goes to the waterfall. Nobody goes there at this hour."

She's right, unless he's about to do what I hope he's not about to do. I don't tell Becca, of course, but something inside me begins to tremble. He looked desperate. No, he looked more than desperate. I've seen that vacant look before, in the ER—along with bandaged wrists or pumped stomachs. I have to make sure he's okay. I have to do it for Noah. He wouldn't have wanted anything to happen to his friend. I get closer to the window and watch the bus drive off.

"Mia, wanna play Scrabble?"

Becca has obviously moved on, but I haven't. I'm focused on how to get out of this house without being seen. The front door is not an option, so I open the window and climb onto the ledge.

"Where are you going?" Becca hops up and down with excitement. "I wanna go too! I wanna go with you!"

I cup her face in my hands again and look steadily into her eyes.

"Becca, listen to me carefully. If I'm not back by dinner, I need you to tell Mr. Rothwell that my doctor called and asked me to take some tests, and that I'm not sure how long I'll be gone, okay? I have to talk to that boy."

Becca gives me a solemn nod and a slight scowl, a sign that she understands and, with a little luck, will remember long enough to cover my back. I cross my fingers and make our sign.

"Hold the fort, okay?"

Becca nods again, and her face breaks into a satisfied smile.

The moment my feet touch the lawn, she shuts the window from inside and gives me a thumbs-up.

What are my options? I don't have a car, and stealing one wouldn't take me very far since I can't drive. Walking would take more than two hours, and the bus passes only three times a day. Becca's Disney bicycle, which is lying on the grass, is my best and only alternative. If anyone from my family sees me chasing a bus into the woods on a bike with pink streamers and a doll basket, they'll call social services and strap me to a hospital bed, so I pray for invisibility.

Hopping on the bike, I start pedaling without looking back.

The bus, already far ahead of me, vanishes around a bend. My thighs burn from pedaling so hard, and I plead with my broken heart to keep up for just a little while longer, to let me accomplish something good—something that will have made my life worth living—before it ushers me off this planet with a final pulse.

I just might make a better runaway than I thought.

KYLE

I'm the bastard who killed his best friend, Noah, a month ago and left his second-best friend disabled. Actually, I just found out about Josh. He left the hospital a week ago, and I didn't go to see him until today. I know I'm a jerk, but honestly, I couldn't even look him in the eye. His mother just told me that he may never walk again. He doesn't know it yet.

I guess that explains why I'm on this bus: I can't go home.

There's no way I'm going to tell my mother. It would crush her. And I can't act as if nothing happened, either, when I've taken one life and destroyed another. It just doesn't work that way.

A bump in the road jolts me out of my hellish thoughts and lands me back here, the last seat in the last row of this rickety bus. My heart is threatening to burst. After checking—for the fifth time—that my seat belt is working, I try to persuade my fingers to stop gripping the seat so damn tight.

I lean my head into the aisle to see where we're heading and catch the bus driver eyeing me in the rearview mirror. His black eyes, bulging under his scowling eyebrows, keep darting back and forth between me and the road. I'm the only passenger on the bus, and the scars on my face and arms are certainly not helping me go unnoticed, but still, that bus driver has some nerve.

I slump back into my seat, trying to make myself invisible, and check the time on my cell phone. It's five-thirty. To be more exact, it's been thirty-one days, twelve hours, and twenty-five minutes since I caused that horrible accident.

My old self hated math, but now I just can't seem to stop adding numbers. Every second, every minute, and every hour that passes is one more second, one more minute, and one more hour that I stole from Noah, not to mention Josh never walking again. *If only it had been me.* And just as the nausea seizes my guts once more, my cell phone vibrates in my hands.

It's Judith, but I let her go to voice mail. Can't talk to her, not now. It sounds ridiculous, but it's as if I would be betraying my old self, the old Kyle. Judith was his girl, not mine.

Needing to do something to stop my mind from going in circles, I take out my sketchbook and draw an outcast sitting on a bus. And for five or six minutes, my thoughts are kept at bay. The drawing is not what it could be, but it almost makes me feel normal again. And just as I start to wish, to pray, to long for the bus to keep going and never stop, the driver veers off the road and slows down. Lately, every wish I make comes crashing down on me. Note to self: scour the internet for *curse, evil eye,* and *Aladdin's lamp in reverse.*

The bus comes to a stop right in front of one of the big

wooden signs that indicates the entrance to the park I've visited so many times: the Noccalula Falls. I grab my backpack, throw in my sketch pad, and make my way down the long aisle. The bus driver, who has opened only the front door, is still glaring at me as I approach, without the least attempt at discretion. He's managed to make my hands clammy. I walk right past him with my eyes fixed on the steps leading off the bus, but he seems in no hurry to let me go.

"Hey, boy. Where you goin' at this hour? Somebody pickin' you up?"

I give him a look as if to say, *What's it to you?*

"Last bus of the day." His knitted eyebrows bunch up even more. "Didn't you know that?"

I try my best to look casual, though I feel like an alien in my own skin. "Oh, that . . . No, don't worry, I'm meeting some friends from the football team." I point to my backpack with the hint of a smile. "We're sleeping in the woods." I show him the scar on my eyebrow, and with a forced grin that belongs to the old Kyle, I say, "But we've learned our lesson, man, I can tell you that much. We're done wrestling bears, and you can quote me on that."

The driver's face is blank, frozen, grave, so much so that it gives me shivers. Okay, he didn't like my joke; I get it. Noah and Josh would have liked it. We would have bust a gut. That's what we did. But that's all over. Noah will never laugh again. The nausea is back, churning my insides.

I race down the steps as quickly as my bandaged knee will allow. The moment I hit the ground and hear the roar of the waterfall from afar, I'm overcome by a moment of clarity I've never known before. In an instant I see it all, and I know that an invisible force has led me here today so that I can pay for what I've done. For the first time in a long while I feel my lungs fill to the brim. A small wooden sign says *Waterfall 500 yards.* I follow the arrow and begin wading into the lushest part of the forest. The bus's engine is still idling behind me, lurking. Almost a full minute goes by before I hear the wheels pull out onto the dirt road and finally head toward the highway.

I zip up my leather jacket. The air is still too cold for spring in Alabama, or maybe it's just me. I look up. The towering trees seem to be eyeing me, pointing at me with their branches, as if relishing being the only witnesses to my demise. The relentless roar of the waterfall draws me onward like Magneto with his superpowers. It's odd, but with every step I take I feel more determined, but also increasingly numb, as if something inside me were already dead. Everything seems to be falling into place, like a puzzle needing one final piece to unveil its most shameful secrets. The green shoots of grass peer through the leaves. One life begins while another ends.

I think of those I'm leaving behind. I know Josh, and he'd do the same thing. Judith will find someone to make her laugh again, a better boyfriend than I could ever be. And my folks . . . well, at least they won't have to live every single day seeing the word *guilty* seared into every inch of my skin, though I know they don't agree with my verdict. They won't have to take me to dozens of shrinks wasting their breath telling me to stop feeling like the piece of shit I am. Might as well convince a flea that he's a superhero. It's not going to happen. I'm a piece of shit, and that's all there is to it. Everything else is a lie.

Deep down, I know I'm going to set them free. Besides, maybe I'll see Noah again. Maybe I can ask him to forgive me. And if he sees me there, maybe he will.

MIA

I don't know how long I've been pedaling, but the rays of the setting sun are still filtering through the trunks of the maple trees when I finally reach the entrance to the park. I've been here before. It was last fall, for a picnic with the Rothwells. The social worker thought it would be healthy for us to do some "family activities."

As it turned out, it was a disaster. The twins got into a fight, Becca got lost in the woods, and while we were all looking for her, a couple of feral hogs took off with our lunch. But having spent two solid hours searching for Becca, I know these woods like the back of my hand now. I lean the bike against the wooden sign pointing the way to the waterfall and set off as fast as I can. My legs quiver from the effort, from lack of exercise, but above all, from fear. I glance in all directions but see no trace of Kyle. I beg my heart to ease up, but it won't stop thrumming against my ribs.

"Kyle!" I yell repeatedly at the top of my lungs in every direction.

The only reply I get is the sound of water plunging in the distance. What if he came here just to take a walk? And what if he just wants to be alone? Or what if he came to pick wild asparagus? Just the other day Mr. Rothwell returned from the woods carrying a bunch of them. And what if he hears me screaming his name and I end up in the local newspaper tomorrow?

When I'm nervous I think too much. Sometimes I even get tired of hearing myself think.

I keep walking, out of breath, and then the shrill screech of a hawk makes me look up. It passes right overhead, as if warning me of something, a bad omen. A sense of menace that I know all too well surges through me. I have a bad feeling about this, and although running is one of the things that I'm strictly forbidden from doing, especially after my last stay in the hospital, I can't help it. Praying for the new pills to do the trick, I break into a run and shout his name over and over again. "Kyle! Kyle! Kyyyllllle!"

I doubt he can hear me. The rush of the waterfall grows more and more intense. I stop thinking and just run and run until finally I glimpse the huge torrent of water cascading between two enormous beech trees.

Oh God, there he is, leaning over the edge and staring at the rushing water, one hand clasping a rickety fence. *No, no, no, please, don't do it.* Gasping for air, I stop in my tracks and take in as much oxygen as my lungs will allow; then I yell, "No!" But he doesn't seem to hear me.

My God. I start running again, but I won't make it in time,

if at all. I have to do something drastic, so I stop, take a deep breath, and beg the wind, the trees, and the entire forest to carry my voice all the way to him, and then I scream, I scream like I've never screamed in my life, like no human being has ever screamed.

KYLE

They say time heals all wounds, but what they don't tell you is what happens when time decides to stop, when every second lasts for hours and every hour lasts a lifetime.

I look down. Ninety feet below my sneakers the water pounds the rocks, as if wanting to turn them to sandstone. Its deafening roar collides with the rush of my thoughts. I'm shaking, and it's not from the cold. I don't even know what frightens me more, turning to sandstone myself or staying alive.

My thoughts spin at a dizzying speed. Some of them yell at me to do it, to let go; others hurl insults, calling me a coward; still others egg me on to pay for what I've done, but my hand must be deaf to them all because it won't loosen its grip on the iron fence behind me.

I think of the devastation I've caused: Noah six feet under, Josh in a wheelchair, the shattered lives of their parents and mine . . . I think of all those I can no longer look in the eye, and my hand slowly starts to ease its grip.

First, my pinkie. If there's a God, I ask His forgiveness. *Next, my ring finger.* Wait, what am I saying? If there's a God, I tell Him to quit His day job. Creation doesn't seem to be His strong suit, at least not the creation of a decent world.

Now my middle finger. I can hear my own teeth chattering.

All I have to do now is separate my thumb and my index finger, and it'll all be over.

I put one foot forward, ready to give in to gravity.

"Help!"

An anguished cry blends with the crashing waterfall. Was that me screaming? My gaze remains fixed on the abyss below my feet. And that's when I hear it again, "Please, help me!"

The words startle me out of my trance, landing me back here—on the brink of a colossal waterfall, dangling by two fingers. What on earth am I doing? My hand tightens around the fence. I back up until I'm leaning hard against the fence and look for the source of the voice.

In the distance, in a clearing between two trees, a girl faints and drops to the ground. I jump over the fence and run as fast as my shaky legs will take me.

As I approach the clearing, there she is, lying on the ground with her arms crossed and her knees folded to one side. She must be my age, maybe a little younger. I kneel beside her. Her gleaming auburn hair obscures part of her face. She looks so fragile. "Hey," I whisper, as if a raised voice might shatter her.

She doesn't react. I part her hair a little and notice she's still breathing. She's wearing a small pendant of the Virgin Mary around her neck, and her complexion is so light that she barely seems real. Her features are delicate. In fact, everything about her is delicate, fine, fragile. If her ears were more pointed, she could be Arwen the elven princess.

"Hey, hey," I whisper again. "Can you hear me?"

I don't dare touch her. I simply brush away a lock of hair that veils her forehead. She inhales sharply and tenses up as if from pain. Her eyelashes start to twitch and open slowly, but she still seems to be somewhere else. She glances in all directions, disoriented, then stares right through me, as if she hasn't yet realized I'm here.

"Hey," I whisper again. "Are you okay?"

Her eyes are wide open now, and our gazes meet. She looks confused, even a little frightened.

"Take it easy. It's all right. You just passed out. You feeling better?"

The elf nods.

"Okay, can you stand up?"

She raises herself onto one elbow and tries, unsuccessfully, to get to her feet.

"Wait, let me help you." I slip my arm under the back of her neck and carefully begin to lift her up. Her eyes avoid mine. She places one hand on the ground, looks at it, and then, just like that, is on her feet in one bound. She backs away, shaking her arm wildly and screaming like she's woken up from a nightmare.

"Get it off, please, get it off me."

It takes me a few glances to see what's going on. A lizard, even more startled than she is, is scurrying along her arm. The poor thing ends up hitting the ground and running off.

The girl goes quiet for a moment, looking flustered.

"I'm sorry. I'm not usually this hysterical," she says. "It's just that when I was a kid a lizard crept into my bed and, well, I guess it doesn't sound like much, but trust me, when you're five years old it can be pretty traumatic, and besides . . ." *Wait, how does one person squeeze that many words into one breath?* She raises her hand to her heart as if she is in pain. "I don't feel very well, and there don't seem to be too many people around here who could help me out, so I really have no choice but to ask you to take me home."

What is with her? Something is off.

"You seem to have recovered pretty quickly, don't you think?" I remark.

"You're absolutely right; that's probably why I feel so dizzy now."

"People don't usually scream when they're about to pass out."

"No?"

"No."

"Yeah, well, I'm . . . epileptic."

Unbelievable—she's making this up as she goes along. You could tell a mile away. She goes on. "And I can always tell when I'm about to faint, and because it scares me and all, I just start screaming. Besides, just imagine if you hadn't found me, I would have been lying here for hours. Pretty sure I would have been devoured by some wild animal. The sign at the entrance of the park says there are coyotes, bobcats, wolves, and even a few alligators around here."

My grandmother always says that if you don't have anything

nice to say, don't say anything, so I just watch her with a steady, icy look.

"Please, I wouldn't be asking you if there was any other way, plus we've never met, and you might be a serial killer for all I know, and I can't make it back alone with my bike."

If her name were Pinocchio, her nose wouldn't fit between us.

"So call your folks," I say, trying to look calmer than I feel.

"I can't. They're extremely poor and don't own a phone."

I've never seen anyone lie this badly, but still, her jacket and pants, which are inside out, do look straight out of the Salvation Army, and I doubt those socks peeking out of the holes in her sneakers are a fashion statement.

"I'll call an ambulance," I say. "They'll take you home."

"No, please don't do that." She looks horrified. "An ambulance costs a fortune."

I stay silent.

"Please, just to the outskirts of town. Then I'll ask someone else to help me out."

What the fuck does she want from me? I'm starting to wonder if she's real or Noccalula Falls' resident phantom stalker.

She chuckles. "Do I really look like a ghost to you?"

Shit, either this chick is psychic or I was thinking aloud.

I catch her glancing sidelong at the waterfall and realize that the spot at which she "fainted" is the only place from which you can see the waterfall, and to be more exact, it's the only place from which you can see the spot *I was in* a moment ago. She notices that I've noticed and bites her lip.

I'm done hiding my anger. Kudos to her power of imagination, no question, and I guess she has good intentions, but right now the last thing I want is company. "Do yourself a favor," I say. "Go home."

"No."

"All right, then." I make my way toward the waterfall. "You can do what you want for all I care; just forget that I exist, got it?"

I need to be alone. I still have no clue what to do or where to go, but going back to town isn't an option. The only thing I want to do right now is hear myself think. Instead, I hear her footsteps rushing up behind me.

"Wait a second, please."

She's really starting to piss me off. "Mind your business."

"You *are* my business. Don't you get it? If I let you do what I think you were about to do, I'll never be able to forgive myself."

"Just go home."

I push her aside and keep walking. I'm a lot taller than she is, and it's not hard to keep her away. And just when I think I've gotten rid of her for the second time, she comes running past me, turns to face me, and keeps talking while walking backward.

"I'm warning you. If you jump, I'm jumping too. And all the pain you will have caused my seven little brothers and sisters and my poor parents—well, that'll be on you."

That's a low blow. "Get lost," I say, with venom this time. "And take your meds."

I shove her out of my path again and continue walking. The waterfall is only a few yards away. And just like that, the Elven Princess Turned Nightmare takes off toward it.

I'm so stunned that all I can do is stop and watch her go.

MIA

Oh God, what am I doing? I've run more this afternoon than
I have in my entire life. As I reach the iron fence that separates
the woods from the perilous ledge of the waterfall, I'm having serious trouble breathing, as if two enormous hands were squeezing
my lungs tight. I look back. Kyle's still standing there, in the same
spot I left him. But judging from the fury in his eyes, he looks
ready to have the last laugh. If he does decide to jump, it will
take only a few seconds for him to reach me at the cliff's edge.
All right, I have to go through with this or he won't think I'm
serious, so I slide down the other side of the fence, lean against
it, and grip it real tight.

Oh my word, the view from up here is as spectacular as it is
chilling. The water plunges from rocks at different heights, merg-
ing into one enormous drop right in front of me. The ledge beneath my feet is narrow, a little too narrow for my taste. One step
would be enough to send me spiraling into space.

I look back at him for only a split second, but it's enough to
read his expression. His eyes are agape, bristling with that eerie

void of one who sees no way out (the same expression I've witnessed countless times in the hospital, when parents are told their child will never wake up again).

I throw him a defiant look, trying to conceal the tremor in my knees.

"Stay away!" I yell, my voice buried under the roar of the waterfall.

Kyle shakes his head, a deep furrow in his brow, and starts walking in my direction.

"Stop right there. If you take another step I swear I'll jump!" I scream with all my might.

And that's when the ground shifts under my feet. The huge boulder on which I'm standing is starting to give way. Before I can jump to one side, the ground beneath me vanishes, dragging me into the void.

"Ahh!"

My fingers clutch the fence, but the fall flings me to one side and my right hand loses its grip. I'm hanging on with one hand.

"Help!" I scream, my throat in shreds, but can't even hear my own voice over the surging torrent. Where is Kyle? I don't see anything except the water and the rocks under my feet. My lungs threaten to shut down again, so I close my eyes and pray.

A deafening howl rises up from my depths as I think of the mother I will never know, and of Becca, and I'm about to burst into tears when a hand grabs me by the arm and I feel myself rise. My eyes open at once. Kyle's are brimming with terror and confusion, but with so much life in them that it hurts.

"Give me your other arm," he shouts.

I latch my free hand onto his. Kyle hoists me up and sets me down on firm ground. Grabbing the fence, he gets to his feet.

"C'mon." He offers me his hand. "Let's get out of here."

He pulls me to my feet, guiding me over to the safe side of the ledge. Once there I collapse to the ground, face up, gasping for air.

Kyle slumps to the ground next to me. I'm laughing and crying at the same time. Kyle is breathing hard.

As my breathing eases and my heart stops racing (thank you, magic pills), I turn to face him. His gaze is lost in the clouds, his chin quivering. I want to help him, to talk to him about Noah, about what happened, to tell him that life isn't a walk in the park but that it has its moments, and that a lot of people would give anything to be in his shoes, to have parents, to have someone who actually cares about you. But after my recent cliff-hanging performance I doubt I'm precisely the kind of person he would want to open his lips to, let alone his heart.

Kyle sits up on the ground and starts rubbing his knee. Without saying a word, he shakes his head and gazes off into the distance.

I scoot next to him, my knees folded to one side. Under the circumstances, bringing up Noah might just be the worst idea ever, so in the most soothing tone I can find, I say: "Wanna talk about it?"

His eyes, a grayish blue that reminds me of the Tennessee River on an overcast day, pierce right through me.

"All right, I get it, you don't want to speak to me, but in that case, you leave me no choice. From now on I'll be watching you."

His jaws tighten visibly, but hey, better angry than sad.

"That is, until you decide to talk to me."

"You are a fucking nightmare, do you know that?" he hisses. This hurts; I can't deny it. It reminds me, for a fleeting instant, that maybe I was a nightmare for my mother too.

He gets to his feet and looks down at me like a giant glaring at a gnat that won't stop biting. "What do you want from me?"

Several things come to mind, some of which almost make me blush, but I don't tell him. Instead, I stand up and stall for time. He's desperate, and I'm desperate to find a solution, something that will stop him from harming himself. And just like that, out of the blue, I get the wildest and most ingenious idea ever.

"Do you have a passport?"

"Excuse me?"

Oh my Lord, I can't believe what I'm about to say.

"Yeah, well, you asked me what I want from you, and until now I didn't realize I wanted anything from you, but now that you've asked, I want you to come to Spain with me for ten days."

"What?"

"A friend was supposed to come but kind of bailed on me and . . ."

"Hang on. You don't even know me, and you want me to go across the pond with you?"

"I *don't* want to, but hey, do I have any other option?"

"Yes, you can mind your own business."

"Well, speaking of business, I won't deny that inviting you on this trip was not quite as selfless as it may seem. Actually, I've been looking for someone to go with me for weeks."

"You're completely out of your mind."

"Maybe, but what would you do in my place? Say your plane was leaving in two days, and you didn't want to tell my folks about it, to spare them even more heartache. Would you go anyway, knowing that I might try to do it again?"

"Do what again?" The quiver in his voice tells me he's not good at lying. "I don't know what fantasy you've got going in that little head of yours, but—"

"I know about the accident, Kyle." I cut him off before he can dig himself deeper. "I saw your picture in the paper."

His gut tightens as the anger flares up in his eyes.

"You don't know a fucking thing!"

"I know that no matter how hard I try I can't begin to imagine what you must be going through. But I also know that you have no right to take your life, that it would leave your mom, your dad, and everyone who loves you in pieces. You just don't! It's not fair on them."

Kyle doesn't make a move. His eyes, gleaming like two waterfalls in midflow, seem to cry out for help. I would give anything to know just how to help this boy.

"C'mon, think about it, all expenses covered. If you still want to kick the bucket after the trip, I won't stop you. Deal?"

"Forget it."

"I understand. You don't have to decide right now. Sleep on it."

"No."

"Oh, and as I said before, until you do make up your mind, I'm going to have to keep an eye on you. Sorry. And by the way, my name's Mia."

I stick out my hand, but instead of shaking it he turns on his heel and walks off. This time, at least, he's moving away from the waterfall.

I feel like jumping for joy, but instead I just follow him, quietly thanking my heart for still beating.

Today is a good day.

KYLE

I've been walking for the better part of an hour now, and this Mia character has been tailing me from across the road the entire time. At least she's had the decency to keep her mouth shut, which is saying something. Along the way, I felt the need to pinch myself a few times to make sure this entire day isn't just one more in the string of nightmares I've been having since the accident. At one point I started wondering again whether the girl wasn't some kind of weird entity (the hazards of growing up the son of a die-hard *X-Files* fan, no doubt). I even thought I might be the only one who could see her, but the moment I heard some truckers honking and jeering at her, it put my doubts to rest. I don't blame them either. A girl with her jacket inside out, riding a bike with pink streamers and a flag sticking out that says *Supergirl* doesn't exactly blend in

I don't know what time it is—my cell phone's dead—but the sun is just setting as I reach the center of town, which means it's not much later than seven. My knee is in serious pain, but if I don't hurry my folks will start to worry, so I pick up my pace.

My folks. A pang of guilt reminds me that my parents were this close to learning that their only child had ended it all. What was I thinking? Alive I'm a burden, but dead? . . . I don't even know what I'd be. The vise gripping my stomach tightens a few notches. I can't take my own life, but what right do I have to keep it after what I've done to the lives of so many others?

I glance off to the side. Mia is still there, lurking on the opposite sidewalk. Now she's walking her bike. Thinking back to what she said at the waterfall, my jaws clench. Did they have to publish my picture in that goddamn newspaper? Now there's nowhere to hide. And was she serious about that trip? And about not telling my parents? There's no way of knowing for sure. What I do know is that I have to find a way to get rid of her. Maybe if I spend all of spring break locked up in my room, she'll give up and go find somebody else to save. Although she doesn't seem the type to throw in the towel that easily. She seems the type to camp out in front of my house, or worse.

As my mind casts about for the best way to lose her, I reach my front porch, turn, and give her a look that's harsher than I actually feel. She stops, too, her gaze intensely serious. She looks exhausted. For a second, I almost feel sorry for her. But there's no way I can let her come any closer.

I walk the last few feet to my front door without taking my eyes off her. She stands there on the opposite sidewalk, silent, motionless, her eyes glued to me. I take the house key out of my backpack and quickly slide it into the lock, as if she might materialize next to me in one giant leap. I think my brain might be suffering from emotional overload (and too many cable series).

After I shut the door behind me, I lean my back against it. Lingering there in the dark for a moment, I dimly observe the narrow hallway that opens onto the staircase leading up to my room. To my left is the kitchen, and facing it to my right is a doughnut-shaped mirror surrounded by golden rays of light. My dad thinks it's tacky, says it reminds him of a fried egg, but my mom persuaded him that we need it in order to spread some kind of healing energy.

It's warm in the house and it smells of recently baked cake, and something with chicken in it, fajitas, I think, but above all it smells of home, a home that I've managed to wreck single-handedly.

"Kyle, honey," my mother calls from the kitchen. Her broken voice is almost too much to bear. "Is that you?"

She knows it's me; who else would it be? It's her way of saying, *Kyle, my dear, what you did broke my heart, but seeing you like this, distant and aloof, hurts me even more.* I hear the sound of frying pans, the refrigerator door opening and shutting. My legs want to follow the sounds, but I'm not so sure I'll let them. I don't deserve it.

"Kyle?" My dad swings the door open, his face broadening into a smile.

The light from the kitchen drives out the shadow sheltering me.

"Hi," I say, trying to look halfway normal. I give him a quick hug and walk into the kitchen.

My mother, who hates to cook, is pulling a cake out of the oven. It just happens to be blueberry, my favorite. I give her a peck on the cheek, avoiding eye contact.

"How was your day?" She tries to look casual as she places the cake on the counter.

My mouth feels like it's sealed shut, so I just shrug.

Dad holds a fajita under my nose as if to tempt me, then draws his hand back with a grin. "I'd give you a bite, but this is just too good."

I manage to crack a smile. God, I can't stand it when they try so hard to lift my spirits, to pretend things are normal when they're not. I know they're doing it for my sake, to make me feel less guilty, but it only makes me feel like shit. I'm a burden; I know it. No matter how much they pretend otherwise, I know they're miserable. My dad's got his sweatshirt on inside out, and the rings under his eyes look like craters. In the thirty-one days since the accident, my mom's lost so much weight she's swimming in her jeans. This morning I saw her popping one of those two-tone pills, the ones she took when Grandma died, and when she was forced to take two months off work because of depression.

"How'd it go with Josh?" my mother asks while my dad brings the fajitas over to the dinner table. "How did he seem to you?"

I freeze. I'm an idiot. Should have been ready for this question. They look at me with raised eyebrows, waiting for an answer that might ease their pain. How am I supposed to tell them that Josh may never walk again?

"He's fine," I lie. "He looks better."

They don't buy it, because my dad proceeds to pull up a couple of chairs and takes a seat in one. "Kyle, wanna talk about it?"

I would give anything to talk, like we used to, the three of us, but instead I shake my head.

"I already ate at Josh's house," I lie again. Why worry them even more? "And, well—"

"You're not hungry," my mother cuts in, her voice edgy. "Yeah, we gathered as much."

My father takes her hand. She takes a deep breath, composing herself, and they both look at me. They try to smile, but their eyes tell a different story. *We feel for you, Kyle, and it hurts us to see you this way. We don't know what to do anymore; let us help you.* But what they don't understand is that it's too late. No one can help me, because no one can change the fact that I fucking killed my friend. I quickly turn away. The last thing I want is to burst into tears in front of them, like a little kid, so I head toward the door.

"Why don't you stay with us for a while?" says my dad.

"I have to shower." I clear my throat to cover the crack in my voice. "I didn't sleep too well last night, and—"

"But, honey . . . ," my mother begins to protest, before my dad cuts her off.

"Go ahead, son; don't worry about it. We'll save you some fajitas for tomorrow, okay?"

I nod without turning around. As I walk out into the hallway my reflection looks back at me from the round mirror, and I almost go to pieces. Just before the door shuts behind me, I see my mother's reflection slumping into my father's lap and burying her face in his shoulder. He hugs her and kisses her hair. The door shuts, and I'm left standing there in the gloom, glaring at my hideous reflection in the mirror, which I'm this close to killing. My mother's sobs echo faintly from the kitchen. I run up the stairs and into my room, hurling my backpack against the bed. I want to break something, to tear it apart, all of it. The need to yell my lungs out is unbearable, but instead, I bite down on my pillow and stifle the sound of my screaming voice.

I have to *do* something, anything besides beating myself up. Picking up my sketch pad, I flop onto the bed and try to focus on something I can draw, but the same images keep hounding me: Noah's vacant eyes, Josh's bloody face, the cars colliding in the curve, the twisted metal, the shattered glass . . . *Enough.* I tear my thoughts away from the scene and abruptly find myself picturing the Elven Princess or, more to the point, the Elven Nightmare.

No, I refuse to have her haunting my thoughts too. But the waterfall . . . I can sketch that. In fact, I'll sketch the entire forest just to keep from dozing off, though there's little chance of that, since I practically haven't slept a wink since the accident. And I've tried everything—counting sheep, counting backward, listening to lullabies—nothing. Apparently, resting is no longer a right but a privilege for someone like me. Plus, even closing my eyes has become a risky enterprise. Every time I start to doze and feel my eyes getting heavy, there's a nightmare lurking, just waiting to pry them open again. And so I prepare myself for another all-nighter.

MIA

By the time I get back to the Rothwell house, they're already finishing up with dinner. I say hi as I walk into the living room, but the TV has abducted them for the evening. Looks like my plan worked; they don't seem to suspect a thing. There's a throbbing pain in my chest, and my entire body is crying out for a rest, but if I don't eat something I'm going to pass out on the spot. And since eating in the kitchen is not an option (and I've tried), I join them at the dinner table. Becca's upstairs, her plate is empty, and the twins are at their weekly anger-management therapy. As I gobble up some low-fat, no-sodium macaroni and cheese, with Sean Hannity droning in the background, I can't stop thinking about Kyle. I wonder what he might be doing right now. Has he had dinner? Is he talking with his folks, or watching TV, or in his room? I just hope he doesn't do anything stupid before I can persuade him to come to Spain with me.

I'm so immersed in my thoughts and my macaroni that when the news cuts to a commercial, the music makes me jump in my seat.

Katelynn, my foster mother, gapes at me as if I've appeared out of thin air. "For God's sake, Mia, you startled me." And once she's settled down, she says, "So, what did they say at the hospital?"

That's odd. "Pass the salt" or "Who'd like to say grace?" are about the only things uttered at our table. I guess it's the fact that I'm due to have surgery in a week, and that my heart has a fifty-fifty chance of coming out of it alive, that has suddenly awakened their interest in me.

"They said everything's fine," I reply. "Thanks."

Mr. Rothwell, as our foster father prefers to be called, peers at me over his glasses, his brow bunched into a frown. "Well, I think it shows a total lack of professionalism, pure and simple," he says, and turns down the TV, which is a bad sign in itself. "They told us they'd already run all the necessary tests. For God's sake, the operation is scheduled for Monday. What do they think they're doing?"

"It was nothing, really," I say, with my best *everything's peachy* look. "They just took a blood test to make sure everything's on track."

"Katelynn, hand me the phone," Mr. Rothwell says. "I'm calling Dr. Rivera this instant. I want an explanation."

My foster mother nods and gets up, covering herself with her cardigan.

"No, no. Please don't do that," I burst out, a little too loudly, and realize my slipup when I see a look in their eyes that says *something's fishy*.

If they find out I've been outdoors the entire afternoon they'll tell my doctor, who will make sure I'm taken directly to the hospital, which will wreck my plans for my escape. *No physical exertion of any kind* were my doctor's orders at my last checkup. Apparently, my oxygen levels tend to drop suddenly and I end up doing stupid things like passing out in the woods at the worst possible time. The Rothwells have been longing for me to get this operation for weeks. I even heard them ask my doctor if I could be kept in the hospital until the day of my surgery. I don't blame them. I can understand their fear that I might die while under their legal guardianship. Too much paperwork, they say.

And now they're staring at me without so much as a blink. I have to come up with something, fast. "I was the one who called the hospital." I shake my head, looking solemn. "This afternoon I started feeling sick." I inhale deeply as if I were short of breath, which, to be honest, I am.

"You're right," my foster mother says, her suspicious face softening. "You don't look well at all."

"Well, I didn't want to worry you, is all," I continue. "That's why I didn't say anything. I'm sorry I upset you."

"Oh please, spare me," says Mr. Rothwell, his frown still intact. "What *I* want to know is what they actually said to you. And why didn't they keep you in the hospital in the first place? That's what they should have done this entire time." He whacks the table with his fist to punctuate his statement.

"No, no, they said that my symptoms today were normal," I lie. "It's just nerves, because of the operation and all."

Katelynn pops a piece of bread into her mouth without taking her eyes off me, as if she were watching one of her sitcoms.

"The doctor said I should go for light walks in the mornings," I lie. "He said my blood needs oxygen."

They exchange puzzled looks. My foster father shakes his head, grabs the remote, and turns up the volume, while she eyes me steadily, as if waiting for my closing act.

"Would you mind if I took a walk into town tomorrow?" I scoop some salad into my bowl to look casual. "I won't go far, just a couple of hours in the morning."

Katelynn looks at her husband, who shrugs without taking his eyes off the TV.

"Well, if that's what the doctor ordered," she says, "I don't see why not."

This is officially the largest number of words we have ex-changed in three years. I'm not saying they're bad people. I think their hearts are in the right place, and they do want to help, but I'm not so sure I'm the one who needs help. The life I've lived has taught me that adults are just kids who happen to have grown in size.

Sean Hannity has recaptured their attention, so I focus on finishing what's on my plate. The searing pain in my chest is getting worse.

Back in my room, Becca assaults me with a million questions. We lie down on her bed, and with her cuddled in my arms she makes me go over and over what happened in the woods. I give her a watered-down version, sidestepping the suicide attempt to spare her any nightmares.

When she finally falls asleep in the crook of my arm, I tuck her in and give her a peck on the nose. That always makes her giggle. If only I could *always* be here to make her laugh.

I go back to my own bed, and although my eyelids are weighing me down, my mind is still racing. Okay, let's say I manage to persuade Kyle to come with me. What kind of parents in their right minds would let their son, in the condition he's in, travel to Europe with a stranger, let alone an orphan, a girl on the run? Besides, if they find out who I am and tell the Rothwells, it's all over. I guess I have no choice but to turn to Bailey, my former foster sister.

I get my tablet from the desk and sit on my bed. While waiting for the two long minutes it takes to boot up, I rummage through my nightstand drawer for my pills. A cold sweat creeps up through my soles, and for the first time in a while, I start to panic. I'm not afraid of dying, but dying when I'm so close to finding my real mother would defeat the very purpose of my life, and that's out of the question.

My tablet finally boots up and I dial Bailey's number, trying to distract myself from my aching heart. Bailey picks up on the fourth beep and appears on the screen, wearing a pink waitress uniform. A jukebox is playing in the background.

"Sis," she says with a beaming smile that instantly turns grave. "Is something wrong? Are you okay? Did they do something to you? Want me to come and get you?"

"No, no, I'm all right," I say with a flustered little laugh. "It's just that—"

"Hold on," she says. "Let me finish serving this table and I'll be right with you, okay?"

I nod. Bailey props up her phone on what seems to be a tabletop, and I watch as she serves pancakes with whipped cream to a family of six. Her smile lights up the entire diner. Bailey is one of those people who can change your whole outlook on the world; at least she did with me. Thanks to her I learned to stop griping about my lousy luck and began to see the glass as half full. Yes, my mother abandoned me, but Bailey's folks didn't even have the decency to do that. Her mother tended to confuse Bailey's back with an ashtray for stubbing out her joints, and her father drank so much he could barely tell whom he was forcing into bed with him. Bailey is a born fighter and, unlike me, she doesn't take shit from anyone (except her shitty boyfriends, but that's another story). She's the example I live by, my very own Wonder Woman.

"I'm back, sis." She picks up the phone as she walks along the counter. "So tell me, how you been? What's happening? You didn't have another attack, did you?"

She moves in close to the camera, as if trying to study me. The rings under her gorgeous emerald-green eyes are even deeper than the last time I saw her.

"Bailey, what about you? Are you okay?" I try. "You still with . . . what's his name?"

"Hey, we'll talk about me another time. Now tell me what's up with you. Why did you call?"

"Okay, I need your help. It's a matter of life and death."

Bailey starts to giggle. "Everything's life and death with you."

"No, I'm serious this time."

"Spit it out."

"All right," I say, leaning hard into my pillow. "You still good at doing voices?"

"Some talents," she says, launching into a Bart Simpson, "are for life, young lady."

That makes me laugh. Bailey always makes me laugh.

"Great. Do you think you can pass yourself off as my mother tomorrow?"

"Of course, darling. Is there anything a mother wouldn't do for her daughter?" she asks, her voice taking on a wise, motherly tone. I can't help but think of my real mother and what her voice might sound like. "But first, give me the rundown."

I tell her everything, about Kyle, my trip, my plans for escape, my operation, and Bailey supports me all the way. Although we lived together for only two years, she's the closest thing to a mother I've ever had. It was in my last foster home that we met, and we had the greatest time ever. But when she turned nineteen they forced her to move out—a younger girl needed to use her bed. And just like that, Bailey was out on the streets with two hundred dollars to her name. She moved to Atlanta, and since then we've hardly seen each other.

Half an hour later we hang up, my heart brimming with warmth and affection. The pills seem to have done the trick, too. Those invisible hands clutching at my lungs seem to have eased off. I look out of the window and find the stars brighter than usual. Venus watches over me from the skies. Inside, I'm smiling. I did a good deed today. Maybe if I manage to save a life, it won't matter that much that I don't care to save my own. I start to reach for my diary, but my eyelids are already giving in to gravity.

KYLE

I'm in the middle of a forest, and I'm looking for something, but I don't know what. The smell of sulfur and burning throws me into a panic, and I try to run, but my legs won't budge. I want to scream, to flee, but I'm speechless and nailed to the spot. I turn and see Noah, right in front of me, wearing black pants, a black sweatshirt, and a red jacket. He gives me a hard stare, unmoving, unflinching. He smiles, but his red eyes are spewing rage. Shaking his head, he takes one step closer to me, inches from my face. Without opening his mouth, he says, "Why, Kyle? Why did you do it?"

Noah's face begins to warp, like a fresh painting splashed with water, and slowly the shapes morph into Josh's face. His right eyebrow is twitching, which always means he's pissed off. "You fucked up my life, you bastard." He opens his mouth, and a gray, molten foam comes gushing out.

Everything around me is going up in flames. The ground, the air, the trees—everything is blazing. And once again it's Noah in front of me, and he says, "You're gonna pay for what you did to us. Come on, I'm waiting for you." I look down at my hands. They're burning, too, and as much as I thrash around I can't shake off the flames. The pain is unbearable.

I'm jolted awake by someone screaming, and it takes me a few seconds to realize it's me. I open my eyes. Everything's pitch black. I'm soaked in sweat and gasping.

"Everything okay, sweetheart?" my mother calls out from the other side of the house.

"Yeah, yeah, I'm fine," I call back. Lately, that seems to be my answer to everything.

Shit, I shouldn't have fallen asleep. I switch on my bedside lamp and check the time. It's 5:06 a.m. My sketch of the waterfall lies crumpled under my pillow. I flatten it out and look closely at every detail: the cascading water, the foam that conceals the rocks, the sandstone, the iron fence . . . every last fucking detail. And now all becomes clear once more—I have to put an end to this nightmare. I will not fail again tomorrow, even if it means tying that girl to a tree if she gets in my way.

KYLE

I tossed and turned in bed until six-thirty this morning, my mind going round and round in circles. Then, after an hour spent trawling through the search results for *death* and *the afterlife* on my cell phone, my body decided to weld itself to the bed. It must weigh a ton. For a second, I wonder what the Hulk must feel like without his powers. Just opening my eyes is a Herculean effort.

A chill ripples through me at the thought that my time is approaching. But for some reason I feel numb and empty. My folks will soon be leaving. On Saturdays they go to Birmingham to get groceries for the week. Mom says that a visit to Trader Joe's and Sprouts makes up for the thirty miles that separate us from the Magic City. That's why I have to bide my time. There's no way I'm going to ruin their Saturday.

While I wait for them to leave, I mentally draw up some farewell messages. (When I manage to budge, I'll put pen to paper.) Because, well, I guess that's what you do in these cases, isn't it?

Nothing elaborate like in *13 Reasons Why*, but something more like, *I'm sorry, I know I've let you all down, but I'm burning alive and all I can think about is how to put the fire out as quickly as possible. It's not your fault. Please don't be sad. I love you.*

I write three letters: one to my parents, the hardest one; one to Josh; and the last one to Judith, because knowing her she'll spend the coming months ravaged by the question of what she could have done to stop me. I also write a mental note to Noah's folks. They deserve an explanation, an apology, *something*. Still haven't had the courage to go and see them. They want to know exactly what happened, how it could have gone so wrong, how I could have fucked up so badly to send my car slamming into Noah's. But I can't help them. My mind shut down the moment I took that fatal curve and deleted it from my memory. And Josh was so wasted that night that he can't remember a fucking thing either.

Knock, knock, knock. Judging by the soft sound of it, it's my mother at the door.

"Kyle?" she says.

Mom pauses for a second, and when she opens the door, I pretend to be asleep. If I see her, I'll chicken out, that's for sure. But this has to be done. It hurts me no end to make them suffer, but to be a burden to them for the rest of their lives . . . that's not going to happen. After gingerly closing the door, she makes her way back downstairs.

A cool breeze wafts through the half-open window when I finally hear the squeak of the front door opening. Mom always says it needs oil, and Dad always says he'll fix it first thing tomorrow. Then I hear Mom speak.

"He needs time, Connor; that's all. Time and some TLC."

"Please, Lisa, it's been a month," my dad says. "And he's getting worse by the day. He won't eat, won't speak. He can't even look at us anymore."

I'm seized by the urge to run to the waterfall, to disappear, to never hear them talk about me again. But I can't move.

"Maybe we should try a different counselor."

Beep. My mother's car door opens.

"No, Lisa, I'm telling you, the last few weeks have put a tremendous strain on him: the police interrogation, the test for drugs and alcohol, the fear that the other parents might press charges. . . . And now that he's been cleared and the nightmare is over, he needs to get his life back together. And that means getting away from here, away from everything, away from *us.*"

I cover my ears but can still hear every word.

"So, what do you propose? That we ship him off like damaged goods?"

"You know it would do him good to spend a few days with my sister and his cousins in Florida. He needs a change of scenery."

"For God's sake, Connor, he needs us now more than ever. Don't you get it? I refuse to abandon him."

"Who said abandon? You're the one who doesn't get it. He's suffocating here, Lisa. We're losing him." It's too much information. I stick my head under my pillow and pull it down over me. And just when my eardrums are about to burst, I hear it, the *last* voice I want to listen to right now. "Hi, I'm Mia, a friend of Kyle's. Is he home?"

I spring out of bed with such force that I slam into my closet. She can't be serious. I head toward the door, but my right foot won't follow and I hit the floor. My knee is in agony. I glance back and see that my foot is tangled in the sheets. I yank it out and limp out of my room barefoot, hobbling down the stairs as fast as I can.

When I storm out the front door and run into my folks, their backs are to me, and in front of them, eyeing me with the look of a Girl Scout, is Mia the Nightmare. I'm about to give her a piece of my mind, but she beats me to it.

"Hey, Kyle, I was about to bring your folks up to speed."

Her words nail me to the spot. My parents turn to me with quizzical looks, and since my brain won't start, I give them my best poker face. They turn back to Mia. With her never-hurt-a-fly smile, she says to them, "Yesterday, as we were leaving Josh's place, Kyle told me he needed to get away for a few days, so my mother's invited him to spend spring break with us in Spain. If that's okay with you, of course. We'll be flying out in the morning."

What? She's out of her mind.

As if they had all choreographed it to a T, three pairs of eyes turn to look at me. I open my mouth, but nothing comes out, at least nothing that makes sense. And that's when Mia rushes over to me, giggling hysterically, puts her hand over my lips and says, "Don't tell me you were going to tell them how we met? It's *so* embarrassing."

I wish with all my heart that looks could kill, maim, strangle. But right now, I have no choice but to follow the lead of this bad elf playing the good girl, so I shrug and make a huge effort to smile. My folks are so floored they've forgotten to blink.

"Son, are you serious? You really want to travel, *now*?" my dad says, a hint of hope in his voice. At least my mother doesn't seem to have fallen for it: the arch in her right eyebrow is proof.

I keep quiet.

"C'mon, Kyle," the elf chimes in. "Tell them what you told me yesterday . . . about wanting to visit Spain and stuff. . . ."

I don't, so she carries on.

"All right, then I'll tell them. . . ."

Shit. I shake my head, stalling, trying to think of a way to shake this girl, but I draw a blank. "Yeah . . . ," I begin. "It's true . . . I have been wanting to see Spain for a while now. Dad, you've always told me about the architecture there, and . . . and . . . well." My words struggle to get past the lump in my throat. "Noah used to talk about how great it was."

My mother, her eyebrow still pointing skyward, says, "Mia, have we met your parents?"

"Not sure. John and Ellie Faith. At church maybe?" My mom shakes her head, so the girl keeps going. "My mother is a psychology professor at UAB specializing in PTSD. She works at the hospital in the afternoons. And my dad is a photographer for a nature magazine. I have no doubts that if you met them you'd hit it off right away."

For God's sake, she's a phony—you can tell a mile away. But as my mother begins to nod, her eyebrow makes its way back down.

"It's just that . . . everything is happening so quickly. I wish we had more time to get used to the idea," Mom says.

"No, please don't worry. Kyle will be in good hands. Plus . . ." The Elven Nightmare looks at me with a broad grin. "I can feel destiny at work here. Yesterday, right after my cousin told me he couldn't go on the trip with me, I ran into Kyle and . . . well, everything fell into place. Isn't it magical?"

More like witchcraft, I'd say. My folks throw me a questioning glance, and with an enormous effort, I manage to crack what passes for a smile. Now it's official: I've lost and she's won.

"Well then, I guess there's no more time to waste," my dad says. "We'll have to speak with your parents and get everything organized."

"Of course. My mom will call you to discuss all the details. I just wanted to meet you in person first. There are a lot of weirdos out there." *You bet there are.* "So I just wanted to make sure you folks were, you know, normal."

My father's face lights up. That's it; he's fallen under her elven spell.

"Kyle, sweetheart, are you sure?" Mom asks.

I nod, trying to conceal the urge to cut and run and never look back. My dad takes a step toward me with his arms outstretched, then pulls me in for one of his bear hugs.

I shoot Mia a vicious glance and mouth the words *I'm going to kill you.*

As if by reflex, she touches her pendant, and for an instant she seems to go paler, wincing ever so slightly as if I'd kicked her in the stomach, but she sure knows how to cover it up—she's still looking at me with a half smile as my dad lets go of me. And yet, I could swear that her eyes weren't that misty a second ago.

My mother walks over to her, and with a sweet maternal air she gently pulls at Mia's T-shirt. "Honey, I think your shirt is inside out."

Mia looks down, feigning surprise. "Whoops, I do that sometimes. Thanks." Then she looks over at me, and there's something in her expression I almost find touching. "Anyway, I'll get out of your hair now."

Before leaving she turns to me, all cool. "Kyle, don't forget. My mom's gonna need your passport details and all that stuff."

I think I'm about to murder an elf. I give a mock smile and watch as the girl walks off, *backward,* her elbow tucked at her side and her hand cupped in a wave, as if she were English royalty. God, the chick gets on my last nerve, but what really riles me is seeing my folks standing there pie-eyed. This is insane. But then my mother turns to me, and there's a different look in her eye, one that I haven't seen in I don't know how long, something that looks suspiciously like joy, or maybe it's hope.

"Are you sure you'll be all right, Kyle?" she says. "I don't know; it seems a little soon and . . . I . . ."

Dad takes her into his arms. "It'll be okay, Lisa."

Mom looks at me, still waiting for my answer.

"I'll be all right, Ma, really. . . . I don't want you guys to worry, but . . . I do think I need a change of scene. Yeah . . . I really need to get away from here for some time. I'm . . . I'm kind of suffocating here. . . ."

Quoting my father seems to have worked because they

instantly share a knowing smile. Then Mom reaches out her arm to include me in the hug—and to hide her tears. "You coming with us? We can pick up a few things for your trip."

Dad looks at me, his eyes welling up. Time seems suspended in air. Everything does. They peer at me, waiting. How do I tell them that I can't go, that I have other less appealing plans? I can't tell them. Instead, we spend the day in Birmingham, the Magic City. As I've mentioned already, my version of Aladdin's lamp works like a charm, just backward.

MIA

It's nighttime, and the lights of the Rothwell house are going out one by one, the last doors are swinging shut, and the final footfalls are receding down the hallway. I look at Becca, peacefully asleep in her bed. There's a faint smile still hovering on her lips from our last moments together. Apart from that episode with Kyle's parents and the call with Bailey, I haven't left Becca's side the entire day. It's been wonderful. A little exhausting maybe, but wonderful.

I sit down at my desk and write her a farewell letter, telling her I love her, that no matter where she goes, no matter what she does, no matter where her life takes her, there will always be someone who is happy she exists, happy she was born. Becca will know what I mean.

I drag my suitcase out from under my bed and take out my pink scarf, which I'd already packed. She's always loved this scarf. I drape it over her nightstand in the shape of a heart and put the letter next to it. Then, after planting a final kiss on her tiny button nose, I open the window, lift my suitcase onto the ledge, and carefully let it slide down onto the front lawn. Then I sling my backpack over my shoulder, climb out, and shut the window behind me. With one last look at Becca, I implore every star in the night sky to watch over her.

When I arrive at the park near Kyle's neighborhood, I look for a safe bench to spend the night on and find one under the branches of a big sycamore. Once I'm sure that my only company is that of the odd squirrel or passing deer, I curl up on the bench and try to get some rest. But all of this is just too exciting to waste one second of it sleeping, so I take my diary out of my backpack and start bringing things up to date.

Back in middle school they had us read Anne Frank's *The Diary of a Young Girl,* and it made such an impression on me that I decided to start my own journal. I'm not comparing myself to her, of course, but I thought that if I should ever find my real mother, she might be curious about my life, about the moments she missed out on. So I started to put them down on paper, to immortalize them, just for her. And, well, if I should die before meeting her and she decides to come find me, my diary will be the only trace of me left on this planet, that and my photoblog. I've filled up three diaries so far. They're packed in my suitcase.

KYLE

Earlier this morning, when the colors of dawn could fool many into thinking that life is worth living, Mia was already on our porch, standing before our front door, with a knitted backpack over her shoulder and a suitcase that, from the looks of it, has seen more places than she has.

My dad offered to drive us to the airport. I guess they've finally given up trying to persuade me to get back behind the wheel. My mother wanted to join us, but she got called away for work at the clinic. A horse at the Sullivan ranch needed emergency surgery, and there was no other vet available.

Mom couldn't stop smiling yesterday. When we got back from Birmingham, she and dad spent over an hour on the phone with Mia's mother. Apparently, Mia's dad, the photographer, has been in Spain for a couple of weeks now, working on a story for some nature magazine. Mrs. Faith also told my folks that they'll be waiting for us at the Madrid airport and from there we'll be heading to our hotel, located someplace in Andalusia whose name

I can't remember. Mia's mom will give a lecture at some university there. So it turns out that Mia's "penniless" parents not only have cool jobs that occasionally involve crossing the Atlantic, but they can afford to take vacations abroad and drag their daughter's hostage along with them. And if we add the fact that the other day at the waterfall she said she'd been planning a trip with a friend before he left her in the lurch, this pretty much makes her the biggest liar in the state of Alabama. This girl has a problem that a simple pill won't fix. Whatever, the plane tickets are real, and so is the smile on my dad's face, so I won't ask her any questions, at least for now.

I have no idea what might happen to me once I meet her folks: being held for ransom by her psychotic family, kidnapped by her cult, or abducted by her alien parents come to mind.

Whatever it is, it will pale in comparison with what I deserve, and what I all too often wish to do to myself.

My dad, who's also had a permanent smile all morning, has put on one of his CDs as we cruise down Interstate 65, and is belting out "Glory Days" by Bruce Springsteen, who, according to Dad, is the hardest-rocking singer of all time. I observe Mia in the rearview mirror. Her elbows are resting on the half-open window, and her hair is billowing in the wind while she's using an old camera to take pictures. Everything seems to fascinate her. She looks like a small animal that's crawled out of its burrow into the light of day for the first time. I notice her clothes—all wrinkled, as if she spent the night with them on. There's even a little moss on the back of her jean jacket, which, in keeping with her style, is inside out. I feel like cleaning the moss off for her but resist the temptation, of course.

I'm not sure how much time I've spent studying Mia when I notice my dad observing *me* out of the corner of his eye, a roguish grin playing on his lips. Great, the last thing I need is for him to think I could be *into* a girl like Mia. I clear my throat, take out my cell phone, and pretend to look something up on Google. But while pretending, I find myself searching for *Ways to end your life on a plane*.

Several minutes and a couple of Springsteen songs later, we get to an intersection. My eyes are still riveted to the screen of my cell phone, and as my dad heads into a curve more sharply than I would like, all the shit comes flooding back, just like that, without the least warning. One by one, flashes of that grisly day begin to assault my memory, blinding, deafening, annihilating me. Everything goes black. When the darkness finally clears, I see a car heading toward us. It's Noah's. We're about to collide. My heart is thundering. I stop breathing. And that's when I feel a hand reach out of nowhere and clutch my arm.

I open my eyes—I didn't even notice they were shut. I draw breath. My rigid hands are gripping the car seat. I look over at my dad, who's no longer smiling. His hand is resting on my arm. He looks at me and nods, as if to say that everything's okay, that it's over, that in some way he understands me.

Still confused, I look straight ahead, expecting to find Noah, his car smashed beyond recognition, but instead I see the tower of Birmingham's airport. It doesn't make sense; it felt so fucking real. I can feel Mia's eyes on me from the back seat, but I don't have the nerve, let alone the desire, to turn around.

"Is that it?" she asks, her enthusiasm bursting at the seams. "That's the airport, isn't it?"

Dad nods, recovering some of his smile. When I finally manage to compose myself, we're heading into the C-shaped road that runs along the departure terminal. As we drive past each gate, Mia reads out the airlines written on the signs, *one by one*. I knew her silence was too good to last.

"United! This is it! This is the one!"

My dad, chuckling at her boundless enthusiasm, pulls up in front of the entrance. Mia jumps out, takes a few pictures, and rushes over to the line of luggage carts.

"I'm happy for you, kiddo. She seems like a really nice girl," Dad says.

I nod. What else can I do? He looks at me for a moment without saying anything. I have the feeling he's trying to read my thoughts. I go stone-faced. He then looks down at the floor and nods, as if answering his own question. Then, after flashing a smile, he gets out of the car. I glance up into the rearview mirror and catch my reflection glaring at me in disgust.

As I get out of the car, I see Mia struggling to get her ancient green suitcase out of the trunk.

"Let me help you with that," Dad says, rushing to her aid.

"That's okay. I can manage, thanks."

Dad helps her anyway and lifts the suitcase onto the cart.

There's gratitude in Mia's smile, but there's something else I can't quite place, something closer to surprise or disbelief.

"Thanks so much for everything, Mr. Freeman." Mia sticks her hand out.

But Dad doesn't shake her hand. Instead he walks over to her, threatening to give her one of his bona fide bear hugs. For a split second, Mia's body tenses up and draws back slightly. She glances at me, and in her pleading eyes I see something more intense than fear. Instinctively, I move toward her, but as Dad wraps his arms around her she seems to calm down. Shutting her eyes, she lets herself go.

I pull my duffel bag out of the trunk without taking my eyes off Mia. When my dad releases her, her chin is quivering. She smiles, overwhelmed, unable to conceal her emotional overload. She turns around, gives a brisk wave, and quickly heads toward the entrance, pushing her luggage cart.

I look at Dad. I want to talk to him, tell him everything, say how sorry I am for all I've put them through, for having sullied our family name forever, but the words remain stuck in my throat. He puts both hands on my shoulders, something he's never done before, and with an earnestness that I didn't know was in him, he says, "Son, I know that what you're going through is not easy, and that we're miles apart right now. Sometimes I feel like that accident put an impenetrable wall between us and . . ." He shakes his head, eyeing me steadily. My whole body is shaking. "All I ask is that on this trip, you try to find whatever it takes to knock it down. Your mom and I miss you terribly, son. Please . . . come back to us."

Every word of his, every syllable rattles me to the core. I want to throw my arms around him and bawl, but I know that if I start

I won't be able to stop, so I just bite my tongue and nod like a heartless bastard.

"Sir, I'll need you to keep moving," says a passing police officer, pointing at the *No Parking* sign.

"Sure thing, just give me a minute," my dad replies. Then he quickly takes out his wallet and hands me one of his credit cards.

"Dad, you don't have to—" I try.

"I'm not asking you." He slips the card into my jacket pocket. "I want you to get the most out of this trip, and if you won't do it for yourself, then do it for your mother and me. It means the world to us."

I nod. The police officer is looking stern.

"I'm goin', I'm goin'," Dad says to him. He pats me on the cheek and heads toward the car.

I want to yell out to him, to tell him I love him, that I'll miss him, but again I just stand there and watch him go. Then I scan the entrance for Mia, and why am I not surprised that people are staring at her? She's standing in front of the door, her arms raised above her head, her eyes shut, and she's *twirling*. Her cheerfulness is painful, agonizing, excruciating to watch. And something tells me these days abroad may prove even harder than I thought.

MIA

We're flying over a sea of plump and playful clouds. It's the most amazing sensation I've ever had. I feel like reaching out and squeezing them, or lying on them and floating around. For a second, they remind me of the nurse at Jack Hughston Memorial and her colorful cotton balls. The sun seems to follow along like a guardian watching over the skies. Is this what it will feel like when I leave this body? Will I soar over the clouds? Greet the sun? Play with the stars?

Kyle is in the seat next to mine, pursuing his favorite hobby: ignoring me. Basically, he hasn't said a word to me all morning. Once we got settled in our seats, he started leafing through every magazine on the plane. When we took off he watched some dull documentary on penguins in Antarctica. And for a while now, he's been reading a comic that he had in his backpack. I guess I don't blame him. If I were in his shoes, I wouldn't be dying to make conversation either.

For the thousandth time he checks the watch he wears on his right wrist. It's the kind of watch that was all the rage sometime in the last century, with a metal band, a dark blue bezel, and three small round chronometers inside. It's nice; it gives him a touch of class, charisma almost. I look at the watch hands. It's noon on the dot, the hour at which, come rain or shine, the Rothwells attend Mass on Sundays. They'll be wondering where I am, and if they haven't done so already, they'll be reporting a missing person—me. But neither the police nor anyone else will find me now. Nothing, and no one, is going to force me to have heart surgery.

For the first time in my whole life, I'm free. All thanks to Bailey. Without her I wouldn't even be on this plane. Her last boyfriend's occupation, among other things, was to help innocent people forge a new identity in order to get around the red tape of a corrupt and unjust bureaucracy. At least that's what he used to say. Until I met him I didn't know you could forge a passport with such ease. I didn't know you could forge a passport *at all*. In the one he made for me, next to the photo, is the name Miriam Abelman. I love the name Miriam. It makes me feel a little more European.

Two flight attendants are approaching along the aisle, pushing a metal cart that, judging from the smell, contains something edible. I'm starving. I haven't had a bite to eat since last night. I look over and see that the other passengers have a kind of tray suspended in front of them. I don't recall getting one of those, so I look under my seat—nope. I check on either side, but there's nothing there either. On the backrest maybe? What an idea. I look at the TV screen on the seat in front of me, in case there are any instructions I'm missing, but there aren't. I just can't seem to find the blessed thing, and the flight attendants are getting closer by the second. And then, just like that, Kyle's hand reaches across me and, flicking a little lever on the seat in front, unfolds the elusive tray.

"Thanks," I say, and ignoring the fact that he's gone straight back to his comic book, I continue. "But seriously, who would have thought it was so simple? Being on a plane like this and all, I would have expected something a little more . . . sophisticated. Wouldn't you?"

He shakes his head with a look that says *This girl's a ditz.* Granted, it wasn't my brightest moment, but I really did expect something more . . . I don't know, just more. The flight attendants arrive. One of them, wearing the cutest navy-blue outfit with one light purple shoulder, gracefully bends down to me and asks, "What will you be having, miss, meat or fish?"

"Neither one, thank you. I'm a vegetarian."

"I'm very sorry, miss, but special meals have to be ordered at least twenty-four hours in advance."

"Oh, well in that case I'll have the fish. At least I know the fish had a good run, swimming around and all, before . . ." I draw my index and middle fingers across my throat. "You know."

The flight attendant looks at me, none the wiser, but smiles anyway. She hands me a tray with something that vaguely resembles food, then turns to Kyle.

"And for you, sir?"

Kyle shakes his head and dismisses her with a wave of the hand. I'm not surprised. The way this fish looks makes me long for Mrs. Rothwell's cooking, which is saying something. I look at

Kyle out of the corner of my eye. He's shutting his comic book. It's the perfect moment to give it another try.

"So," I begin, "considering we'll be spending the next ten days together, I think we should get to know each other a little better. Ask me anything and I'll tell you. Go ahead, shoot."

He doesn't shoot. Instead, he leans forward, slips the comic book into his backpack, and starts rummaging. As he straightens up, I see what he was looking for—his earphones. Nice, a really subtle gesture, but I'm not giving up just yet. "Seriously? You don't even want to know where we're headed, what we're going to do, *nothing*?"

I pause and wait, but he doesn't bat an eyelash, so I carry on.

"You're not planning on spending the whole week without saying a word to me, are you? I don't think my failing health could deal with that."

Kyle seems to have gone selectively deaf, because instead of replying he puts his earphones on, shuts his eyes, and crosses his arms. Fine, that'll just give me the chance to study him up close.

It doesn't surprise me that he drives the girls wild. His black hair falls in waves over his gorgeous features, lightly dappled with freckles. His lips are so fleshy that, were it not for his chiseled jaw and muscular arms, he would look too feminine. And then I see it protruding just below the sleeve of his T-shirt—a deep scar sewn shut, a faithful symbol of his suffering. If only his other wounds could be treated with a few stitches.

I leave half of my meal unfinished, and while taking in the spectacular view from my window, I begin to imagine what it will be like to meet my mother for the first time. Instantly my thoughts start to race. Does she ever think of me? Has she forgotten I exist? *Boom, boom, boom,* my heart warns me that I've gone way beyond my daily quota of intense emotion. I heed the warning and lean against the window, hoping I can get some sleep. Tomorrow is my birthday and my second day of total freedom, so I plan on being fully awake for every second of it.

KYLE

The sun is beating down so hard in the airport parking lot that my eyes can't stop squinting, even with my shades on. Twenty-one hours without sleep doesn't help either. Spent the whole trip *pretending* to sleep while listening to the loudest music I could find. No way was I going to risk dozing off, then waking up the entire plane with my post-nightmare screams. That would have been a real show. Plus, after downing four strong coffees in a row I'm not only exhausted but totally wired.

Mia is ahead of me, pushing a luggage cart. She seems to be looking for something, or someone. She reads a printout she's holding, then keeps walking. I follow her, keeping a safe distance. I have no idea what we're doing here, but I don't ask her. Right now, I'll do anything to avoid talking to the elf. Her parents are nowhere in sight, but I couldn't care less, to be honest. The only thing I do care about is getting to the hotel and hitting the hay.

She seems to be waving to someone in the distance, but the only thing remotely resembling a person is a shirtless dude with dreadlocks walking around barefoot, his body covered in tattoos, his beard grown out of control, and jeans so tattered you can see right through them. As we approach the man I see that next to him is a van, the flower-power type they used last century. One half is fuchsia, the other is fluorescent green, and to top it off there are huge daisies painted on in screaming colors. The side of the van has a hand-drawn message on it: *Life is about the journey, not the destination.* I don't know what we're getting ourselves into, but it doesn't look good.

"Hi," says Mia as we come to a stop in front of the guy. She extends her hand, playing the responsible adult.

"Hey," he responds in a strong Spanish accent. "Namaste."

He gives her a quick hug.

"Namaste," Mia replies, breaking into a toothy grin.

"Say, you wouldn't happen to have the contract with you?" the dude says, scratching his head. Something tells me you could grow potatoes under that mass of knotted hair. "I don't know what I did with my copy. Must have dropped it somewhere."

Mia nods and shows him her printout. The guy takes it and reads it carefully.

"Okay, I'm with you now; you're Miriam Abelman. The girl who booked my little Moon Chaser two years in advance, but suddenly moved it up by a year. You're lucky we could change your reservation on such short notice."

And now her name is Miriam. She's a compulsive liar; there's no other term for it. Mia or Miriam, or whatever her name is, gives the guy a blushing smile and says, "What can I say? I'm a lucky girl."

Oh, c'mon, next thing you know she'll be hooking up with this dude.

"You said it," he replies with a chuckle. And then he turns to me, as if he overlooked something important.

"Greetings, man," he says, sticking out his hand. I don't know why, but I shake it, and for an instant he frowns at me.

"Whoa, you're in bad shape, buddy. Your aura's got a super-dark cloud over it."

Mia clears her throat nervously. I clench my fist, ready to pop this guy in the mouth.

"I'm telling you I can *feel* something," he goes on. "Something, I don't know, *karmic* about the way you—"

"Okay then," Mia cuts him off. "We're kind of in a rush so if you don't mind . . ."

"Hey, guys, speed kills," the Rasta announces with a furrow in his brow.

"No, dude," I say, about to snap, "the only thing that kills is wasting our fucking time listening to your karmic crap."

The Rasta bursts out laughing.

"All right, all right, I'll get those keys for you, and I'm gone."

And while he heads toward the driver's door, I turn to Mia. She's looking something up on her phone. I glare at her, my eyes seething.

"What the fuck is all this about?"

Mia stares at her phone and pretends not to hear.

"Hey, I'm talking to you."

She looks up, wide-eyed. "I'm sorry. Did you say something?"

I shake my head in disbelief.

"Thought you weren't speaking to me," she says.

"Well, I am now. Tell me what on earth we're doing here, and what *this* is." I point at the van.

The weirdo with the dreads comes back, tosses a few sheets of paper onto the luggage cart, and says, "Just sign here, sweetie."

Mia scribbles a signature.

"All right, then. She's all yours."

Ours? He hands Mia the keys. This can't be happening. Oh wait, I get it—I'm still asleep on the plane and about to wake up screaming any second now. But then the guy comes over and pats me on the shoulder, and it's as real as it gets. This isn't a nightmare. It's worse.

"Back here in ten days, got it?" he says, holding up two fingers in a peace sign while walking off barefoot on the scorching asphalt.

Mia opens the back door and starts loading her suitcase.

"You must be mental if you think I'm getting into that thing, and even more deranged if you think I'm getting into any vehicle with you behind the wheel."

She slowly turns to me, and in a tone so composed it makes me want to throttle her, she says, "Oh no, don't worry about that. I don't have a license."

"What the fuck are you saying?"

What is she saying?

She shrugs, a picture of innocence.

Then it dawns on me. "No fucking way, don't even think about it. *I'm* not driving that piece of junk anywhere."

KYLE

So here I am, behind the wheel of this clunker, driving down a highway, following the directions my abductor has kindly put into my cell phone's GPS. If I don't play along, she's perfectly capable of telling my folks about what happened at the waterfall. The cars overtaking me—which is to say all of them—are honking at me, flashing their headlights, or both. I don't blame them: I'm stuck at twenty-five miles an hour. What they don't understand is that every time the speedometer inches upward, so does my pulse, which must be at two thousand beats a minute by now, no joke.

My fingers are squeezing the wheel so hard they've gone numb. I'm barely breathing. My eyes dart from the side mirror, to the rearview, to the other side mirror, to the highway, and back again. But it's only my eyes that are shifting, as if the slightest movement of my head could throw the whole car off track. This is worse than my first day at hockey tryouts.

I'm getting cold sweats at regular intervals; my back is

drenched and sticking to the old leather seat. Mia has been oddly quiet for the last few minutes but is far from sitting still. I don't know what she's up to, but from what I can gather out of the corner of my eye she's fiddling with her phone.

"Got it!" she squeals as if she's reached the Himalayas. "I bought a SIM card at the airport. They say roaming charges are way too expensive. Wanna buy one too?"

My mind is too busy to register what she's saying. I can't shake the feeling that we're about to crash, that any second now something is going to jump out in front of us and that'll be it. God, the tension is unbearable.

"Okay, your loss," she says. "But don't come crying to me when you get your phone bill."

A sleek sports car passes me, honking like a lunatic. And although my attention is split four ways—side mirror, rearview, side mirror, highway—I could swear the driver's holding up one particular finger for my benefit.

"Hey, Kyle, check it out!" Mia blurts, and she sounds so hysterical that I skip one of my mirror checks to cast a sidelong glance at her.

She's pointing at the side of the highway. "That turtle is gaining on us."

I'm gonna kill this girl. I hold my tongue and save my best put-downs for when we get to wherever we're going.

"On second thought," she says, "I think we should renegotiate the terms of our agreement. At this rate I'll need a month to hit all the places I want to visit."

"Forget it!" I thunder, my voice rivaling Thanos's on a bad day.

"He speaks. It's a miracle. But I didn't quite hear what you said. Could you repeat that?"

If I give her a piece of my mind, she's going to regret asking. Luckily for her she doesn't insist, and after a few minutes of silence she's fidgeting in her seat again. Great, she's not only a basket case but has ADD as well. Seems to have rearranged her position and is now leaning her back against the passenger door, because I can feel her eyes glued to me. That's all I need, a spectator watching my pathetic performance at the wheel. I snort.

"Am I bugging you? I can stop if you like, but it's something they taught me back at St. Jerome's. The grown-ups used to say that if you focus your attention on something you want for long enough, you'll get it in the end. And there are two things I want right now: I want you to talk to me, and I want you to rejoin the world of the living."

St. Jerome's? So now it turns out she's an orphan. A psychiatrist might be the best thing for this girl.

"Oh, c'mon," she says. "You mean you're not going to ask me *anything* about this trip, or about me? Nothing? At least ask me where we're going."

She doesn't get it. I'm on the verge of a freak-out here, and she wants to chat like old pals. She's shifting around again; I'm not sure what she's up to, but she's putting her cell phone on the dashboard. We're approaching a tollbooth. Harry Styles launches into "Adore You" on her cell phone. It's one of Judith's favorite songs, and it's the last thing I need right now. As we come to a stop in front of the barrier, I turn to look at her. Her eyes are shut, and she's dancing in her seat, hugging an imaginary partner. Good Lord.

I have to flex my hand a few times before my tense, swollen fingers can slide my credit card into the tollbooth slot. While we wait for the barrier to open, I reach over and turn the damn song off. Mia opens her eyes, indignant, and with a defiant look, she turns the song back on.

I put my credit card away, and before pulling out of the toll booth I try to reach for her phone again, but she slaps my wrist in midair and, grabbing it firmly, places my hand back on the steering wheel. For some strange reason, the feel of her fingers on my skin sends a tingle up my whole arm and ends up right in the middle of my chest. I'm going to chalk it up to the effects of not sleeping, and not eating.

"Nobody *ever* turns off my favorite singer in the world," she says, wagging her finger in my face.

I hope this is the extent of her dark side. I couldn't deal with her having an aggressive streak on top of everything else. The car behind me is honking, so I pull out of the toll area. Mia's watching me like a hawk, so I resign myself to listening to this mushy crap as background music to our imminent car crash. Could things get any worse? I doubt it.

MIA

It's been two hours since we left Madrid, and I've taken so many pictures I'm going to need another memory card. The landscape here is something else. Right now, to my right there's a sea of centenary olive trees and a stream of clear water wending its way through them. To the left is a stone monastery that must be several centuries old. And nestled in bell towers, in trees, and even in some electrical towers, are enormous storks' nests. It's like a fairy tale, only better—there are no witches, no princes, or anyone else who can ruin the magic for you.

Kyle doesn't seem to share the sentiment. For someone who slept through the entire trip, he looks frazzled. And he's gripping the steering wheel so tightly his fingers have gone white. For an instant I recall that those hands once gripped another steering wheel and caused Noah's death. I'd give anything to be able to help him, but I don't know how. I've tried cracking jokes, being serious, singing, dancing, whistling, reading aloud, anything that comes to mind. At least I got him to drive, which is something. I read it online in some self-help guide for people dealing with trauma after an accident. I haven't told him this, but driving is an essential step in his recovery.

Turning in my seat, I take a picture of him, but it only makes him grit his teeth harder. He's even more attractive in profile. His nose looks sculpted by a Greek artist. A tiny scar in the middle of his rounded chin gives him an alluring, enigmatic look. But his eyelashes are his best feature. How many girls would kill to have them that long and shapely? If there were a contest of profiles, he would win hands down. I take another snapshot. That profile is too good not to immortalize. He huffs.

"Bet you're wondering why I'm taking so many pictures," I say.

He doesn't reply, so I carry on. "Well, I'll tell you. They're for my photoblog—*Expiration Date*."

Nothing. Seriously, I don't get it. *I'd* be dying to know more.

"Expiration date, you know, like a metaphor . . ."

Not a flicker of interest. Looks like I'm going to have to change tack.

"Okay, how about this? I'm starving. You?"

I'll take the rumbling of his stomach as a reply. Since we started the trip he's eaten only a couple of granola bars and a pack of peanuts. I don't know how he's made it this far without passing out. I have to find a place where we can stop and eat but am not about to settle for some gas-station restaurant. I want something special, with atmosphere, something typical of the area.

Ever since I found out that my mother is Spanish, I've tried to soak up everything I can about this country: its customs, its cuisine, its people . . . And now that my life is entering its final chapter and I don't know if I've got days, weeks, or, with a little luck, a few months left, I don't plan on leaving this country. It's strange, but being in the land of my ancestors makes me feel closer to her, closer to myself.

A sign along the highway indicates the next exit: *Alcázar de San Juan, 1 km.* I look the name up on the web and find that not only is it a picturesque little town with historic buildings and narrow cobblestone streets, but it has several restaurants with great reviews. Perfect. I choose one.

"Take the next exit," I say to Kyle. "There's a restaurant a couple of miles from here that's got four point seven stars."

But he doesn't seem to hear me, his eyes fixed on the highway.

"Kyle?" I say a little louder. We're coming up to the exit. "Get off here. Here!"

He looks dazed. We're right at the turnoff, and he's still not responding.

"Kyle!"

I grab the wheel and yank it toward the exit. The camper van nearly swerves off the road.

"No!" he yells as he tries to straighten the wheel. When he gets it under control, he's out of breath and livid. Then he unleashes a booming voice on me, every word seething with fury. "DON'T EVER DO THAT AGAIN."

The venom in his voice leaves me shaking.

"I'm sorry, really. I thought—"

"JUST STOP," he bellows, gripping the wheel, his eyes glued to the road. "PLEASE, just stop thinking, stop talking, stop *being who you are.*"

That hurts me, bad, worse than bad. I slump down in my seat

and look out the window as we drive down a country road that runs along a river. Two or three minutes go by in silence, and then I see a stork lifting off from a nest in the distance and taking to the sky. It's a sign; it has to be. It's life reminding me that I'm free now, that no one can do me any harm, that I don't have to take anything from anyone and certainly don't need to feel like this. So I think of my mother and the joy it will soon bring me to meet her; of Becca, because thinking of her always makes me grin; and of Bailey, who wouldn't let anyone's remark ruin her day, much less her birthday. And I force my lips into a smile. Maybe that'll persuade my heart to stop crying.

MIA

As Kyle continues down the dirt road that leads to the restaurant and finally parks in the shade of an aspen, I carry on taking snapshots: of the white tavern with blue wooden shutters; the two huge earthenware jugs on either side of the carved wooden entrance door; the leaves of the aspen, which when bathed in the sun create a silver glimmer; and a windmill, one of those old ones with a white cylindrical base and a black conic roof. I've been transported into a different era, a world apart, one that dreams are made of.

I would gladly spend the rest of the day taking pictures, seizing moments, capturing beauty. That's how I met Noah. We attended the same community photography course a couple of years back. Noah was really good. He knew how to bring out something special in people, in places, even in ordinary things. We'd planned this trip down to the last detail, except his death.

Kyle kills the engine but doesn't get out of the car. He rolls down the window, letting the breeze in, and looks straight ahead. Maybe it's his way of telling me that he needs a moment alone.

"I'll go in and order something, okay?" I say, as tactfully as I can. "What do you like? Do you have a preference? Any dietary issues? Allergies? An intolerance to something?"

"Yeah, to this trip."

Okay, well, at least he's making jokes.

The restaurant is even prettier inside. Noah would have loved it. There are whole cured hams hanging from the dark wooden beams above. On one side, next to the entrance, there's a selection of cheeses on display that are begging to be devoured. The dining area is bustling with people chatting and eating heartily around rustic wooden tables covered with blue-and-white-checkered tablecloths. But what strikes me most is the smell of the place. I don't know what it is, I guess it must be the blend of cheeses, hams, and the dishes they're serving. Whatever it is, it's making my mouth water.

I approach the bar and pick up one of the menus. It's laminated, and one side says *Raciones* while the other says *Bocadillos*. The restaurant door opens. It's Kyle. My heart leaps for joy. I'm convinced that this place, with its people, its warmth, its enticing odors, won't leave him indifferent, will get him to react and lure him out of his shell, if only for a while. But as he walks right past me as if I weren't there and heads toward the bathrooms at the back, I realize it's not going to be easy. I'd give the world to know what he's thinking, what I should say to him, how I can help. I watch him until he disappears behind the men's bathroom door.

At the other end of the bar there are seven or eight waiters, all wearing black pants and white short-sleeved shirts. Some are making coffee, some are serving beer, and others are going in and out of a door at the back carrying plates to and from the tables at a dizzying pace.

I lean farther over the bar and raise my hand, trying to catch somebody's eye. I must be doing something wrong because nobody's paying any attention.

"Excuse me," I say, waving to one of the waiters.

Nothing.

"Excuse me," I call, singling out one of the taller ones.

No luck. Obviously this approach won't work, so I get on one of the stools and, shooting my hands into the air, holler, "EXCUSE ME."

A particularly young waiter with short, spiky hair turns and smiles at me.

"Americana, no?"

"Yeah, well, it's just that . . . Never mind, can I get two cured-ham-and-cheese sandwiches, please?"

This sandwich happens to be number five on my list of things to try in Spain.

"Marchando," he says with a grin. He faces the kitchen door and calls out, "Dos bocatas, Tere; de jamón y queso." He turns back to me. "Something to drink?"

"Yes, water, please, and do you have a tarta de Santiago?"

He raises one eyebrow.

"No, señorita, you're in La Mancha. The tarta de Santiago is from the north, from Galicia, I believe. But we do have a lemon pie that my mother makes." He leans in close as if sharing a secret. "The recipe has been in our family for three hundred years."

"I see," I say, giggling. "Well, unless you're afraid I'll steal your recipe and sell it to an American restaurant chain, I'd love to try some of that pie."

The waiter laughs and walks over to a fridge at the other end of the bar. I take the opportunity to get in a few snapshots of the barrels of wine, the carved wooden door with its iron lock shaped like a heart, the framed photos of bullfighters, the people around me, and the classical guitar propped up in a corner. Then I turn my camera on the waiters. One of them looks at me and, elbowing one of his colleagues, says something in Spanish I don't quite catch. And suddenly they're all striking funny poses in front of me. They make me laugh, and I take as many pictures of them as I can before they're called back to their tasks.

The waiter with the spiky hair comes back with a slice of lemon pie. It looks so good that I can't resist taking another snapshot. There are little wavelets of meringue covering the surface, and the yellow cream beneath has that citrusy yet sweet smell that is so addictive. I'm not sure I'll be able to stop at one slice.

Looking at the pie, I'm seized by the urge to cry again, but I hold back. I feel angry but don't show it. Yet another birthday goes by, with me wondering whether there's anyone that actually cares about me. No, I refuse to go down that road right now. I'm zooming the camera in to capture every detail of the pie when I sense someone walking up to me from my left-hand side. I swivel around so quickly that I'm still holding the camera up to my face and find a magnified version of Kyle the Furious glowering at me. Oops.

KYLE

Unbelievable—I leave her alone for a minute and she's already chatting with half the staff. And now she's fixing me with that old camera, which she won't put down for a second, not even to go to the bathroom. I cover up the lens with my hand—who knows what she plans to do with all those pictures?

If I don't put something in my stomach right now I'm going to pass out, so when a waiter comes our way carrying a couple of sandwiches and a bottle of water, my belly rejoices. While Mia takes a bill out of her wallet, I ask the spiky-haired waiter for something a little tastier with which to wash down the sandwich.

"One orange juice," I say.

The waiter grins and says, "Sorry, orange press broken, but we have mosto if you want."

I have no idea what that is, but I nod.

"No *please* or *thank you* for the waiter?" Mia whispers to me under her breath, a chiding tone in her voice.

I'm too hungry to respond. I grab one of the sandwiches as if it were my last and take a huge bite. Mia picks hers up leisurely.

"I'm starving," she says, and opens her mouth wide. As she raises the sandwich, the two slices of crunchy bread part slightly and I see even more proof of her lying ass—a couple of slices of cured ham.

"Aren't you supposed to be a vegetarian?" I say. She stops mid-bite and looks up at me. "Jesus," I mutter. "Does anything you say remotely resemble the truth?"

She puts the sandwich back on the plate. "Well, that depends on whom I'm talking to. And no, I'm not a vegetarian, but I only eat animals that haven't spent their life suffering for our pleasure. Have you ever stopped to consider how much of the meat you eat comes from animals who've spent every waking hour crammed into cages and exploited?" And without giving me time to reply, which I didn't intend to do anyway, she carries on. "But as you can imagine—and if you can't, then I'll explain it to you—I'm not trying to lecture you or anybody else, but the fact is that people don't want to hear the truth. And for your information, this is authentic Iberian ham, and the Iberian pigs range freely in the pastures of central Spain. It's right here in my guidebook."

I've had about enough of her bizarre and never-ending rants, so I don't bother answering. Instead, I dig in to the sandwich while I wait for my drink to arrive. I'm not in the mood for small talk, so I focus my attention on the collection of wine bottles displayed on the shelves against the wall. Right next to the shelves is a mirror, reflecting the image of Mia biting into her sandwich. She closes her eyes and chews extra slowly, as if she were savoring something divine. In fact, she's so ecstatic it looks like she's on the verge of an orgasm.

I study my own sandwich for a moment. It does smell pretty good, I'll give it that. I take another big bite and chew more slowly, relishing each flavor and texture. I bring it up to my nose and inhale its fragrance. Wait, what the fuck am I doing? Don't tell me that on top of everything else, this Mia character is *contagious*. I look for a ten-euro bill in my pockets. Are those the blue ones or the red ones? Mia places her hand on mine.

"I told you, the meals are on me."

Again, her touch sends a tingle through my fingers and right up my arm, but a million times stronger this time. *What's wrong with me?* As soon as the waiter brings my mosto, I leave the restaurant, determined to preserve what little sanity I have left. I walk outside, keeping my fingers splayed, as if they'd touched something highly toxic.

I finish my sandwich, standing as far away as possible from our rickety flower-power van. My cell phone begins to vibrate. It's a message from Mom, asking how the trip is going. I'm torn between sending her a picture of the van and letting her draw her own conclusions, and telling her a white lie. I opt for the second and send three emojis: a thumbs-up, a kiss, and a blue heart.

I check the time. It's almost three in the afternoon, and according to my GPS we still have two hours to go. I haven't even checked where we're going. The only thing I care about now is getting there and hitting the sack (and with a little luck never waking up again). I drain my glass in one gulp and head back into the restaurant to get Mia.

And just as I'm crossing the threshold, fate gives me a huge kick in the ass, one that I clearly deserve. I see Mia, alone at the bar, sitting on a high stool. Her shoulders are hunched over a slice of pie. One single birthday candle, looking as forlorn as she does, flickers before her. Mia seems to be singing. I get closer without her seeing me and listen in.

"Happy birthday, dear Amelia," she sings softly, her voice breaking. "Happy birthday to me."

I'm rooted to the spot. She looks so frail, so lonely. I can see her face in the mirror. Her eyes are welling up, trying to hold back the tears stored up over a lifetime, like a dam fit to burst. Her small and fragile body resembles a minefield, where year after year someone must have been planting one explosive after another. There's something in this scene that is too painful to watch, like a knife through my gut. My tears are pleading to be let out. Until this very moment, I never actually *looked* at her; I saw only what my rage allowed me to see. I back up slowly, as if the slightest noise could break her, as if the slightest shift might shatter the fine glass sphere that keeps her isolated from the outside world. As I back away through the door, she blows out the candle and I hear her:

"Happy birthday, Amelia."

I've never heard three more anguished, crestfallen words in my entire life. Those are not the words of a girl, but of an old soul too tired to keep fighting, of someone whose heart is too heavy to keep beating.

I stand outside, watching the door swing shut in front of me, unable to move, powerless, and yet with the glimmer of something new, something humming inside me. God, how could my own suffering have so blinded me to someone else's pain? This is not me, goddamn it. This is not who I am.

MIA

I open my eyes in a daze, as if a cloud of smoke were shrouding my memory. And although I can't remember why I'm sitting here, I vaguely recall popping one of my pills, the ones I take when things get rough. They always knock me out. I'm sitting on my side, with my knees tucked under me and my head leaning against a backrest. And as the world parades before my eyes, I begin to remember the trip, the van, the restaurant, and Kyle. *Kyle!* I recall leaving the restaurant and finding him asleep in the van's driver's seat. I didn't want to wake him, and so, after updating my diary, I let myself doze off too. But I must have been out cold, because I didn't even notice Kyle starting the engine and getting back on the road.

And I must have slept awhile because now the sun is already setting behind the mountain peaks, a glowing shade of fuchsia lighting up the sky. For a second, I'm assailed by doubts—is Kyle driving us to where we need to go, or is he going rogue? Then I chuckle. If he were going rogue, I'm the last person he'd take along for the ride. Besides, he's driving way too slow for that. I just saw a guy on a bicycle pass us, and he wasn't even breaking a sweat.

I straighten up in my seat a little to relieve my sore neck, but I don't turn around. Better to keep my back to my supersociable driver. I know myself; if I face him, I'm going to want to talk to him, and to be frank, I'm not in the mood for his gibes, or worse, his silent treatment. I pick up my cell phone, search for the latest Harry Styles video, and press play, but instead of hearing Harry's sexy voice, I hear an even sexier one behind me.

"So aren't you going to tell me what this trip is all about?"

I freeze, trying to process what I just heard. Did he say what I thought he said, or was that my imagination conjuring up a birthday present for me out of thin air?

"Mia?"

I spin around, gaping at him, and reach over to touch his forehead.

"Oh my God, are you *okay*? You must be delirious. I'm calling an ambulance."

While I pretend to dial a number, Kyle just about cracks a smile and gives a tiny shake of his head. Then, without ever moving his head, his gray eyes glance in my direction for a fraction of a second. He must have serious neck issues.

"Well?" he insists. "Are you going to spit it out, or do I have to beg?"

"Begging is a good start," I say, trying to sound indignant. "Why don't you begin by telling me why you changed your tune?"

Of course, I'm thrilled to pieces, but I can't go easy on him. He swallows hard, as if eating his own words, and maybe a slice or two of humble pie.

Still playing the offended card, I say, "And what if now *I* don't want to talk to *you*? Maybe the moment's gone and I don't feel like telling you *anything*. Maybe I don't even feel like taking this trip with you anymore."

All right, I may be pushing it a little, but Kyle is too busy keeping tabs on a truck that's passing us to notice.

"Fine, I'll tell you," I say, caving way too fast—can't help it, I'm too soft. "This trip is about finding my mother."

Kyle gives a slow nod, like someone trying to put pieces together. "And exactly which mother are we talking about here, the professor? Or the one who is so poor she can't even buy you a cell phone? Or the one who made you an orphan?"

"None of the above, actually."

"Uh-huh," he says, his head seesawing again. "Or maybe it's the other mother, the one who'd be all torn up if you died because of me."

I straighten up, dignified. "I'm sure she would have been crushed."

"She *would have been*? You're saying she's dead? Don't tell me we've traveled thousands of miles to look for a gravestone."

"Well, here's the thing. . . . I don't know her; she had to leave a couple of days after I was born."

I sense that my words have made his stomach seize up. Maybe I'm not the only one who has lost the desire to laugh. Body language is always blunter than what comes out of someone's mouth, and I guess I've become something of an expert in this area over the years. When you look at someone, when you look really close, you learn a lot. Like the nurse who tells you you're going to get better but turns away just enough so you don't see her chin quivering. Or the doctor who says the operation is straightforward but can't keep his hands from sweating. Or your brand-new adoptive mother who says she's really sorry, but something terrible has come up, and they won't be able to keep you, while her dilating pupils give her away.

Observing people has helped me survive, no question, but it has its downsides, like realizing that most *I love you*s are formalities devoid of emotion, and most *I hate you*s are wretched cries for attention that really mean *I hate you for not loving me.*

Kyle clears his throat and resumes his cross-examination. "Wait, your mother had to leave, as in leave for *work,* or as in . . ." He lingers on the last word, as if waiting for me to finish his sentence.

"I don't *know,*" I say, now almost wishing he'd go back to ignoring me. "That's what I'm here to find out."

"And have you had any news from her or from your family over the years?"

I shake my head. I've never spoken to anyone about my mother, except to Bailey, and I'm starting to think it was better that way.

"But she did send you a letter, or called you at least, right?"

"Enough," I say, putting my fingers over his mouth. "You know all you need to know."

I withdraw my hand slowly, hoping he doesn't say anything

— 87 —

else, and notice his cheeks are flushed. No wonder; although the sun has set, the thermometer still reads seventy-seven degrees. I see he's about to say something, but I beat him to it. "Besides, guess what? Today's my birthday. Wouldn't it be cool to find her on the same day I was born?"

"Happy birthday," he says, and puts his blinker on. We get off the highway and onto a secondary road. "May I ask how old my kidnapping psycho is today? I wouldn't want a minor on my hands."

"Don't worry, I'm turning eighteen today," I lie. And even if in Alabama we have that ridiculous law that says you're not an adult until you're nineteen, here in Europe that makes me an adult. Free and independent.

"That's a relief."

"And I brought a candle along, in case you wanted to sing me 'Happy Birthday,' but it's too late now; I already blew it out. And you blew your chance, amigo."

His belly tightens up again, but relaxes more quickly this time.

"It's never too late," he says, trying to look casual.

"Oh yes, it is." I pat my stomach. "You missed out on the best lemon pie in the *whoole* country."

"My loss. So tell me: Where does this mother of yours live?"

"No clue."

"What?"

Kyle turns to me, glaring (not sure if it's because he's regained the use of his neck or what I said about my mother), and then immediately turns back to the road. "So where the fuck are we going now? For God's sake, can't you talk straight for once and tell me what we're doing here?"

"All right, all right, don't freak out. It's bad for the heart. I'll begin at the beginning. Two years ago, I got my hands on my adoption papers and discovered my mother's name—María Astilleros—and that she was from Spain. Luckily, Astilleros is not a very common name, so while I waited to be able to make the trip, I looked up every woman between the ages of thirty-six and sixty-six with that name. And came up with a list of thirteen possible maternal candidates."

"Maternal candidates?"

His tone makes it sound silly, so I ignore him and carry on. "The first mother on my list lives in Granada, a city in the region of Andalusia. That's in the south."

"Well, you're going to meet her real soon." He points to a sign on the road. I almost jump out of my skin. It says *Granada, 15 km.*

"That can't be right," I say, already verging on hysteria.

I check the GPS—we're ten minutes away from our destination. "Oh-my-God-oh-my-God-oh-my-God, and I look like *this*. Why didn't you say anything? Couldn't you have woken me up? I have to brush my hair and change my clothes. You don't get it; I can't show up looking like this."

His quizzical expression says it all—he doesn't get it. I stand up and pray for time to slow down, just for a few minutes. I can't believe it's about to happen. My whole life hasn't been enough to prepare me for this moment. God help me.

KYLE

Mia springs to her feet in a flash and, leaning her hand on my shoulder, starts to move to the back of the van. That brief touch of her fingertips is enough to set my whole body tingling again, and for a microsecond, I wish she'd never take her hand away. While she slips through the front seats and vanishes into the back, I try to make these wild thoughts of mine vanish too.

Okay, I need to get my brain back into my default Kyle-mode *right now,* so I focus on the road ahead. It doesn't work—that tingling feeling won't leave. I inhale deeply, hoping that breathing out will ease the sensation, but no luck.

A moment later, the ancient city of Granada emerges on the crest of a hill. It has an impressive stone palace in the Moorish style surrounded by a high wall and several towers. Beyond the walled city, the snowy mountain peaks rise like majestic guardians against a bloodstained sky. This place is incredible. I read something about the palace in the in-flight magazine. *Alhambra,* I think they call it. The pictures were nice, but seeing the real thing takes my breath away. It's like being transported to another time, another place, where friends don't die because of what you did and tragedies don't wreck your life without warning. My folks would love this place. Noah would have too.

And then I'm struck by something very odd—Mia has been quiet for longer than a minute.

"Hey, Mia, everything okay back there?"

No reply.

"You're missing the best part. This place is unbelievable."

She's still not answering, and it's starting to worry me. I can't imagine her passing up a chance to get a word in, so I check on her through the rearview mirror. She has her back to me, naked from the waist up. She's luring me like a magnet, and as much as I command my eyes to look away from the mirror, they just won't obey. She's cute, even cuter than I'd like to admit. I take my foot off the accelerator, even more than usual. She bends down and takes a T-shirt out of her suitcase. A car behind me honks. *All right, all right.* I look back at the road and speed up just a little. When I check the rearview mirror again her T-shirt is on—inside out, of course—and she's putting a cardigan over it. I'm so spellbound I don't even notice that she's turning to face me. *Shit.* I look away as fast as I can.

Jesus, what is wrong with me? Must be some short-term side effects of losing my shit back at the waterfall the other day, or something. Have to look it up online. Could be one of those conditions like Stockholm syndrome, except you start having strange feelings for the person who prevented you from taking your own life. No idea. Whatever it is, the moment she sits back down in the passenger seat, my cheeks are burning.

"You hot?" she says, so casually it kills me. "Want me to turn up the AC?"

"No, of course not. I don't want you to get cold. Seriously, you don't have to put that cardigan on for my sake."

"Oh no, it's not that. I like wearing it," she says while buttoning it up. "It makes me feel . . . I don't know . . . safe."

I cast a sidelong glance at her. Visibly worried, she is trying to hide the edges of her discolored T-shirt under the collar and sleeves of her cardigan.

We come to a stop in front of a traffic light.

"In three minutes, you will reach your destination," the GPS announces.

Mia's breathing is jagged; she's almost panting. She wipes her hands on her jeans and tries to take a deep breath. Pulling down the passenger mirror, she inspects herself, puts her hair up, lets it down, and then puts it back up again. In less than a second, she clears her throat, glances in the mirror again, scratches her head, and looks over at me without saying a word. I hold her gaze, her eyes alight with terror. She takes my hand and, turning my wrist, checks my watch.

"It might be a little late, huh?" she blurts out. "Yeah, it's kinda late. You can't just barge in on people at this hour uninvited, you know? Besides, she might be having dinner and—"

"Oh, c'mon, it's still daytime," I say in a soothing voice. "Plus, I read that people here have dinner real late."

"No, no, no," she says while picking up my cell phone from the dashboard. "It's been a long day, and I'm exhausted." She stabs at the phone. "Yeah, let's start bright and early tomorrow morning."

Suddenly, she looks drained. Her skin has a bluish tinge, and two dark circles have appeared under her eyes. She places my cell phone back onto the dashboard. She's typed in a new address.

"I booked us a place for tonight," she says. "All you gotta do is ask at reception."

Before I can say anything, she gets up and slips through the seats to the back. As the traffic light turns green, I press the gas pedal, looking at her in the mirror. Once again, her shoulders seem to be bearing more weight than she can stand. With visible effort, she opens the bed and lies down, her clothes still on.

There's a lump in my throat. I accelerate a little bit. All I ask is to get where we're going and, with a little luck, for her to let me stay by her side.

KYLE

When we finally get to the campgrounds and pull into the site they've assigned to us, Mia is fast asleep. It's getting dark and the first stars are emerging overhead. The spot they've given us is ample, protected by bushes and trees with lush green leaves and tiny white blossoms. Mia will love it. I turn to her.

"Mia," I whisper gently, but she's light-years away.

It's been hours since we last ate. When she wakes up she'll be starving, so I decide to grab something to eat from the campground restaurant. As soon as I open the car door, I hear the warble of hundreds of birds, blended with an orchestra of crickets, cicadas, music, and children laughing. The breeze is laden with a sweet and penetrating scent of orange trees in bloom. Makes me think of Grandma and her house in Florida. We used to visit her at this time of year, and her whole house smelled of orange blossom and cinnamon cookies, her specialty.

I find myself smiling at the thought of Mia waking up to this. Here I go, thinking of Mia *again*. I try to convince myself that it's that weird syndrome that gives you a one-track mind. Must be, because I've got only one thing on the brain right now, and that's Mia.

As I step out of our site, I walk along a gravel path. On each side, bushes and olive trees shield the tents—of all shapes and colors—and a few campers from prying eyes. With our fuchsia-and-lime-green van, nobody beats us for discretion. Some spots have families with kids, some have couples, while others have friends, shooting the breeze and cracking jokes.

I pass one neon-red tent with three guys chugging beers, listening to rock music and roaring with laughter. I slow down, and just like that, without warning, a rush of anger surges up into my jaws. I want to yell my head off, to start breaking shit, to stop that fucking music and wipe those stupid grins off their faces. Christ, doesn't anyone see through the bullshit? How can they even crack a smile knowing that life will always have the last laugh? Then I take a deep breath and picture Mia back in the restaurant, slumped in front of her slice of pie. I remember her peacefully asleep in the van, and my rage turns to shame. Shit, sometimes I think I'm going insane. But maybe it's me finally waking up from what was a lifelong insanity to begin with—the insanity of living as if nothing could ever change, of taking things for granted, when those things can crumble in the blink of an eye, pulling the rug out from under your feet.

I put my musings aside for the moment and, looking discreetly at the three friends, I mouth an apology. Then I pick up my pace. The last thing I want is for Mia to wake up and have another panic attack, or worse, think that I've up and left her.

The restaurant terrace, with its wooden tables and blue-checkered tablecloths, is packed. Luckily, inside it's empty, apart from a TV presenter droning on a channel no one's watching. An older woman with a yellow apron comes in from the terrace and walks over to me.

"¿Puedo ayudarle, joven?" she says with a broad smile.

"Oh, I'm sorry. I don't speak Spanish. Do you speak English?"

"A little."

"Great," I say, slowing down my speech. "I'm looking for a dish for a friend of mine who enjoys traditional food. Could you recommend something?"

She's frowning and biting her lower lip. I guess "a little" English was meant literally.

"Typical Spanish," I say, and raise an imaginary fork to my mouth. "Typical. Eat."

"Ah, típico, claro." The woman nods, her face aglow.

She gestures for me to follow her to the bar and points to what looks like a big, round yellow pie.

"Omelet. Potatoes. Good." She makes a sign as if to say that we're in for a treat. "Good. Good."

I nod and motion for her to give me two portions of that, plus two slices of a cheesecake I see in the dessert display. It's not a lemon pie, and probably not the best dessert the country has to offer, but at least it's a cake, which means that we can celebrate Mia's birthday in some small way.

While the woman prepares my order and places everything on a tray, I take a few pictures and send them to my mother. Five seconds later I receive a selfie of her and Dad, together with a kiss and a couple of red hearts. I smile to myself.

It's already dark when I get to the Moon Chaser, our flower-power camper van, carrying the loaded tray. Looking at it now, in the dim light, the fuchsia on this side is toned down and the flowers aren't so loud. Just when I start to think that maybe the van isn't as bad as all that, a flash from behind me lights up the whole vehicle. I spin around and see a couple taking pictures as if it were a tourist attraction. Then they smile and wave as if we were old friends and walk off. I chuckle to myself, surprised that I'm not pissed off by this little incident. Another symptom of my current syndrome, no doubt.

"Mia?" I approach the van's side door and wait a few seconds, but there's no sign of movement inside. I balance the tray on my good knee and manage to slide the door open. Mia hasn't budged; she's sleeping in the same fetal position she was in a half hour ago. I step into the narrow space between the bed and the front seats and set the tray down on the counter that doubles as a kitchen surface.

"Hey, Mia, brought you some dinner," I whisper. No response.

How can someone sleep so soundly? The breeze wafting in through the van door is fresher now, so I rummage through the cabinets looking for something to keep her warm. I carefully bundle her up in a couple of light blankets and brush away the hair that's fallen over her face.

For some strange reason, just looking at the elf girl relaxes me, lets me forget for a few moments that I'm the prick who killed Noah. Sitting here watching her sleep all night long would be creepy, though—syndrome or no syndrome—so I get up and slide the door closed from the inside, trying not to make noise, but end up stumbling over her open suitcase, which is sticking out from under the bed.

I lean down to nudge it out of the way and notice that the few clothes she's brought with her are all worn, threadbare. And it sure as shit isn't the type of clothing a girl like her would choose to wear. Next to her clothes there are three diaries, the leather kind, tied with a ribbon. I pick one up. The front cover says *Diary I. By Amelia Faith.* I untie the ribbon and open it to the first page. It's decorated with hearts and unicorns drawn with colored pens. At the top of the page it says *All the things I will ask you when we finally meet.*

Shit, what am I doing? I shut the diary with a flush of embarrassment and put it back where I found it, but as I do so I see a bundle of colored pens held together by a rubber band, and I get an idea. At first it strikes me as outrageous, even a little cruel, but it might be the only way to solve her wardrobe issues. It would also be a gift to make up for being a jerk to her.

I leave the suitcase open, just as I found it, and turn on the range-hood light. I remove the plastic covering from the lights, pick up her colored pens, and hold the tips up against the warm bulbs. Now all I have to do is wait.

MIA

There's a ray of sun frolicking on my closed eyelids, but I wait a moment before opening them. The dawning day is just too delicious for me not to savor every second of it, and that includes lazing in bed for a while. Today just might be the day I meet my mother. My goodness. I sit bolt upright, feeling more rested and refreshed than I have in months. And to mark the occasion, I rush over to look out the window and am greeted by a landscape that nearly puts me on my butt. This place is heaven. I roll down the window and breathe in the air. It smells of flowers, freshness, felicity, of all that's good in this world. Kyle has to see this.

"Kyle?"

He doesn't answer, and who can blame him? He must be exhausted. I get up and slide the bed back into its sofa position, flip my suitcase shut with my foot, and push it to one side. Last night I was so out of it that I just left it lying on the floor any old way. Kyle must think I'm scatterbrained. On the kitchen counter there's a paper plate with a slice of cake on it, and a second one with what looks (according to my guidebook) like an authentic

Haverstraw King's Daughters
Public Library

potato omelet. It's cold but smells irresistible. Kyle must have brought it last night. Maybe he was full and let me have the leftovers. Then it occurs to me: Could it be for me? Not just a leftover, but actually *for me*. Silly, I know, but my eyes get misty at the thought.

Taking a few steps back, I check the rooftop bed, but it's empty.

"Kyle?" I say again, leaning forward to check the driver's seat. No one there either.

Okay. I try to calm down, thinking that he's probably in the bathroom or has gone out to get some breakfast, but I can't avoid the sinking feeling in the pit of my stomach. What if he's *really* gone and has left me here alone? After all, I was the one who forced him to join me on this trip, against his will. I threatened and manipulated him so that he wouldn't be left to his own devices. Sure, my intentions were good, but maybe I pushed it a little too far. Maybe more than a little.

My heart is going full tilt now. *No, no, no.* I rush over to the back door and check the luggage compartment behind the sofa bed. His duffel bag isn't there. He's gone! I'm an idiot; what did I expect? In the end, everyone leaves. And it's not like we were friends or anything; we barely knew each other. This was supposed to be the best day of my life, and all of a sudden, I'm all alone, stranded in the middle of nowhere in a van I can't drive. I'm starting to pant.

All right, there's no time to whine. I need a plan *right now*. I slump down on the sofa and pick up my cell phone. I have a van and my list of potential mothers, so all I need now is to learn how to drive. Hey, millions of people do it every day; it can't be that hard. There must be an online tutorial for this kind of thing. While my cell phone boots up, I run through all the possible scenarios. One of them, the worst by far, would throw a monkey wrench into my whole operation: if the police catch me driving without a license, they'll identify me on the spot and ship me back to Alabama, straight to the hospital. Okay, need a plan B. It can't be that complicated. I just have to find someone willing to drive me around for a week, *for free*. And just when my heart is about to burst from anxiety, the handle of the van door starts to jiggle.

Great, all I need now is to get robbed. I jump up and grab the door handle, ready to give the intruder a piece of my mind, and yank the door open.

"Hey," Kyle says with a smile, oblivious to my paranoia. "Well, look who's up. It's about time."

I'm flustered for a moment, not knowing whether to have a hissy fit or weep for joy. His hair is wet and his duffel bag is slung over his shoulder. In one hand he's got two greasy paper bags that smell delicious, in the other he's holding two paper cups of something that smells like hot chocolate.

"Where *were* you?" I ask, sounding a tad more hysterical than I'd like. "Why did you take your bag with you? What were you doing?"

He raises one eyebrow, amused. I don't see what's so funny.

"Well, good morning to you, too, Miss Mia Faith. I took a shower is what," he says, as if I were missing the obvious. "And on my way back I got us something for breakfast." He raises both of his arms. "Hungry?"

"You took all your stuff with you? You expect me to believe that you took all your things just to take a shower?"

"What's eating *you*?"

I don't really know the answer myself, so I shake my head.

"You were out cold," he says. "I just didn't want to start pulling stuff out of my bag and making noise."

"Are you serious?"

"Is that so hard to believe?"

I don't answer that.

"So you weren't planning on taking off and leaving me here?"

His expression tells me that my question saddens him. Is he sad *for me*?

"Of course not," he says, with what I could almost swear is affection. "A deal's a deal, right?"

I feel like crying and laughing and screaming at the same time. Instead, I jump out of the van and wrap my arms around him. He laughs and raises his laden arms out to the side.

"Thank you," I say. "Thank you for staying. I know I've been a pain in the ass, but really, I was only trying to help."

"Hey, hey," he says with a chuckle. "You're spilling it."

I let go of him and see half a cup of hot chocolate dribbling down the sleeve of my one and only cardigan.

"Oops, I'm so sorry," he says, and the look in his eye tells me that he is.

"Don't worry," I say. "It's not your fault."

Kyle is here now, and that's all that matters to me. And I get the feeling that it doesn't matter to me only for fear of being left stranded. Just the thought that I might be getting used to his company makes me dizzy.

"I brought you these," he says, raising the greasy paper bags. "They call them churros. I've already tried a couple, and they're not to be missed."

"Churros. Right, my guidebook says they're made with a blend of flour and sugar, fried in vegetable oil. They're heavy, practically indigestible, super high in cholesterol and sugars and bad for the heart." He gives me a funny look, one corner of his mouth rising. "But I'm dying to try them, thanks."

Kyle gives a shrug. "Whatever you say." I take one of the paper bags and the half-spilled cup of hot chocolate and quickly head back into the van. He laughs, but doesn't move.

"Aren't you coming in? I'm famished," I say.

"Nah, it's getting late. Plus, today is Tuesday and it's the perfect time to visit your first maternal candidate, don't you think?"

I nod, my spirits so high they're floating on a cloud of all the prettiest colors.

"Same address as yesterday, right?" he asks, showing me his cell phone with a smile that makes my knees weak.

I nod again, still floating on cloud nine.

"Okay then, I'll let you get changed."

I'm still so cloud-ridden that I forget to answer him. Offering me another grin, he slides the van door shut. I quickly take off my cardigan and check the extent of the damage. The hot-chocolate stain has bled right through to my T-shirt.

Kyle climbs into the driver's seat and starts the engine. I

glance at him, and for some reason it no longer matters to me how I look when I show up at my mother's doorstep. After all, I've never heard of any mother withholding her love because of what her kid looks like or what she wears. I take a deep breath, letting my mind give shape to my wishful thoughts. I'll wear my blue T-shirt, the one with the faded rainbow on the front; worn inside out the rainbow is hardly visible.

I kneel, and when I open my suitcase, my heart does a triple backflip. This can't be happening. All my clothes are covered in colored ink. I feel a scream rising up from my very depths.

KYLE

Around five o'clock this morning, I was already wide awake. I sketched for a little while and then searched online for some decent clothing stores on our route. I know I went a little far by spilling the hot chocolate on her and making her think it was her fault, but I guess it's one of those times when the end justifies the means. And in my defense, before spilling the drink on her I took two laps of the campgrounds, blowing on it till I was sure it wouldn't scald her.

Before starting the engine, I angle the rearview mirror so that I can see her without turning my head when she's in the passenger seat. I drive to the exit of the campgrounds and, following the GPS, turn right. And just as I'm getting onto the highway that leads to the city's old quarter, I hear Mia shriek as if she'd seen Thanos in the flesh.

"Ahhh!"

Jesus, her voice is so shrill it makes my hair stand on end. For a second, I really do think that Thanos is in the back of our van. I don't dare look at her in the mirror. I knew the stunt I pulled with her clothes might upset her, but I didn't think the loss of a few tattered pants and T-shirts would send her off the deep end. Pangs of guilt already have my stomach in knots when Mia barges through the front seats and slumps down next to me.

"Look," she says, with more desperation in her voice than I've ever heard.

I give her my best it-wasn't-me glance and look back at the road. She pulls down on the hem of her T-shirt to show me the damage in all its glory—ink stains everywhere.

"Well," I try to joke, "at least this one's not inside out."

"I'm such a klutz," she says, glowering at the T-shirt.

"Don't say that."

"But it's true," she says with a groan. "I left my colored pens in the suitcase with my clothes, *all* my clothes. And now look." She looks straight ahead and frowns, lapsing into silence. Then she shakes her head. "I don't get it. I used those pens yesterday, and they were fine. And it's not as if the weather now is hot enough to make the ink run."

"Yeah, well," I say, making an enormous effort to cover my tracks, "that happened to me a couple of times. Maybe your suitcase was exposed to the sun or was too close to the engine; who knows? Might have something to do with global warming . . . you know, that kind of thing."

She looks at me as if I were not quite right in the head. And she has a point. *Global warming?* Seriously? My brain must be offline. The knot in my stomach still won't let up, and I just hope my clammy hands don't give me away. Mia reaches into her backpack and takes out a wallet with unicorns on it. She opens it while biting her lower lip. She's on edge. And here I was thinking I was going to surprise her so that she'd feel more at ease meeting her mother for the first time, and I'm already blowing it big-time.

We're getting into Granada's old quarter. No matter where I look, I see ancient stone buildings and white houses fronted by balconies. It's mind-blowing. Noah would have loved photographing all this stuff. Shit, the nausea is back, letting me know I have no right to feel this good. For a few minutes there I almost felt like the old Kyle, the Kyle who hadn't killed anyone, who hadn't ruined so many lives. But this is no time for wallowing in self-pity, so I look at Mia and see her counting her money with one hand and biting the nails of the other.

"Hey, c'mon," I say, trying to sound reassuring. "It's not that bad, could happen to anyone."

We're approaching the clothing store I picked out, but I don't say anything just yet.

"It's not *that bad*? So, what am I supposed to do now? I can't show up at my mom's place looking like this."

Bingo. Her timing couldn't be more perfect.

"Are you really gonna get your panties in a knot over *this*? All right, so your colored pens sprang a leak and your clothes look like modern art. Maybe it was a blessing in disguise, ever think of that? Like maybe it was time to change your wardrobe. We'll stop somewhere and get you some new threads. End of story."

I watch her in the mirror as she shakes her head and starts counting what little money she has for the third time. My GPS tells me to turn right in its jarring and bossy voice, but I go straight ahead, thrilled that I get to ignore its orders, just this once.

"What are you *doing*?" says Mia, abruptly raising her head. "The GPS said to turn right."

"Yeah, I'm not deaf, but I saw a couple of shops up ahead and—"

"No. Please, just keep driving."

I pretend not to hear her and pull up in front of a sleek, modern-looking shop nestled in a building that must be at least three hundred years old. The contrast is so stark it makes me want to grab my sketchbook and start drawing. Mia doesn't look so impressed. While I park the car in the only spot left on the entire street, she glares at me with her arms firmly crossed.

"Oh, c'mon," I say, trying to lighten things up. "You said yourself that you can't show up at your mother's place looking like that."

"I'll think of something."

"You'll think of something? If you're planning on borrowing my clothes, you've got another thing coming."

She starts to smile, then hunches her shoulders and starts to fidget. "I can't, okay?" she says softly. "I'm on a really tight budget here."

"Great," I say, a little too keenly. "That solves both of our problems."

She eyes me as if suddenly doubting my sanity. I pick my backpack up off the floor and, placing it between us, take out the credit card my dad gave me and show it to her.

"My dad, also known as Mr. Bear Hug"—this makes her smile—"gave me his credit card for this trip and asked me, no, wait, he *begged* me, to max out. If I don't buy something, he'll think I'm having a miserable time. He's capable of sending a team of shrinks out to find me. I'm dead serious." She's gone a little pale. I continue, "You wouldn't want him to call up the embassy and send out a search party, would you?" I'm not prone to exaggeration, but the situation calls for it. "Because he's perfectly capable of doing that." She shakes her head, her hazel eyes wide open, as if picturing something unspeakable. "Besides," I say, "you can consider it a belated birthday gift."

She studies me, mulling it over. For a second it looks like she's about to give in, but when she raises her chin I realize I couldn't be more wrong. "Thanks, but I can't accept that," she says with a haughty air.

"Of course you can."

Mia shakes her head and looks out the window.

"C'mon, don't be so high and mighty," I say.

She ignores me.

"Fine." I shrug. "Then don't come crying to me when I get you something you don't like." I shove the credit card into my pocket, grab a couple of churros (good thing I already ate a whole bag of them at seven o'clock this morning), and get out of the van.

I want her to follow me, but the only thing following me is her gaze. She doesn't realize it, but I can see her reflection in the shop window, and for some reason, I'm liking what I see more with each passing hour.

MIA

Leaning on Kyle's backpack, I watch him until he disappears into the shop. Is he really doing what he said he was going to do? If he has to use his dad's credit card, then why not buy something for himself instead? It doesn't make sense. And although it seems absurd, I get the feeling we didn't end up at this shop by accident. Kyle is a lousy liar, but I'm no straight arrow: I haven't even told him yet that Noah's the one who was supposed to join me on this trip. I prefer not to dwell on that. If I start obsessing over it I won't be able to stop, and knowing that in a few minutes from now I may come face to face with my mother already puts me over my daily recommended intake of excitement.

I have to distract myself, so I look at the clothes displayed in the shop window, and what I see brings a smile to my lips. They're pretty, beautiful, in fact, as if something or someone had arranged them there just for my benefit.

I straighten up in my seat and in doing so knock Kyle's

backpack over, spilling its contents all over the driver's seat. *Oops.* It's one of those backpacks with brown leather straps and lots of pockets.

I quickly start gathering up all his things: a pack of very unhealthy gum, a pair of sunglasses, a box full of pencils, two erasers, a pencil sharpener, a blue cap, a leather wallet, and a cell phone charger. On the floor next to the gas and brake pedals there's a book and a notepad.

I pick up the book. On its worn leather cover is a title in gilded letters: *The Complete Poetical Works of Rabindranath Tagore.* Running my fingers over the soft leather, I bring it up to my nose. It has that antique, intimate smell of a library. I open it. On its yellowed pages are several underlined verses. One of them catches my eye.

Do not keep to yourself the secret of your heart, my friend!

Say it to me, only to me, in secret.

You who smile so gently, softly whisper, my heart will hear it, not my ears.

It's as if the letters formed more than just words and the words more than mere phrases, as if something beyond language were speaking to me. I might have judged Kyle too harshly. I didn't think he was the type to read this kind of thing. I read the verse over again and find myself wishing that he would do exactly that—open up to me and share the secrets of his broken heart.

I turn to look at the shop, but there's no trace of Kyle. I slide the book into the backpack and pick up the notepad. It's one of those sketchbooks we used in third grade. It's fallen open to the last page he used, a drawing of an elven girl with her back turned. Wearing jeans, she's naked from the waist up, and her hair is up. I study the sketch closely and have the impression that it may be *me*. In fact, if it was not impossible to begin with, I would even swear that it was me. God, I shouldn't be doing this. My heart is starting to pound.

I look over at the shop window again, and even if this time the guilt is needling me, I can't help leafing through the sketchbook. The drawings are gorgeous; some of them are depressing, others upbeat and playful, but all of them are stunning. They convey something different, something that goes beyond the lines and shapes. The trees, the rocks, even the buildings seem to spring from a single soul. The gazes are full of profound longing, brimming with secrets that yearn to be told. I look once more at the drawing of the girl, and I long to be her.

My pulse suddenly quickens, as if sensing danger, perhaps the danger of falling for a side of Kyle that I'm just beginning to discover. But when I sense a shadow looming in front of the passenger window, startling me half to death, I realize it's not that kind of danger.

"Ahh!" I can't help letting out a hysterical shriek.

A woman in a navy-blue uniform is looking steadily at me from the sidewalk. Oh God, I hope the Spanish police don't punish indiscretions. I look at her, not able to hide my guilt, and when she motions for me to roll down the window, I do so without a murmur.

"Está en una zona regulada," she says.

"Sorry, but . . ." And then in my lousy Spanish I venture, "No hablo español." After an entire year of Spanish tutorials on YouTube, all I can manage is that I don't speak Spanish, adding "muchas gracias" and "de nada." Turns out it's not only my heart that has a genetic defect; it's my tongue too.

The woman points to a parking meter a few yards down the sidewalk and rubs her thumb and index finger together.

"Oh, right, sorry," I say with a sigh of relief. "My mistake, we didn't get a parking slip, is that it?"

The officer nods with a half smile and makes her way to the next car without taking her eyes off me. I swiftly slip the sketch-pad back into the backpack and shake out my hands as if that could remove evidence of my crime. Then I grab my wallet and step out of the van. The officer keeps her eye on me until I've inserted the coins into the parking meter. I feel a chill at the thought that it could be her.

While I wait for the meter to issue my ticket, I take a look at the other women on the bustling sidewalk. Any one of them could be my mother, walking right past me at this very instant. A thunderous pang in my chest lets me know I need to stop thinking. Dr. Bruner, the child psychologist at Hughston Memorial, used to say that thinking too much causes anxiety: a weak heart's mortal enemy. He told me that in these moments I should make my mind a blank canvas. I know he was right; it's just that my head is a swarming hive of colors at the best of times.

I write a note to Kyle on the parking slip, telling him I'll be back in a few minutes, and place it on the dashboard. Then, with my camera hanging from my shoulder, I plunge into the throng of people on the street.

For the very first time in my entire life, I am, and feel, utterly free, but for some weird reason it's not what I imagined it would be. Instead of happy, even ecstatic, I feel strange, out of sorts. A stifling sadness reminds me that I won't be able to enjoy this freedom for long, and for a moment I wish it could last. *No.* That wish is off limits. I've lived enough. More than enough. And once I meet my mother, all I want is to stop suffering, stop fighting. Being alive is exhausting. To snap out of my train of thought, I fill my mind with dazzling colors and focus on exploring the old quarter, taking snapshots of anything that grabs my attention— which is more or less everything—in order to post it later on, in my photoblog. I capture the narrow cobblestone streets, the traditional shops selling handmade leather wares and wicker baskets, several stone churches that are centuries old, the river that winds around the city, the pigeons fluttering to the rhythms of bread crumbs tossed by tourists, the rustic wooden doors, the steep inclines, and the whitewashed houses with balconies boasting colored flowerpots. As I breathe in the rich scent of the blossoms, finally I feel the pulse of my heart begin to ease.

The clock on the church bell tower tells me it's been half an hour already! My internal clock must be on the blink— I could swear only five minutes have gone by. Our parking slip must be about to expire, so I rush back through the maze of side streets.

When I finally get to the steep hill that leads down to the

street where our van is parked, I spot Kyle coming out of another store with both arms full of shopping bags.

Has he totally lost it?

I confess to feeling more curiosity than anger, so without dropping my frown, I make my way over as quickly as my lungs will allow.

KYLE

In the end I paid with my own credit card; good thing it was still in my jeans after buying dinner last night. My folks insist I should never keep a credit card loose in my pocket, but I just can't get used to carrying a wallet. And although it took me less than half an hour to burn through a whole year's savings from waiting tables at the Cheesecake Factory, I couldn't care less. You can't put a price on the joy it's bound to bring Mia. Plus, my parents would be extremely concerned about me buying clothes for a girl whose wealthy parents invited me on a trip in Spain. Had they known this would happen, the trip would have ended before it began.

The moment I step out of the shop, after spending ten minutes choosing a pair of sunglasses she might like, I see Mia rushing over like a whirlwind. I slip the wallet I bought her into the bag with the sunglasses and quickly toss the bag between the front seats. But before I have time to throw the other bags into the back of the van, she's at my side, scowling at me. In a hiss that verges on a screech, she says, "What did you do, clean out the entire boutique?"

I can't help laughing. She looks livid, but I think it's more from exhaustion than from rage: the gleam in her eye tells me she's not quite as pissed off as she wants to be.

"Sorry, I couldn't make up my mind," I say.

Her eyes dart from one bag to another as if she's counting them. "This isn't all for me, is it? Please, tell me it's not all for me."

"Hey, I can try these things on myself if you like, but I doubt they'd suit me."

"You're being silly."

"I don't think so. So anyway, do you wanna see what I got you or not?"

Her eyes are screaming *yes*, but her hard head will have none of it. She sticks out her chin and shakes her head ever so slightly, while stealing furtive glances at the bags.

I slide the side door open and put the bags inside, next to the sofa. "Okay," I say with a shrug. "If you really prefer to meet your mother looking like that . . . be my guest."

She looks down at her T-shirt as if she'd forgotten about the enormous ink stain splattered across the front. Crossing her arms in a vain attempt to hide it, she looks around sheepishly.

"C'mon," I say. "It's getting late. Just get in and at least try the stuff on. If something doesn't fit, or you don't like it, we can come back and exchange it this afternoon, after you've met your first maternal candidate."

"What part of *I can't accept this* did you not understand?" she says with a blend of frustration and feigned anger.

"What I don't understand is that you insist on rejecting my offer when you know you don't have a better option. Besides, it's not as if I'm buying you a villa." And with a light smirk, I add, "And may I remind you that you hired your wonderful driver for just ten days, so unless you want to stand here wasting precious time . . ."

She opens her mouth, at a loss for words. Huffing, she climbs into the van and, before sliding the door closed, says, "But I'm paying you *back*." And as the door shuts in my face I hear her holler, "Every last penny."

I burst out laughing. For some strange reason, this girl makes me laugh. But her elven spell is lifted as soon as I get back behind the wheel. Nausea and fear begin to claw at my insides again. They won't let me forget, as if I ever could. The worst part is knowing that this shit will haunt me forever. Every day I wake up from a nightmare, only to realize that the nightmare is as real as it gets and won't ever go away. What I wouldn't give to never have to drive again, never to set foot in a car again, never to wake up again.

But an "Oh my God, this is awesome" from Mia brings me back to the land of those who want to live to see another day.

I retype the address into my cell phone's GPS and select the longest route; that'll give her time to prepare. For a few minutes I hear her exclaim "ooh," "wow," "awesome," "I love it, I love it, I love it," not to mention a few more *oh my God*s. The more I listen to her, the more I smile and the more bearable my nagging nausea becomes.

"I cannot *believe* this," she says, slipping through the front seats. "Everything fits like a glove."

I'm as close to feeling good as I've been in a very long time. Then Mia slides into her seat, and as she starts to fasten her seat belt, a kid comes charging into the street out of nowhere, chasing a goddamn soccer ball. *Shit! I'm going to hit him!* He looks up at me, terrified. I reach my hand out to protect Mia as I slam on the brakes. That look of his, *Jesus,* it's all Noah. It all comes rushing back full tilt like a train off the rails, plowing straight into my chest. I scream inwardly, stomping on the brakes. The van comes to a screeching halt—just an inch away from the kid.

"Are you okay?" It's Mia, but her voice is distant, drowsy as if in a dream.

The kid waves an apology and takes off.

"Kyle?"

I turn to her, but I'm still not all there. She looks worried. I shake my head, then nod, not sure what I'm doing. Then I focus hard on her. She's beautiful. She's wearing the new T-shirt with the sunset on it, inside out, and the jean shorts. I realize I'm breathing heavily. I inhale deeply and blow out hard.

"Hey," I say, pretending I don't want to disappear off the face of the earth. "You can't sneak up on me like that. You dazzled me. You look stunning." *She does.*

"Yeah right," she says. "Sure you're okay? You can talk to me, you know."

"As soon as my heart recovers"—*from its urge to stop beating*—"from your dazzling new look, I'll feel better, I promise."

She shakes her head, a little disappointed. My legs are still shaking from the near miss, and my foot refuses to press the accelerator. But I pretend everything's fine and check the rear-view mirror. At least no one's behind me. I clear my throat. I feel Mia's eyes on me and can sense her shrugging her shoulders.

"Turn right in three hundred feet," the GPS announces.

"So, what's the deal?" she says. I look at her, and something in the warmth of her gaze gives my foot the courage it needs to step on the gas. "Do you moonlight as a personal shopper or what?"

I almost manage a smile. My racing pulse slowly subsides, though my desire to end it all is still hounding me. "My girl-friend, Judith . . . ," I begin, as I lean my foot on the pedal. "I mean my *ex-girlfriend* Judith. She was constantly threatening to dump me if I didn't go shopping with her." It takes me a moment to gather my thoughts as the van picks up speed. "And believe me, that girl liked to shop."

"Well, kudos to her. It's so nice when a guy's been properly prepped and trained."

"Prepped and trained?" I say as I slowly head into a curve. "What am I, a pet?"

"Well, pets and boyfriends have a lot in common, don't you think?"

"Tell me you're joking."

"Think about it. You can take both of them for a walk; both of them keep you company; they both like to be stroked, in dif-ferent areas if I'm not mistaken; both of them need to be trained so they'll behave, although it goes against their nature. The only real difference I see is that pets tend to be more faithful."

Any other girl would have made this sound like a put-on, but she looks dead serious about it, and this brings a smile to my lips. I don't think she realizes how funny she is.

"Sheesh," I say. "For the good of my sex, I hope not all girls think like you."

"Nah, *I* don't even think those things. Don't you sometimes get ideas in your head that are so *out there* that you just have to tell somebody, even if they make no sense?"

"No."

"Well, I do. Don't tell me you weren't impressed."

I was, but I don't say so, because at this moment my GPS is trying to kill me with all these narrow streets. I can't figure out where it wants me to turn, and I have no desire to get lost in this maze of ancient alleyways. When I finally get my bearings, I look at her through the mirror. She's petting her T-shirt as if it were a stuffed animal.

"I love it," she says. "I've always wanted something in this color." And I can see why; that T-shirt is made for her. "This blue reminds me of those clear nights, when the moon and the stars are so bright they even manage to keep the darkness at bay." She seems to be thinking aloud. "Those nights are the best, when fear doesn't even exist, when everything seems calm and at peace. Those are my favorite nights."

And I thought I was poetic. I have no words. And she seems to have lost them too. She gazes up at the sky with such intensity that it's obvious she sees much more than an average joe like me.

I let her bask in her vision, and once we turn onto a broader avenue, I ask her, "Hey, so tell me, what's the deal with you always wearing your clothes inside out?"

She answers with a mischievous grin, "As opposed to wearing them outside in?"

"Uh, yeah. Like everybody else."

"Well, there you go. Not interested in being like everybody else."

We come to a red light. I ease on the brakes and look at Mia, ready to give her a witty reply, but hold back, because although her body is still here, she seems to be somewhere else entirely. She's observing people in the streets with a wistful gaze. Some are strolling on the sidewalk, others coming in and out of shops, still others sitting leisurely at the cafés. She seems to look intently at each person, as if each of them means something to her, as if something in each of them is a cause for sadness. Her eye falls on two girls our age who are staring at their cell phones as they walk, oblivious to everything around them. Then a hipster catches her attention, with earphones on, looking straight ahead as he walks, as if no one else existed, as if he couldn't care less if they did. Then she looks across the street, at a couple seated at a café table. The woman is reading a menu while the man steals glances at the waitress. A few tables down is another couple, bored, exchanging no words, looking everywhere except at each other. For a moment it all looks like a movie to me, a movie in which everything that matters no longer does. I think I'm beginning to understand Mia, if only in my own small way.

I observe her. There's a profound sorrow in her eyes, the sorrow of an old soul. I sense that Mia feels things with more intensity than others do, that she feels the sadness of humanity as a whole, and that it pains her that she's powerless to help. But who's helping *her*?

KYLE

I've got just enough time to reply to a message from my folks before the light turns green, allowing my lips to speak again.

"Hey," I say. "It looks to me like there's one shopping bag left for you to open."

Narrowing her eyes, she glances around. Within seconds she spots the bag from the eyeglasses store between the seats, where I dropped it.

"What's this?" she says.

"Open it."

Mia gives me a sidelong glance, and slowly her lips curl into a ravishing smile. She runs her fingertips over the bag and unties the ribbon like a princess in a fairy tale. It's one of those stylish ones in navy blue with a silver ribbon. She peeks inside and takes out the red leather wallet without uttering a sound, though she doesn't have to say a word—her eyes tell me just how thrilled she is. After opening every single one of the pockets and compartments, she gives me a look of sheer gratitude. Then she reaches back into the shopping bag and pulls out the sunglasses case as if it were a diamond-studded Rolex. She parts her lips, ready to protest, but I beat her to it.

"Yeah, yeah, I know, you can't possibly accept it. But I've got two good reasons you can. One . . ." I put on my sunglasses, and as if I were reciting a romantic poem, I declare, "Every time the sunlight bounces off your big hazel eyes, it dazzles me while I'm trying to drive." This draws a giggle from her. Then, looking deeply concerned, I continue, "And two . . . if someone sees you with that Toys 'R' Us wallet of yours, I just might get arrested for abducting a minor."

She bursts out laughing. Then, raising an eyebrow, she says, "Looks like we're making progress. You're still driving like an old lady, but you're a smooth talker today, that's for sure."

"There you go. I'm not only a safe and cautious driver, but I'm also well spoken. A steal—two for one."

Mia puts on her new sunglasses and takes a peek in the mirror with a satisfied smile. They look huge on her.

"Shit, it seems my skills as a personal shopper don't apply to sunglasses." I put on my blinker. "We'd better go back to the store and exchange them."

"No way." She switches the blinker off. "I love them. I've never had a pair before."

"Ray-Bans? Really? Can't get more classic than that."

"No, dummy, *sunglasses*."

My stomach tightens. I'm an idiot. It didn't even occur to me that someone from our town might never have owned a pair of shades. I know it's stupid; it just never crossed my mind.

We fall silent for a moment, the only sound coming from the

GPS spouting directions. In the mirror I see Mia turn and stare at me in total silence. At least a minute goes by like this. Even my eyelashes start to sweat, I swear.

"What?" I blurt out, wishing she'd stop doing that.

"Does it bother you when I look at you?"

"Maybe. Don't tell me you're using that Jedi mind trick they taught you at the orphanage again."

"Oh, c'mon, everybody knows that orphanages don't exist in our country anymore. St. Jerome's was a group home, and no . . . as it happens I was just observing you."

"Wow." I feel my cheeks burning. "You really know how to make someone feel uncomfortable, I'll give you that."

She chuckles, then eyes me steadily and starts making all kinds of faces—crossing her eyes, sucking in her cheeks like a fish, knitting her eyebrows, then raising them. And then she comes up real close to me with her eyes wide open, and when she's so near I can smell the scent of her shampoo, she says, "You're a good guy, Kyle. I hope you know that."

This catches me off guard. I find myself shaking my head without meaning to.

"All right, you're a total jerk, if that's what you want to hear. It's your call." She laughs. "Now that I think about it, you're pretty good at that too."

"Thanks, pal."

"No, it's true," she says. "But it's also true that no one has ever done anything like this for me before."

"I bet," I say, without thinking.

But when she slumps back down in her seat and leans her head on the window, looking off into space, I realize I've put my foot in it again, *way in* this time. She wasn't just teasing me; she was serious, goddamn it, dead serious. I keep my mouth shut to keep my tears in check. God, how can someone reject a girl like Mia? Now I'm itching to meet her mother and tell her a few things she needs to hear.

Not even a minute has gone by when we head down a steep side street flanked by old houses. The GPS announces, "In three hundred feet you will have reached your destination."

I ease up on the gas until I see house number seventy-eight. Mia is studying every detail of the wine-red house. It's two stories, with windows and a door made of lustrous dark wood. Above the entrance is a coat of arms carved in stone. It looks like one of those properties that are passed on through generations, like in those cable series on the British aristocracy, but much smaller. Must be centuries old. I park the van a few yards away from the entrance. Mia's gone pale. She turns to me but doesn't say anything.

"Hey, I can come in with you if you want."

She shakes her head. I get it. Well, actually, I can't possibly understand what she's going through. But I guess it's one of those things that you have to face alone.

Mia opens the van door, clutching one of her diaries, and gets down. She shuts the door in complete silence and looks at me from the other side of the window. I nod with an encouraging smile. Staring at me, she takes a deep breath, and only after exhaling does she nod too. Then she turns toward the house.

I don't let her out of my sight. For a brief moment she stands still, looking at the house. She raises her shoulders, then lets them fall before taking a step forward and advancing slowly. She reminds me of a kid on her first day of grade school, but instead of clutching her mother's hand, she's gripping her diary. The moment Mia reaches the front door, she rings the bell. The door opens almost instantly, revealing a balding man, midforties, with a white shirt and jeans. They're talking, but I can't hear what they're saying. I lean over the passenger seat and roll down the window, but I still don't catch a word. The man nods and goes back into the house, leaving the door open.

I'd give anything to be beside Mia right now. God, even *I'm* sweating, and I'm just sitting here.

Mia turns to me, still clutching her diary. I give her a thumbs-up that makes her smile. A tall, slender woman with chestnut hair appears at the door. Mia says something to her. The woman smiles and shakes her head repeatedly. Mia nods and takes a step back. It looks like Mia says something to her before turning around and heading back my way. The woman lingers in the doorway, looking at Mia, and although I can't make her out distinctly, there's a note of sadness, of compassion, in the way she's standing there. Mia fixes her eyes on me as she approaches, shrugs her shoulders, and gives me a wistful smile, her fragility no longer hiding itself. I open the passenger door. She gets in and shuts it without looking back.

"Okay," I say. "One down. Which means we're one mother closer."

She nods, visibly grateful, but her emotions must be so keyed up that although her mouth is open, nothing comes out. She looks off into space.

"Next address?" I ask. "It's still early, and we have a lot of rounds to make."

Without uttering a word, she takes a notebook from her backpack and opens it to the first page, trying to force a smile. But her quivering chin tells me more than her dejected smile. She hands me a list of all the prospective mothers and their addresses. The second one lives in a place called Úbeda. I type in the address and start the engine. And although driving through these convoluted streets is a challenge in itself, even for the old me, I grab the wheel with one hand and take Mia's hand with the other. Still staring straight ahead, she lets a single tear roll down her cheek.

Her hand is warm, soft, brittle. It feels familiar, as if my hand and hers have already met. She's shaking. I run my thumb over the back of her hand, keeping my grip firm, unwavering. Then a voice inside me says, *I won't abandon you, Mia.* I say the words to her over and over again, without ever speaking them aloud. Then I drive for miles until she finally falls asleep.

MIA

We spend the next two days looking for my mother throughout the south of Spain. Kyle is being a true friend to me. There are moments when his pain returns, clouding his gaze, but he tries hard not to let on. Then there are times when he's calm and the real Kyle seems to come out, and I'm delighted by what I see. One thing hasn't changed—he still drives like an arthritic turtle.

When I get a free moment, I take the opportunity to bring my mother up to speed in my diary.

March 28

I keep looking for you but still haven't found you. This morning, after leaving Granada, I slept a while, and when I woke up we had already reached Úbeda. It's beyond wonderful, and I would have loved it if you happened to live there. It's such a picturesque little town, and we had fun too. A man answered the door, and when I asked after María, he said that he was María. He was transgender and had changed his name to Mario ten years ago. It was as if life itself was giving me a little wink, something to bring a smile to my lips and make my heart less heavy. He wound up inviting Kyle and me to lunch and told us his life story. It was fascinating. Remind me to tell you about it one day, okay? Our next stop is Baena, but I'll keep you posted (in person maybe?).

7:00 p.m.

Kyle is driving and we still have an hour to go, so I thought I'd dash off a few lines. After Úbeda, as I mentioned, we went to Baena. Wow, what a spectacular place. But I didn't find you there either. This particular María was a very kind lady, a schoolteacher. We didn't get to talk much, because she had to organize a children's festival for something they call Semana Santa, but I was happy to have met her.

Little by little I'm starting to feel more at ease, and Kyle has a lot to do with it; he's been supportive the whole way. Who would have thought? I really want you to meet him. You're going to fall in love with him. Well, not in love, but you know what I mean. He's adorable. He's been through a lot, but I touched on that a few days ago. I have to confess that I've had a few sleepless nights wondering how I'm going to tell Kyle what I've been hiding from him all along: that Noah was supposed to be on this trip with me. I just don't have the guts to come clean, not yet.

Anyway, how about we lighten things up a little? Now we're heading to a place called Nerja, which my guidebook says is worth the visit. We'll spend the night at some campground in the area. I'm dying to see the sea. It will be my first time, you know?

9:00 p.m.

We just had dinner on a restaurant terrace overlooking the Mediterranean. Kyle's in the bathroom, so I'm using the time to write to you. I know it's my third entry in one day, but it's all so exciting . . . Seeing the sea for the first time was . . . I don't even know how to describe it. There aren't enough words. The moment I saw it I was so blown away I started to cry. Poor Kyle kept asking me what was wrong and if there was anything he could do to help. Just seeing all that water in one place, the immensity of it, made me think of space, the universe, life, Venus.* The waves were crashing onto the sand with such force, almost a kind of fury. It's no wonder; if I were the sea I'd be more than pissed off at the human race too. I wish you'd been there to witness it with me.

One of the waiters was so sweet to us. He used a napkin to make a list of all the things worth visiting before we head back to the campsite tonight. I can't wait.

*By the way, rereading this entry I realize that I never told you why I have this thing for Venus, and come to think of it I haven't told anyone. It all started with a book I found in the library when I was living with the Yang family in Phenix City. It was called Alliance: Message from the Venusians to the People of the Earth. Have you read it? It's incredible, and it changed my life, literally. Did you know that on Venus there are no illnesses, no misery, no parents who aren't cut out to be parents . . . ? (Anyway, I'll finish this up another day. Kyle is back from the bathroom in the restaurant.)

11:00 p.m.

I didn't want to mention it, but my heart has been giving me problems in these days. For now, I'm just taking the pills they gave me for when it gets bad. I'm not supposed to take those for more than three days in a row, but I don't think that matters too much anymore. What does matter is finding you and getting to know you a little, before we part. Good night, Mom.

March 29

As soon as we got up this morning we set off to visit two more Marías, but neither of them was you.

Now Kyle is driving us to a place called Ronda. Is that where you are? I hope it is.

I can sense we're close. There are even moments when I think I can feel your heart beat next to mine. I can't believe that before long we might be reading these lines side by side, laughing and crying over the time we've lost. Will you enjoy what I've written? Will it interest you to read it? Will you want to know things about me? Sometimes I'm afraid I won't have enough time to find you; sometimes I'm afraid you might not even <u>want</u> me to find you after all, and it crushes me.

5:00 p.m.

Kyle is on the phone with his folks. They called him, so I'm taking a moment to bring you up to date. When we got to the house belonging to the last María on today's list, the one in Ronda, it was horrible. The woman had recently died. I almost flipped out thinking it might be you. Kyle was there for me again. He didn't stop asking around till he found someone who could tell us something about her. Fortunately, this María had never traveled to the US.

How fleeting life can be, right? Here one moment, gone the next. And how many people are totally unprepared to make the great leap. Do you feel prepared, Mom? I'd love to be able to talk to you, to listen to your stories, your opinions, to discover what you like, and what you could do without. Will you like _me_?

10:00 p.m.

Kyle is asleep, up on the rooftop bed. We decided to skip the campsite tonight and instead set up on a wonderful spot along the sea. I can stargaze from the window as I write to you. You might be watching the same stars at this very moment. And speaking of Kyle, do you know what? I think I'm growing dangerously "accustomed" to his company. I don't want to get too attached to him, or for him to become too attached to me. He has no idea about my problem. And I'm even starting to doubt whether I'm doing the right thing. He has a right to know, but I can't bring myself to tell him. I don't want him to leave, and they all leave once they find out. Maybe that's why you left too.

Anyway, my heart is begging me to give it a rest, so I'll sign off now. I'll be sleeping under the stars, looking up at Venus, and thinking of you.

We'll be up bright and early for our trip to Córdoba. I saw some pictures of it in my guide, and I can't wait to see the real thing. Above all, I can't wait to see you. Sweet dreams, Mom. See you tomorrow?

KYLE

This morning I set my alarm for six o'clock just so I could capture on paper this spot we spent the night in. It's called Maro, and it left me in awe. It's an extraordinary place, untamed, with a beach of fine sand mingled with rocks and vegetation. As I was sketching, the sky was suffused with the most vivid colors I've ever seen at dawn. It almost looked unreal. Mia got up late, around nine, and the moment she stepped out of the van she ran over to the shore and dipped her toes in the water. Without her seeing me, I managed to sketch her as she played in the waves like a little girl. It was awesome. As time goes by she seems much more relaxed, a little tired maybe—that could be the search for her mother taking its toll—but more at ease.

We had breakfast, sitting on a couple of rocks, and after she persuaded me to write our names in the sand with sticks, we got onto the highway in the direction of Córdoba.

The next maternal candidate lives at the heart of an area called the Judería. Apparently, it was a Jewish quarter during the Middle Ages. It's in the old town and is pedestrianized, which means we had to leave Moon Chaser parked outside the city walls and continue on foot. Mia insisted I didn't need to go with her and that I should do a little sightseeing instead, visit a museum or something, but she's wrong if she thinks I'll let her go it alone at a time like this.

"This is it," she says, pointing to a cobblestone street so narrow it won't fit more than two people at a time. Over the white-painted facades and narrow iron balconies hang scores of indigo flowerpots, all identical. Mia takes a deep breath. She's nervous.

"Call me if you need anything, okay?" I say. "I'll wait right here."

She gives me a grateful nod and starts walking. Without losing sight of her, I sit down on the edge of an octagonal stone fountain, the enviable witness to a few centuries of history and hordes of tourists that never cease. Mia comes to a stop in front of a house. Its door is arched and bordered by small mosaic tiles. She rings the bell and waits. This whole place is magical, as if lifted from the pages of a book, but with elven Mia in it, that magic takes on new proportions. I just *have to* sketch the scene.

Without taking my eyes off her, I grab my sketchbook and pencils from my backpack. A woman with long curly hair opens the door to the house. I start drawing Mia in broad strokes. They're talking. I sketch Mia's silhouette, fun-size and foxy, her hair up in a ponytail; I widen her already gaping honey-colored eyes and take the liberty of adding elven ears and an elven crown. And just when I start feeling slightly guilty for committing her to paper without her permission, the ring of my cell phone makes my heart hit the roof. A quick check of the screen shows me it's Josh. Shit, he doesn't even know I'm in Spain. My heart is thrumming against my rib cage. I want to answer the phone but can't, not until I know whether Mia needs me. With each ring I feel more guilty, more rotten, and yet I don't have the guts to send him to voice mail. I send him a photo instead: I couldn't even begin to explain the situation to him otherwise.

I zoom in on Mia with my cell phone camera, and just as I shoot the picture, she turns to me. *Oops.* I bring the phone down to my side and wave, looking like an idiot for good measure. She says goodbye to the woman and heads back in my direction. I send the photo to Josh as fast as humanly possible and write, *In Spain. Will explain.* Mia approaches.

I need an excuse; there's no way I'm letting her think I was taking snapshots of her behind her back (even though I took a bunch of her yesterday on her first encounter with the sea). What she needs right now is a good friend, not a creep.

Asking her to pose would be the sensible thing to do, but I'd feel awkward somehow, plus I don't want her to get the wrong idea. At night, while she's asleep, I use the photos of her as a model to draw from. For some strange reason I feel better as soon as my pencil hits the paper, as if I were stepping into a parallel dimension where I never killed my best friend and where Josh can still walk. I can't and won't stop drawing her.

"No luck?" I ask as she approaches.

She shakes her head, obviously disappointed. "The woman hardly speaks English, and from what I understood, she's never been outside Europe."

I show her the snapshot I took of her and, putting on a

blameless face, say, "Sent this to my folks. They asked me for some pics, and this street is just amazing, isn't it?"

God, I'm a lousy liar.

"Oh," she says, slightly put off. "And here I thought you wanted to immortalize me in one of your drawings and needed the picture as a model."

Gulp. Oh, shit.

"What?" she says with a sly look. "You didn't think I noticed?"

Oh crap.

I must be making a stupid face because she giggles and says, "You really don't think I see you?"

The blood is rushing to my head. And now she's going to tell me she knows I secretly draw pictures of her and that I'm a weirdo for doing it.

"With your *sketchbook* . . . in bed. I know that instead of sleeping, you spend hours drawing every night."

"Oh," I say, forgetting to conceal my relief. "You mean *that*."

Now it's her turn to look confused. "What did you think I meant?"

"Never mind . . . ," I say, praying my face doesn't reflect how dumb I feel.

Looking baffled, she shrugs. Then, pointing to my sketchbook, she says, "Mind if I have a look?"

No way. "Some other time, maybe," I say, trying to stay composed. "Right now, there are more interesting sights to see. Besides, we have to think about where we're going to eat."

"You're acting strange this morning." She raises an eyebrow.

"Something up? Maybe you're on the man rag. I read it in *Cosmo*. Irritable male syndrome, I think they call it, and you guys get it once a month because of low testosterone or something. I didn't catch all the details. I didn't think I was going to suffer the consequences so soon."

"Ha ha, my testosterone levels are fine, thank you very much. I just get like this when I'm hungry."

She seems to buy it and says, "All right, then, let's deal with that first. According to my guide, we're not far from a tapas bar where they make the best sandwiches in the city." She takes out the booklet they gave us at the tourist office and, pointing to our left, adds, "I think it's this way."

I follow her lead as we join a flock of tourists through the narrow, serpentine streets of the Jewish quarter. Nothing we see is wasted on us. Mia takes snapshots of everything as if she were wandering through a dream. I take mental pictures of her so that I can draw her later on. We pass houses with arched doors and windows, stone fountains of all shapes and sizes, handicraft shops, restaurants, and even small art exhibitions hidden away on the patios of some houses. As we walk, I run my hand along a wall, envious of the centuries of history these stones must have witnessed.

The narrow street we're on opens onto a rectangular square of whitewashed houses. In one corner is a restaurant with a terrace; in another a guy with a ponytail is standing in front of an easel, drawing. While Mia takes a photographic tour of the whole square, I walk over to the artist. He's doing portraits of tourists but also has some incredibly good drawings of the city and of other places I'm not familiar with. On the ground beside him is a set of paints in a case that's covered with stickers of flags and names of places.

"Isn't it amazing?" Mia says as she sidles up to me.

I turn to her without knowing what she's referring to.

"Living like *that*," she says, pointing at the stickers. "I'm sure he traveled to all those places just with the money he made from his artwork." I raise an eyebrow, but she doesn't notice, and then, as if it were the most sensational idea on earth, she says, "Have *you* ever thought of doing that?"

I laugh as if, besides being the most sensational idea in the world, it's also the dumbest. From her sudden glare I take it she doesn't agree.

"Come *on*," I protest. "You can't be serious."

"I don't get what's so funny. You like drawing, and unless you're faking it, you like traveling too."

"Yeah, but that doesn't make me a globe-trotting hobo."

She eyes me for a moment without concealing her disappointment, and then, while taking a photo of the artist as if he were the coolest thing since sliced bread, she asks, "So, what does the good Mr. Kyle plan on doing with his life?"

I chuckle and shake my head. "Mr. Kyle was accepted at Auburn University. He will study architecture and go on to lead a normal life, with normal people, in a normal place."

"*Architecture?*" She says it as if I were studying to become an executioner.

"Is that so strange?"

"Well, if architecture was really your thing, I imagine you'd be walking around admiring buildings and structures and, you know, *talking* about that kind of thing. If you were really passionate about it, I would have noticed."

"I'm not passionate about it, but it's a good profession, and it'll pay the bills. Besides, it worked out well for my dad."

She laughs. "Pay the *bills*? Do you hear yourself? You sound like my last foster dad, a real old-school type—sad, responsible, and bored to death."

"No," I reply. "What I *sound* like is a sensible person who plans on buying a house before he turns thirty."

"I don't get it, Kyle," she says, suddenly looking dejected. "You like to draw."

"Yeah, but that's just a hobby. It doesn't put food on the table."

"Apparently it does." She gestures toward the young artist, and I can see from the look in her eyes that she's dead serious.

"Well, you know what I mean."

She shakes her head. "What *do* you mean, Kyle? Do you mean that you could live the same empty shell of a life as everyone else? Do you mean that you would prefer to spend years and years studying at college, wasting thousands of hours glued to a computer screen only to spend thousands more working at a mind-numbing job and missing out on all of this?" She opens both arms wide. "Missing out on *life*? You know, enjoying life isn't only something you do on vacation or on weekends." Now she *has* left me speechless. And she's not finished. "We're all deranged. Don't you see that?" There's an odd intensity in her voice as she says this, one that lights up her eyes. "Are you going to be like all of those people who spend their lives *waiting*? Waiting to finish high school so that they can go to college, waiting to finish college so that they can start a career and get married, buy a house; waiting to have kids, waiting to finish paying the mortgage; only to find out that while they were waiting their dreams passed them right by and their whole life slipped through their fingers?"

She says this all in one go, almost without breathing. I don't know whether to laugh or cry. "Wow, that was the most intense and depressing thing I've heard in a long, long time."

"And the most honest, Kyle," she says, more disheartened than disappointed. "It's too bad that you're just as asleep as the rest of them."

These last words are like getting doused with a bucket of ice water. She starts walking, but I don't budge. I look at the young artist and try to imagine myself in his shoes. I try to picture that kind of freedom, the freedom to spend however much time I want just drawing, the freedom from work hours, from things tying me down, from being chained to a computer, and just like that, something inside me detonates, something that says *yes, yes, yes*, and I feel happy, actually happy, with no stress, no pressure, no competition, no demands. God, this girl is wreaking havoc on me. My life before Mia suddenly seems hollow, bland, meaningless— a mistake.

MIA

I had trouble getting up this morning. The pressure on my chest was so intense I had to take two pills at once, and even then, they were slow in taking effect. A whole hour passed before I was able to breathe normally and leave the van. I guess that explains why I'm feeling so touchy; these pills always leave me drained and a little depressed. I'd give anything to be able to rewind and take back all the things I said to Kyle. I shouldn't have brought up such delicate subjects, not yet.

I suppose that being born with a looming expiration date makes me see things from a different perspective, and no matter how hard I try, it's still difficult to understand other people's points of view. I admit that when I care for someone I can get a little vocal, but I would like so much to be able to help. Noah used to call me the alien, but he also told me that he appreciated my quirks. It was thanks to him that I started *Expiration Date*, my photoblog. He once read that people are much more willing to make a change when they are—or think they are—the ones to come to a realization, rather than having that realization thrust upon them. He told me that my photographs were like bread crumbs left along a trail, helping others find their way back to their own heart. I think it was the most beautiful thing anyone has said to me, ever. Today, I miss him like crazy; he would have loved to see this place.

So here I am, wandering around this square, trying to get to grips with my guidebook. The tapas bar is supposed to be on a street right off the square, but for some reason I don't see any street signs anywhere. Till now I've just relied on how the streets look on the map. I search for someone who might be able to help me, but all I see are tourists who seem as lost as I am. Kyle is walking over from the other end of the square when a sales clerk comes out of a handicraft shop carrying wicker baskets.

"Excuse me," I say, showing her the name on the map. "I'm looking for this street."

"Careful, it might bite you," she says, wiggling her eyebrows.

Okay, I don't get it. But then she points to the small square tile up on the wall of the house in front of us. No way. It's the street I was looking for. Here, they write the street names on tiles. Sweet. I'll have to tell Kyle about this.

"Muchas gracias," I say.

The woman smiles and is turning to another customer when a marvelous odor makes me wheel around. Oh my God, the restaurant opposite is serving a dish of paella, the authentic kind, to one of its outdoor tables. It's exactly like the photo in my guidebook. The rice is colored a yellowish orange and served in a low, spacious frying pan, mixed with strips of bell peppers, shrimp, mussels, and lots of other things I've never tried before. When I finally manage to drag my eyes away from the dish, I realize that Kyle is standing next to me, studying me in silence.

Trying to convince myself that the world won't come to an end if I don't try that paella this instant, I say, "So I think I've found the tapas bar; it's down this street. What kind of sandwich would you like?"

"Are you serious?" he says, his brow furrowing in protest. "Tell me you're not keeping me on a steady diet of sandwiches for the whole week. One more of those and I'm going to lose it."

What? In organizing this trip, I didn't think for a second there would be an antisandwich rebellion by any of the members of our party. And before I can think of what to say, Kyle makes his way over to the restaurant opposite and sits down at one of the free tables.

"Let's have a nice lunch." He flashes an enticing smile. "My treat."

I want to say yes, but my head keeps telling me it's too much and that I can't accept it.

"C'mon," he says, pleading with me. "Do it for my folks."

But in that instant, something in his gaze tells me this is not about his folks, or about the credit card, or about him. . . . He's doing this *for me, just for me.*

"All right." I take a seat at the table to stop from falling over. "But for the record, I'm accepting only for the sake of your parents."

"Deal."

I stare at Kyle intensely, hoping that my smile conveys the

sheer gratitude I can't put into words. But I seem to fail big-time, because instead of smiling, he blushes and averts his eyes, turning solemn.

"Anyway," he says, regaining some of his confidence. "Getting back to our earlier conversation, you still haven't told me what you plan to do with *your* life."

Since he brought it up, I say, "Kyle, about that. I'm sorry for being so—"

"Intense?"

"Yeah, I guess. I know I talk too much sometimes. My former foster sister Bailey used to say so all the time."

"What are you talking about? In less than a minute you cleared up more things than my school counselor managed to do in a year. I should be paying *you*."

"Are you serious?"

"Totally. I can't promise I'll turn into a drifter overnight or travel the world collecting stickers of the places I visit, but yes, what you said hit home."

I smile on the inside, on the outside, and everywhere at once.

"But," he says, "don't change the subject. You still haven't told me what your plans are after you graduate."

I don't want to lie to him, so I stretch my arms out to the side and say, "To fly, fly to the stars."

"Okay," he says with a chuckle. "Anything more concrete? From what I hear, astronauts have to spend quite a few hours in front of a computer screen before taking off."

I burst out laughing. "Right, so maybe I could be a tourist guide; what do you think? Or an investigator of missing mothers, which of course will depend on the success of this first mission. As you may know, a bad report can sink a career."

He laughs. I love to watch him laugh. His whole face seems made to smile—it's like all his features fall into place when he does. A waiter with a mustache and a friendly air approaches us with a wicker basket of bread that looks crunchy and delicious. As he hands us the menus, I hand mine straight back and say, "I already know what I want, thank you."

The waiter nods and looks at me expectantly. Kyle looks at me too. Discreetly, I point to the table nearby and whisper, "The paella and the red cream that those people are having."

"Excellent choice," the waiter whispers back with a wink. "Paella and salmorejo for the lady. The paella is for two people minimum, I'm afraid."

"No problem," Kyle says, handing back his menu. "I'll have the same."

The waiter, with an elegance I've seen only on television, lowers his chin to one side while gently closing his eyes, then glides away.

"Thank you," I say to Kyle without disguising my emotion. "I've always wanted to try paella."

What I really want to say is that I've always wanted to feel this way in somebody's company, but it's just that I didn't know it, or didn't want to know it, or deep down suspected it would always be something extremely dangerous, and, in my case, would cause untold suffering.

KYLE

While we wait for the paella, we plan our itinerary for the next two days. This afternoon we'll be heading to a place called Sevilla, so for today there are no more potential mothers to visit. Mia is busy with the bread and the olives they brought us as an appetizer.

The sun is beating down hard today, and even under the awning the heat is becoming unbearable. I take off my hoodie, and as I toss it onto the chair next to me, I catch Mia inspecting my arm. It takes me a moment to realize she's looking at my freaking scar. I pull my sleeve down in a useless attempt to cover it up. No luck, the scar has her spellbound. She reaches over as if she wants to touch it. I feel like a block of steel, unable to move. The instant she grazes my scar with her fingers, my body is jolted by a kind of electric charge.

"Don't," I say, tearing my arm away.

Mia braces herself as if I were about to hit her, her eyes going wide.

"No, no, no. Look, I'm sorry," I say. "It was a reflex. I didn't mean to scare you."

She shakes her head and lowers her chin, her breath still coming fast. "No, Kyle, *I'm* sorry, I shouldn't have . . ."

The waiter arrives with our drinks, forcing us into a moment of silence. When he leaves, Mia looks again at the scar, then up at me, and asks in a hushed voice, "Does it hurt?"

I want to say no and change the subject, but my head beats me to it and nods. Trying to keep my turmoil in check, I say, "Some scars never heal, they say."

"Yeah, but they also say that pain eases with time. And I can tell you from experience that it's true."

From experience? Is she so blind she can't see that her experience and mine are polar opposites? She was hurt by someone, and that's something she might be able to put behind her. I caused someone's death, and that will be seared into my guts forever.

"Is that why you were at the waterfall the other day?" Her question hits a nerve.

I shrug and sigh, trying not to let my irritation show, hoping she changes the subject, but she doesn't.

"Noah would not have wanted you to do that. He loved you very much."

Her words set off a depth charge, roaring in my ears till I can't hear a goddamn thing.

"What are you *talking* about? What the fuck are you talking about, Mia?" I ask her, more fiercely than I mean to.

She bites her lip, nervous, and blurts out, "I'm sorry; I know I should have told you this at the start, but I was afraid that if you knew, you wouldn't have come, and it's not like you were dying to come in the first place, you know? And—"

"Wait, hold it. You *knew* Noah? Is that what you're trying to tell me?"

She gives a tiny nod. "Remember at the waterfall I told you that a friend was going to join me on the trip, but something came up?"

I nod in turn, afraid of what she's about to say.

"That friend was Noah."

For a moment I'm at a loss for words. This is surreal. It can't be happening. "He never mentioned anything about a trip to Spain."

"I know. I made him swear to keep it under wraps. I didn't want anyone finding out. And by now you know how persuasive I can be."

I don't get it. Noah was my best friend; he would have told me. I suddenly feel betrayed. I know it sounds ridiculous, but I feel like I got played, as if it was all a lie, as if Noah had been leading a double life behind my back, and with Mia of all people. I even feel a trace of jealousy. Christ, I think I'm heading for a straitjacket.

"We met in a photography class a couple of years ago," she says, oblivious to the struggle within me. "And we hit it off instantly. As you know, he was very reserved, didn't like to talk, but from the little he did say, it was clear that he loved you like a brother."

That hurts me more than a knife through the gut. I betrayed

him. I took his life. I face Mia squarely, unable to speak, to see straight, to hear anything but my own pulse pounding in my ears, and that's when I remember.

"*Amy?* You're Amy the Alien, the friend we never got to meet because she was never allowed out of her house?"

She nods and shrugs.

"Amy?" I frown this time.

"Well, sometimes I'm Amy, sometimes Mia, other times Amelia or Lia or Mel, or even Mila. I feel different depending on whom I'm talking to. We shouldn't identify with a single name anyway, don't you agree?"

I register her words, but my brain can't seem to process them. "In other words," I say, looking around at everything I stole from him, "it's Noah that should be here, right now, with you."

"Yes." And as if she were reading my mind adds, "But he would have been delighted that you joined me. He wouldn't have wanted me to go alone. I hadn't told him anything about my mother; I thought it was better to wait until we were here together, but . . ."

Then she launches into a drawn-out explanation, but I tune her out. As her lips move I realize that not only did I kill my best friend: I robbed him of this trip with Mia, and for all I know he liked her as much as I do. So why the fuck didn't he say anything? Why didn't he tell me about this trip? And why didn't he want me to get to know Mia?

She's gone silent. In her expression there's the same concern and powerlessness that I see in my folks, in Judith, and in everyone else for that matter. For God's sake, not her too. There's a lump in my throat that's suffocating me, and I don't know whether to fly off the handle, apologize, or break down.

"Excuse me, I have to . . ."

Unable to finish the sentence, I get up and head into the restaurant.

I walk straight through the dining area with my eyes fixed on the bathrooms at the far end, without even noticing if there are people seated at the tables. I enter, shut the door behind me, and start pounding the walls with my fists until my fingers go numb. *Shit. Shit. Holy shit.* Leaning on the sink, I glare at my reflection in the mirror. It disgusts me so much that I lower my gaze. No, I can't do this to Mia. For once in my fucking life I'm going to do right by someone. Looking in the mirror again, I almost feel sorry for myself. I shut my eyes, take a deep breath, and walk back out.

Mia's sitting sideways, fidgeting. She looks worried, or scared, or maybe both. I hate that she hid this bombshell from me, but it pains me to see her like that. And it pains me even more that I'm the cause of it. As I walk over to our table she looks up at me pleadingly. "I'm sorry, Kyle. I know I should have told you before, but please don't be mad, don't be mad at me."

I feel like wrapping my arms around her to calm her down. "Are you kidding? Of course, I'm not mad, Mia. Not at you."

An awkward silence passes between us. She gives me a pensive look, as if she is still grappling with the issue, looking for a way to help me. She's about to speak, but I cut in. "You know, you still haven't told me how you came up with your hit list of . . . *maternal candidates,*" I say, doing an impression of her.

Granting me a wistful smile, she shrugs. "Well, if you really want to know, I guess I've always wondered who my mother was, what she was like, and above all, *why* . . . you know, why she did what she did. For years I tried to get information, but they always told me the adoption papers were confidential, or that I would have to wait till I turned nineteen to request them. So a couple of years ago my foster sister, Bailey, introduced me to her new boyfriend. She said he was a hacker and might be able to help."

Mia takes out a piece of paper from her backpack and puts it on the table.

"This is what he found," she says, pointing to what appears to be an official document. "These are my adoption papers." Mia indicates a line that reads *María A. Astilleros.* "It says here that she was from Spain. Bailey's boyfriend discovered that she was an exchange student at the University of Alabama. I wanted him to keep investigating, to hack into the college server and find out more details, but he was caught in some operation or other, and . . . after spending three months in jail he decided to dedicate himself to safer pursuits—forging IDs."

I chuckle. "Yeah, a lot safer."

Mia shrugs with a hint of a smile.

A guitarist with long sideburns, dressed all in black, and a woman wearing a polka-dotted dress come to a stop in front of the restaurant. They remind me of those flamenco gitanos I read about in the in-flight magazine.

"At which point," I say to Mia, "you tracked down every woman in Spain with that name."

Mia nods and says, "Not only in Spain, in the States, too.

Luckily, her last name isn't very common. That, and the fact that Spanish women never lose their maiden names."

"So why didn't you call them? That would have been much simpler than coming all the way here."

She pauses before answering. Biting her lip, she looks at the ground, and as she raises her head again, she says in slow, measured tones, "Because if it turns out that she doesn't want anything to do with me, at least I'll be able to look her straight in the eye and ask her why . . . why she didn't love me." Her eyes have the glow of someone demanding justice. "If I'm right there in front of her she'll have to answer, and if she doesn't . . . Well, the answer will be written all over her face; you can bet on that."

She's managed to give me goose bumps. As the man starts playing his guitar and the woman starts to sing, Mia's gaze turns to them, though her mind is elsewhere, perhaps adrift, returning to that somber, secret island of hers. The song's plaintive melody is the perfect soundtrack to this moment.

MIA

I just took the last bite of the second-best dessert I've ever tasted, after the lemon pie, of course. They call it gachas cordobesas, and it's a cream that tastes of lemon, cinnamon, and aniseed, sprinkled with small chunks of fried bread. It's to die for. Kyle ordered a custard dish. I don't think I've ever eaten this much. I even had to unbutton my fabulous new white pants to avoid bursting the seams.

Kyle spent the entire meal listening to me talk, grinning every time I thanked him for the delicious meal and, above all, trying his hardest to look in good spirits. But his eyes don't know how to lie—he's in bad shape. It's no wonder; talking about Noah must not have been easy for him, but I had to try, and more importantly, I had to tell him about the trip. Still, there were some moments, however brief, when it seemed to me that his smile was real.

I'm itching to get on the road to our next destination, and besides, the town square is getting more crowded by the minute, and I miss the quiet of the van, so I take Kyle's wrist and turn it over to check the time on his classy watch. But before I even get the chance to look, something odd happens the moment I touch him. The warmth of his skin sets off a current that crackles up my whole arm, and I feel as if I were riding a roller coaster. I look at him, startled, and see the same amusement-park expression in his eyes. *Oh boy,* this was not part of the plan. I look away, as if I hadn't felt anything remotely electric and say, "I think we should go. If we leave now, and knowing how slow you drive, we'll get there just in time to miss dinner."

Kyle gives me a mock smile and shakes his head as if to say, *Not funny.* Then, raising a hand to ask for the bill, he starts to wave down one waiter after another, but the place is so full that they seem more intent on welcoming new customers than charging old ones.

"I'll settle the bill inside," he says, getting up. "If we wait any longer, and considering how much you talk, your poor driver won't make it by supper in one piece."

Ingenious. As he turns around and heads into the restaurant, I catch myself checking out his ass, but not just in a "cute ass" kind of way, but really lingering over it. And once I manage to tear my eyes away from that portion, it's only to move on to his back, then to his neck, to every nook and cranny, every twitching muscle. I can even detect his scent, the warmth he exudes, the texture of his bronze skin, and just like that, out of the blue, I want to wrap my arms around him. My breathing quickens so abruptly I think I'm going to pass out. For Chrissake, what am I *doing*? This isn't me. Mia Faith does not fall for a perky butt, or a back, or any other part of the anatomy, no matter whom it belongs to, period. End of story.

I obviously need to distract myself, so I spring to my feet, knocking my chair over with a huge clatter in the process. Great, now I've managed to attract every single person's attention, no kidding, every single one, with no exception. I'm flushed with embarrassment, as if everybody noticed my little episode of "posterior hypnosis." I'm not sticking around here a second longer, so I grab my backpack and start walking as fast as I can.

As I cross the square, I take out my camera and wedge my eye into the viewfinder. I can't think of a better way to stop my gaze from wandering to highly treacherous places. But while I'm walking, I can't stop thinking about his neck, his back, and everything south of that. I feel a tingle starting from below my belly button, rising up through my breasts, and reaching the top of my head. Must be the butterflies they talk about in books. *Oh boy.*

Suddenly I realize I'm still walking around with one eye glued to the camera, not having taken a single picture or even focused the lens. I must look like a total dimwit. I clear my throat, trying to look halfway normal, and start firing off snapshots at everything I see: the street, the tiles, anything that comes my way. I notice a stone on the ground, one darker than the rest. I take a picture of it for my photoblog, and just as I'm thinking of titling it "the ugly duckling of Córdoba," I raise the camera and through the lens I see a woman with dark, wrinkled skin; black hair tied up in a bun; and long gemstone earrings. She's eyeing me steadily. I put the camera away in a flash.

The woman gives me a sprig of something that looks like the rosemary my former foster mother used to grow in her orchard. I smile, thinking that this gesture must be an example of the friendly Spanish character mentioned so often in my guide.

"Thank you," I say, smelling the herb.

"Son cinco euros bonita," she says.

"I don't understand," I reply, shrugging.

The woman, in a movement so swift that I have no time to react, takes my hands, turns them around, and stares at my palms so insistently it makes me uncomfortable. I feel an unpleasant chill. I try to pull my hands free, but she's gripping them with such force that I can't budge. I feel like shouting, calling for help, but then she looks up at me and her glare is so intense, so peculiar and penetrating, that I can't fight her. Without loosening her grip, she peers down at my palms and starts reading the lines. She shakes her head, wrinkles her brow, glances at me, then back down.

"Tienes el corazón roto," she says, following the brief trajectory of one of my palm lines.

"I've already told you that I don't understand," I protest.

The woman places a finger at the center of my chest and says, "Corazón." Then she takes the sprig of rosemary and snaps it in half. She nods, as if asking me whether I've understood.

This is a waste of time. If only I could explain to her that I'm the last person who needs her fortune told. I want to get away from her, but her feverish eyes are so overwhelming they keep me rooted to the spot, depriving me of the will to resist.

She fixes me with a stare and, in a loud voice, as if raising it will make it any clearer, says, "Un corazón sediento sólo se cura siendo fuente."

Why bother repeating that I don't speak her language? Instead I recite her phrase to myself over and over again, until I've got it down. She still won't budge. I sense she's waiting for something, but I don't have a clue what. She shows me the palm of *her* hand. Really? I don't know the first thing about reading palms, but if she insists. But as I'm about to take her hand, she gives me a scowl that frightens me, and says, "Money, money."

Oh, silly me. I take out a few coins from my wallet and hand them to her. And as she walks off in search of the next clueless tourist, I keep repeating that phrase to myself.

"Who was that?" says Kyle as he joins me. "What was she saying to you?"

"No idea, but I need to write it down. Quick, I need a pen."

Kyle takes one out of his backpack and hands it to me. I don't know how to spell that phrase, so I start looking for someone to help me. Most of those around us are tourists, and I doubt their Spanish is any better than mine. A boy about our age is opening the door of a house in front of us, so I run over to him.

"What are you doing? C'mon, let's get out of here," Kyle says.

"Excuse me," I say to the boy, "could you write these Spanish words down for me?"

He shakes his head, as puzzled as he is amused. "No hablo inglés, lo siento."

Kyle looks a little less amused when I hand the boy the pen and motion for him to write on my arm. The guy nods, holding up the pen with a grin so bright it could light up a toothpaste commercial.

"Tienes el corazón roto," I dictate. "Un corazón sediento sólo se cura siendo fuente."

And my pronunciation must not be half bad, because he scribbles the words with no problem.

"Gracias," I say, delighted.

The boy smiles again, waves, and disappears into his house. I turn around, ready to tell Kyle all about it, but his sulky stare takes the wind out of my sails.

"I could have done that for you, you know," he says. "No need to ask a total stranger to write stuff on your arm."

I can't help giggling.

"Since when do you know how to write Spanish?"

"I took a year of Spanish in elementary school and . . ." Even he seems to realize how dumb that sounds. He shrugs and mumbles, "Anyway, it can't be that hard."

I giggle again, to myself this time, and start walking.

"This way," I say, pointing to a street that leads off the square to our right. "I'm dying to get to the nature reserve. Tripadvisor says it's unmissable."

Kyle takes the lead. The street is too narrow and busy for us to walk side by side, and looking around, I'm not entirely sure this is the street we took on our way in. They all look so alike that I stop for a second to check my map. Okay, we're just walking in the wrong direction.

"Kyle, hold on, it's the other way," I call out, but amid the bustling crowd he doesn't seem to hear me.

I pick up my pace through the crowd and grab his arm. As he turns to me, that current jolts me again, but this time it's twice as strong. Kyle looks at me without a word, but those Tennessee-blue eyes of his speak for themselves—he felt it too. *No, no, no.* I have to nip this one in the bud.

"Let's go," I say, forcing a smile. "I'm dying to find my mother, and most of all to free you from the burden of this trip."

Kyle goes pale, his eyes lowered. It pains me to say this to him, pains me so much I feel my heart implode, but it's the best thing—no—it's the *only* thing I can do. I don't want to hurt him, to give him false hope. And although I wish this trip could last forever, it can't. In my life, there are no forevers. Besides, I know it won't take him long to forget me. A boy like Kyle can have any girl he wants.

And so, we wend our way through the narrow streets, one behind the other, in total silence, a silence fit to burst, a silence that says it all without saying anything.

KYLE

It's been an hour since we left Córdoba, and Mia has been glued to her cell phone trying to get a signal so that she can translate that precious little phrase the gitano said to her. And although I've tried to convince her that those women are no fortune tellers, just con artists, she won't listen. She insists that things happen for a reason, that life gives us signs and that it's our duty to heed them. In that case, I hope this particular sign wakes her up to the fact that I'm more than just a traveling companion.

When I'm with her, all is well, things fall into place, the stars align, or *something*. There are moments when I manage to forget about everything else, forget my hometown, forget the past, and sometimes I even think I could return to a halfway normal life. But when she turns cold and indifferent on me, like when she said that she can't wait to be done with this trip, and I remember her hiding the planned trip with Noah from me, I feel lost, as if she'd pulled the rug out from under me, and I start to sink. I get that she wants to track down her mother; that's understandable. What I don't understand is why she insists so much on wanting to free me, which sounds more like she wants to be free *of* me. I just don't get it. We've been having a great time, we get along, we laugh together. To be honest, I would give anything for her not to locate her mother just yet, for her real mother to be the very last one on the list, which would give me that much more time to be with her. But what if it's the very next one? Would she call off the trip and send me packing like a lowly hired driver who's served his purpose?

I haven't even asked her what she plans to do once she does meet this woman, and I'm not sure I want to know—I'm not sure I could take it. It's all so confusing. There are moments when I think she's not indifferent to me in the least, when I could swear she feels the same way I do, but then, as if on cue, she says or does something that tells me she couldn't care less about me, at least in that way.

"Finally!" she says. "I've got a signal." She hastily types something into her phone. "Okay, I found it. Let's see, here it says: 'A broken heart can only be cured by being the source.'" She looks at me and frowns. "By being the *source*? What do you think she meant by that?" I shrug. "It doesn't make sense. . . ." She takes her diary out of her backpack. "The source of what?" She writes down the phrase in her diary and looks off into the distance, pensive.

"Next time you might want to ask life to send you something a little less cryptic," I suggest.

"The signs are always clear, Kyle. We're the ones with veils over our eyes that prevent us from understanding. Whatever it is, I'll figure it out—you can count on it."

She rubs at the letters on her arm, but they don't come off. Then she tries with the little hand wipe they gave us to clean our fingers after the paella. No luck. She looks closely at the letters and rubs harder, over and over again. "They won't come out," she says.

"Maybe life is sending you a sign it doesn't want you to forget," I say with a note of sarcasm.

"Not funny. I'm serious; it's not coming out."

Oh, shit. I forgot to take the indelible pens out of the backpack after helping Judith doodle on her Easter eggs. My face must be giving me away because Mia suddenly says, "What?"

"I think . . . ," I say, scratching my head, "I gave you a Sharpie."

"You're kidding," she says, her words coming faster now. "So how am I supposed to get this out? I can't meet my mother like this; she'll think I got a tattoo, or worse. And the letters are not even in color; they're in black. That's *so* not me. What do I do now?"

The wail of a police siren cuts her off, sending me back for an instant to the fateful day. I glance up in the rearview mirror, short of breath. Two police officers on motorcycles are approaching us. One of them motions for me to pull over. I do, next to some bushes on the side of the road. The same officer walks up to my window and gestures for me to roll it down. I do so as fast as I can.

"Señor, va por debajo de la velocidad mínima."

"Sorry, sir. I don't understand."

With a strong Spanish accent, he says, "Minimum speed. Forty-five kilometers per hour. You, too slow."

It takes me a second to process this. He can't be serious. "Oh, okay," I say. "Sorry, I didn't know."

"First time, warning. Second time, fine. Okay?"

I nod, still dazed. They start their motorcycles, and as they peel out, I hear howls of laughter coming from the back of the van. I spin around to see the passenger seat empty. "What the . . . ?"

Mia slips through the front seats, still cracking up, and sits down. "I bet you're the first person under eighty who's ever been stopped for driving too slow."

"What were you doing back there?" I ask, but she doesn't answer. She's too excited, looking at something outside while she rolls down the window. "Seriously, Mia, what were you doing? Were you *hiding*?"

And as if I weren't even there, she points at something outside and says, "Look, wild strawberries, *real* strawberries! Oh my God, I have to try some."

She opens the passenger door and rushes out. Perched on the stone wall are a bunch of strawberry plants. She plucks one and holds it up to her nose, inhaling as if it were a divine nectar. Then she walks over to the passenger window and shows it to me.

"Come and give me a hand. There are loads of them; we can pick some for dinner."

And as she says this her attention is drawn to something else, a stand of trees farther up the road.

"Look! Cherries! Hurry, I need something to put them in. Where is that bag they put the sandwiches in yesterday? You put it away, right?"

I open the glove compartment and hand it to her.

"What are you waiting for? Come with me."

But I don't move. I prefer to observe her from the safety of the van. I watch her picking cherries from the tree like a kid opening presents at Christmas. She looks blissful. I don't ever want this moment to end. I don't ever want *Mia in my life* to end.

KYLE

The sun is beginning to set as we approach the spot where we'll be spending the night. Apparently, it's a nature reserve where camping is allowed. After a half hour of trying to persuade me to drive through the night, Mia found this place by chance. On the way here, she made me stop at a bakery where, according to her, they make the best empanada in the entire region. An empanada is a kind of pastry stuffed with I'm not sure what, but it smells so good it must be a fucking sin.

Mia lifts a corner of the foil it's wrapped in, and sniffing the doughy scent, says, "I'm starving. You sure we haven't passed the campsite?"

I shake my head.

"You're paying attention, right?"

"I'm paying attention."

"According to the map, it has to be around here somewhere," she says. She's been saying that for the last half hour. "Stop. Stop the car!" she shrieks, as if we were about to crash into an alien aircraft.

"Now what?"

"Back there, I think I saw a sign."

"I told you I've been paying attention, and I didn't see any signs."

"I said *stop the car*."

I slow down, and checking twice to make sure no one's behind us, I pull over.

"What are you waiting for?" she asks. "Back up."

"Are you seeing straight? We're in the middle of a road. I can't just put it in reverse."

She looks at me as if I've just said something incredibly stupid and shakes her head. Then she leans all the way over me and sticks her head out of my window.

"You're right; there's an anthill causing a huge traffic jam, but if you put your flashers on I'm sure they'll let you through."

Having her lean so close is making my heart race. I have to hold myself back from wrapping my arms around her.

"Ha ha," I say.

"C'mon, Kyle," she says, drawing away a little. "We haven't seen a single car for over an hour."

I guess she's right, and for the old Kyle it would have been a piece of cake. He wouldn't have thought twice about reversing up a country road, but *this* Kyle sees danger wherever he looks. I put it in reverse, look two dozen times in all three mirrors, and slowly step on the gas. When I've backed up about a hundred and fifty feet, she says, "Stop, stop here. Look."

On the side of the road there's a wooden sign that says *Free Camping Area.*

"What do you say to that?" She crosses her arms and gives me a sidelong glance.

"I say that what you're looking at isn't an official road sign. How was I supposed to see it?"

"Giving credit where it's due isn't your thing, is it? I was expecting a 'Yes, Mia dearest, you were right all along, I didn't see the sign.'"

"Yes, Mia dearest," I mimic, "when you put your mind to it you can be a real pain in the ass."

"Typical sore loser."

Unbelievable. I don't answer. I put the van in drive, and following the small wooden arrow, I turn onto a dirt road flanked by olive trees, oaks, and some pines. A few minutes later we reach a clearing. A creek of crystalline water runs along one side. On the other side there's a barbecue grill. The spot is idyllic, as if lifted from a tourist brochure.

"Oh my Lord, this place is *perfect*," she says, opening her door and scrambling out.

With her arms stretched out to the side and her eyes shut, she takes a deep breath as if she wanted to inhale the scenery, as if she wanted to drink it all in and take it with her. I find myself wondering where she would take it.

I put the hand brake on and get out.

"Can you smell that?" she asks when I'm at her side.

I inhale deeply. There's a scent of wild herbs, flowers, and pine resin. The sky seems somehow *closer* here, as if you could reach out and touch it. It's already dappled with stars, but the towering moon refuses to give way to the darkness. *Jesus, now I'm starting to think like her.*

Mia lies down faceup on the sandy ground and stretches out her arms. "I've died and gone to Venus," she says.

"Well," I say with a chuckle, "you're not from *this* planet, that's for sure. I should have known it was Venus."

Mia opens her eyes and bursts out laughing. "Are you saying I'm weird?"

I put my index finger and thumb together as if to say *just a tad.* Mia sits up.

"Good," she says solemnly. "Normal is overrated. Go to school, get married, have kids, work, work, work, shop, shop, shop till you drop, watch TV, and then wait till you die." How graphic. She gets up and shakes the dirt off her clothes. "Thanks, but no thanks. Normal is for those who've been given the gift of life and don't know how to use it."

"Okay, I'll get dinner ready. No point in getting all philosophical on an empty stomach."

"All right, and don't forget the empanada. I'm dying to try it."

And as I turn to go get our things, I notice her staring at the van. Who knows what she's up to?

I slide open the side door, climb in, and start rummaging around for the table and a couple of folding chairs. They're in a small compartment under the bed. And as I'm kneeling to pull them out, I hear a loud thud and a scream.

"Ah!"

I jump down from the van, and despite the sharp pain in my

knee I run to the other side of the van at warp speed. When I get there, Mia is lying on her back with her legs raised and pressed against the door. I don't know whether to laugh with relief or have a panic attack.

"What the fuck happened to you?"

"They make it look easy in movies," she groans. "Someone should sue Hollywood for false advertising."

I help her to her feet and shake my head, chuckling under my breath. Mia, in pain, clutches her butt.

"There's supposed to be a meteor shower tonight. Should be awesome. I just wanted to climb onto the roof to be a little closer to the stars."

This makes me smile. "Like I said, an extraterrestrial. Wait here; I'll get something to hoist you up." I take out the folding table and set it up just behind the van. "All right, climb up. I'll hold you."

I offer her my arm and, leaning on it, she lifts herself onto the table. Then on tiptoe she struggles to climb onto the roof, but it's too high and her arms are too weak.

Her butt is right at eye level when she says, "Push."

I look for a different portion of her body to lay my hands on but honestly can't find one.

"Come on, push me up," she groans. "What are you waiting for?"

And so I do. I plant both hands on her ass and very gradually move her upward, not only to make the moment last, but because she's so dainty I'm afraid I'll send her flying.

"Okay, I'm almost up," she says, grabbing the metal bars on the roof. "A little more, just a little."

I give her one last shove, and with great effort she clambers to the top and lies down.

"Woo-hoo!" she shouts once she's on her feet again.

I'm flushed, and it's not from the effort. I can't stop staring at her up there, with the clear, star-studded sky as a backdrop. She's a beauty, plain and simple.

MIA

The view from up here is exactly what I hoped it would be—perfect. The stars that are already out seem to be calling out to me, saying, *We're here; we're waiting for you.* And for the first time in my life I'm exactly where I need to be, at home. I revel in the moment, taking it all in, hoping the memory will stay with me, wherever I end up.

An alarm on my cell phone breaks the spell, reminding me that we're about to witness the big event. According to what I read online, the meteor shower is supposed to start now, at eight. According to the rumblings in my stomach, what should have started a while ago is our dinner. My plan, had we followed it, was flawless—first, eat a generous portion of that empanada, and only then come up here and enjoy the show. But who could wait? Not me. I was dying to look at the skies from this height.

I hear Kyle below, bustling around. He must be getting dinner ready. Watching the stars from the roof of the van must not be his thing, plus he looks exhausted. And as much as I would have liked to visit Seville at dusk and get to Cuenca bright and early tomorrow morning, that would be asking too much of Kyle. Driving at night when you're that tense behind the wheel can't be easy. Besides, I'm not in great shape either. For some reason, the pills are no longer as effective at easing that crushing grip on my ribs. There are moments when my strength begins to fade, as if my body were turning to mush. I lean over the edge to ask him for a slice of the empanada and see two blankets flying up at my head.

"Careful," says Kyle, a fraction too late.

I try to catch them in midair and manage to get one, while the other lands on my head. Peeling it off, I peer over the edge of the roof, still wondering what's going on. Kyle is beaming up at me. In one hand he's holding a plate with the empanada cut into pieces of different sizes; in the other is a bowl of cherries and strawberries, rinsed and served with a couple of napkins. "Got room up there for me?" he asks, raising the plate of empanada.

I freeze for an instant, not knowing whether it's because my brain has decided to go on strike or because I'm still taken aback when someone is too kind to me without ulterior motives. Kyle chuckles, still holding out the plate.

"What's wrong, too tight up there for two?" He gives me a hangdog look. "C'mon, I promise I'll stay in my corner."

"No, no, there's plenty of room," I say, rousing myself from my mental strike.

I take the empanada, then the bowl of fruit, and make way

for Kyle as he grabs the roof railing, hoisting himself up next to me as if it were the easiest thing in the world. Muscles are unfairly distributed on this planet. As he gets to his feet, I notice he's wearing my jacket, the yellow one with colored buttons, tied around his waist. I gape at him, so surprised I forget to close my mouth.

"Oh, right, your jacket," he says, as if he just remembered. He unties it and hands it to me. "I thought it might be chilly up here, so . . ."

I'm still gripped by an emotion I don't understand, and again I'm at a loss for words. Did he really do this all for me? Truly? Then why is it so hard for me to believe? Instead of feeling overjoyed, why do I feel like someone has their hands around my throat? And as if a voice were dictating the answer without uttering a word, I hear it resound within me: if someone is *this good* to me, I might be forced to face the fact that others haven't been, that my mother never was, and that maybe, just maybe, she doesn't care to be.

Poor Kyle clears his throat, suddenly uncomfortable, and averts his eyes. That's when I realize I'm still gawking at him with my mouth open, as if I'd had a vision.

"By the way," he says, spreading out the blankets side by side. "We'll have to improvise some kind of table. Lugging up the table and the folding chairs was a tall order." He takes the plate and the bowl and sets them down between the blankets. "You're starting to worry me," he says. "I've been here all of, what, sixty seconds? And you haven't said anything about the meteor shower, or the empanada, or the starry sky, or anything at all. Did I do something wrong? Or did one of your alien friends get your tongue?"

I giggle, and doing so I see a shooting star, the first this evening, lighting up the dusky sky for a fleeting moment, as if showing me the way, my way.

"Look," I say.

"Cool." Kyle takes a seat on one of the blankets. As soon as his butt touches the roof, he springs back to his feet as if he'd sat on a dozen rotten eggs. "Shit," he says, taking two smooshed chocolates from the back pocket of his jeans.

"Since I didn't know how long this legendary meteor shower was going to last," he says, sitting back down, "and because I know you can't go for very long without eating, I brought you these. Better to eat these chocolates before you start hallucinating and mistaking me for roast chicken. Free-range, of course."

I laugh. Kyle looks up at the vast, shimmering night sky. He's so enthralled his breath catches in his throat for a moment. Then, trying to play down his sensitive side, he grabs the plate of empanada and says, "So how hungry are you?"

"What a question."

He chuckles, scoops up a huge portion, and places it on a napkin. Handing it to me, a corner of the napkin protruding from his hand starts to give.

"Careful," he says, putting his other hand underneath to stop it from falling.

His hands are so close to my cheek I can feel their warmth. I accept the napkin and quickly take a bite of the empanada.

"Hmmm," I say, resisting the urge to graze his fingers with my lips. "Wow, this is *so* delicious."

I focus on the empanada stuffing. It looks like a mix of peppers, onions, fried tomatoes, and something that resembles tuna. It's so good it makes me swoon. Kyle, who seems to be observing me, starts cracking up.

"What?" I ask.

He shakes his head, amused, and picks up a piece for himself.

Side by side in silence, we scan the skies, hunting for falling stars. And as we feast on the empanada, I get swept up in a stream of racing thoughts.

I've never felt so at ease with a person, not even with Bailey, and it's messing with my head. In the past, I couldn't stand being in someone else's company and not talking. It was unthinkable. After five minutes I'd be on edge. With Kyle it's different. I can talk for hours, or say nothing at all, and it's okay. And although it sounds insane, at times I can't even believe I *had* a life before I met him. Plus, he seems to get me better than anyone else, and that's without knowing about my defective heart. He gets my jokes—as weird as they may be—and my erratic moods; he even seems to like my endless rants.

And if I hadn't been born with my days numbered, Kyle would be exactly the type of guy I've always dreamed of, and I doubt that even my dreams could have conjured up someone like him. I steal a glance at him. His eyes, reflecting the glow of a million stars, speak to me of a warmth, a gentleness, and a rare depth, one that even he may not be aware of. Each time he looks at me, I lose myself in those blue-gray eyes of his, as if an entire universe shone behind them. Oh boy, here comes one of my poetic streaks, which means I'm only digging myself deeper.

Why do I *do* this? I have to stop thinking of Kyle in this way. Can't do this to him and don't want to. But how it *hurts* to have to put a stop to whatever this is. It hurts *too* much. It creates the kind of void in me that I know only sadness will fill.

MIA

I remember one day at St. Jerome's. I must have been six or seven. It was Christmas, and the families in town had decided to donate the toys their kids no longer used. It was a wonderful day. The Destiny's Child Barbie dolls must have been all the rage at the time because there were lots of those. The older girls fought over who would get one of the few Kens available for their Barbies. I already knew that my Barbie would never have a Ken, so it didn't matter. I never really cared about that kind of thing. Until now. At this moment, sitting next to Kyle, I do care. I feel like running away, but now I know there are invisible strings attached, and they won't let me go.

"I have to say, this meteor shower of yours seems to be missing a few drops," he says, completely unaware of the emotions running riot inside me. "I haven't seen more than, what, four or five falling stars?"

"Good things come to those who wait."

Kyle looks as if he is trying to pick up on a double meaning in these words, but doesn't find one. "All right," he says, putting the empty plate and bowl aside, next to the chocolates. "If that's the case, why not get comfortable while we wait."

And so he does—he lies down on his back, *really* close to me. I think this is more romanticism than is good for my mental health, so I do my best to remain sitting, but before long I find myself sliding down next to him, giving in to the exhaustion of my ailing heart. I'm doing exactly what I promised myself I wouldn't do.

"Hey, look, look!" he says, pointing up at the sky.

Suddenly, dozens of stars burst in all directions, like fireworks. Seeing him this excited brings a smile back to my lips.

"Amazing," he says, and subtly moves his arm so that his hand grazes mine. I feel a burning urge to take his hand, but instead I just let mine rest there, and he just lets his rest there. For a whole minute we lie in the stillness, gazing skyward. The crickets and a few birds go out of their way to ease the silence our words can't seem to fill.

Then, out of nowhere I'm gripped by an urge to scream at the sheer irony of this moment—why is this happening *now*, when my time is running out?—to scream at not being able to take his hand, at being forced to part with him within days, at being incapable of telling him . . . Well, I don't even know *what* I would tell him. I'm furious at life, at Kyle for being so amazing, for having appeared in my life, and although I never curse, I find myself mumbling a few zingers—*Crap. Fudge. Fiddlesticks.*

Kyle must feel my churning thoughts, because he shifts onto his side with his head leaning on his arm and says, "Hey."

I turn to face him.

"What's wrong? You look bummed," he says.

"Not at all, I was just thinking . . . about my mother and . . . it's nothing, forget it."

Before going on he studies me for a moment, his features turning earnest. "Thanks," he says. "If it hadn't been for you, I would have missed out on all of this." He points upward. "And lots of other stuff."

I feel myself giving in, his lips drawing me in like magnets. His eyes come to rest on my mouth. I have to do something, say something, *now*. "What's your favorite place in the world?" I don't know where this question came from, but it'll do.

Kyle knits his brow, shrugs, and with a hint of a smile says, "Six Flags?"

I smirk and shake my head. *Boys.* "Mine would be . . ." I point to the brightest star in the sky. "Venus. That's where I plan to be born in my next life."

"You believe in reincarnation and all that stuff?"

"Some things you don't even have to believe," I reply, as if stating the obvious. "Whatever you feel deep within you. That's what it's about."

Looking off into the distance, he says, "What if what's deep within me isn't the same as what's deep within you?"

"Oh, c'mon, you're not telling me you're one of those who thinks the only planet with life on it is Earth?" I turn onto my side to face him. "We humans think we're so important, but really we're groping around in the dark. I have no doubt there are other worlds out there, better worlds than ours, worlds without disease, pollution, war, hunger, without parents who don't love their kids, or even without—"

"Death?" His expression goes cold, pained, with a tinge of anger.

"Death isn't a bad thing, Kyle."

Clenching his jaw, he sits up, staring straight ahead and breathing hard. I sit up too, hoping I haven't put my foot in it again.

Kyle picks up the piece of foil from the empanada and crushes it into a ball. "Once you're dead," he says, "you don't laugh anymore, or go out with your friends, or fall in love, or eat a fucking hamburger." He turns to me, his face livid. "And if you're dead, you can't hug your mother and say, 'Don't cry, Mommy; everything will be all right.'" He jumps to his feet and, striding to the edge of the roof, hurls the ball of foil into the night air. "Death fucking sucks."

I get up, but I don't dare get near him. I'd give anything to be able to ease his pain. I can't stand feeling this powerless. "Kyle . . . It was an accident. It could have happened to anyone."

He shakes his head, and with his gaze lost in the vast canopy of stars above us, he begins to speak, his voice ragged. "I can't even remember what happened. Even that's beyond me. I must have lost control of the car. I don't know. What I do know, and what I can't change, though I'd give my life to be able to, is that it was my fault. It was me behind that wheel."

I want to reach out and touch him, hug him, tell him it's okay, but I can't bring myself to do it and don't even know if I should. So I walk over and stand beside him. "Noah wouldn't have wanted to see you like this," I say. "He wouldn't have wanted you to punish yourself. If it had been him behind the wheel, and you had died, would you have wanted him to suffer so much? I don't think so, Kyle."

He drops his gaze and takes a deep breath. "It's not just Noah," he says. "Josh was in the car, and . . . they don't know if he'll ever walk again." He turns to me, his eyes like two open wounds. "Who can fucking live with that?" He looks back up at the stars and, almost in a whisper, says, "I can't."

His pain is tearing me up, and I suddenly feel my heart splitting in two, literally. It hurts me, it hurts me beyond what is bearable, but I can't leave him like this. "Kyle, God wouldn't want you to punish yourself this way."

He spins around, glowering. And though he's looking at me, he doesn't seem to see me. "Give me a break. *God . . . ?* There's no such thing. What kind of God allows things like that to happen?!"

I beg my heart to grant me another minute, just one more minute with him. "No, Kyle," I say, with the little strength I have left. "I'm not talking about *those* gods, from the holy books, with fire and brimstone. I'm talking about the kind you don't even have to believe in." I point to my ailing chest. "Because that God lives right in here. That God *does* exist. That God *has to* exist, because when neither your father, nor your mother, nor your adoptive parents love you . . ." My words make him go pale and are excruciating for me to utter. "There has to be something or someone out there who is glad that you were born."

Kyle takes my hands, and I realize only now that his breathing is erratic and his cheeks are moist. "Mia," he says, and there's something beyond friendship in his eyes. "I'm glad you were born."

I'm finding it hard to breathe. I don't want to hear these

things; I don't want him to care for me in that way. Not now. It's too late now. I feel light-headed. I'm seeing stars. Is it me, or is Venus shining brighter than usual? She is calling to me; I can feel it.

"Mia? Mia, talk to me. What's wrong?"

"Kyle . . ." I hear myself from afar.

I'm terrified. I look at him. No, not now, not yet, please, not yet.

I feel a pair of arms latch onto me. They must be his. And slowly, I start to black out. Venus looks down on me from above.

"Mia!"

His words are receding, as if I were no longer in my body but far, far away. Little by little the lights go out, and everything fades, except the pain.

KYLE

I've been in this damn waiting room for two hours now. They're supposed to let me know when they find out what's wrong with Mia, but for the moment they haven't told me shit. It's torture. I never thought I'd be back in a hospital so soon. In fact, I swore I'd never set foot in one for the rest of my life, and yet here I am, praying to a God I no longer believe in to let Mia recover, without even knowing what's wrong with her or how bad it is.

I'm sitting next to a chubby guy who's been watching TV for an hour. With my head in my hands and elbows on my knees, I start brooding over the whole situation. I should have known something was wrong; she looked exhausted the whole afternoon. She seems to tire so easily. Could just be a virus or something. But what if it's not? What if it's serious? I can't stand to see her suffer. Are they taking good care of her? They don't know how fragile she is. My nerves are killing me. I can't lose her, not her too. I have to get up, and although they told me to wait in here patiently, I leave the room for the twentieth time and check in with the nurse at the information desk.

"It's been two hours," I say sharply as I walk up to her. "When the hell are you going to tell me something?"

The nurse gestures for me to wait while she answers a call on her headset. Great. The lack of empathy in the medical profession obviously knows no borders.

"Habitación ciento cinco," she says in Spanish, taking her precious time. "Sí, claro, le paso."

I consider roaming the halls again to find Mia's room, but the security guard has already threatened to throw me out of the hospital, twice. So I'll be good and wait. But still, I have to do something, so I stand here and stare at the nurse, hoping it makes her uncomfortable enough for her to tell me something. No chance. This woman has all the compassion of a steel vault. A printer on the desk right under my nose is printing out a sheet of paper. At first the sound of it annoys me and I feel like giving it a good whack, but then, as the letters appear, it catches my eye. The first line reads *MISSING PERSON REPORT*. But it's odd, because it seems to be a US document. The second line slowly emerges. That can't be right. It's *her*. The name appears in large black letters—*AMELIA FAITH*.

The nurse wraps up her phone call, then turns to me as if I were a chore she'd like to get over with as soon as possible. "As I told you before, until the doctor comes out I can't provide you with any information."

I nod. "Of course, I understand," I say, taking a gentler

approach. "It's just that there's an unpleasant odor in the waiting room, and I'm guessing that the man next to me hasn't washed in months." The nurse looks puzzled. "You don't mind if I just stand here for a second, do you?"

She shrugs and turns back to her desk to take another call. "Hospital Sierra Norte," she says in Spanish. "¿En qué puedo ayudarle?"

I look around. The sheet of paper has just finished printing. Behind me, the security guard is making his rounds down the hallway. The nurse moves to one side to open a drawer. I swiftly snatch the paper from the printer's tray and stuff it into my backpack. Before I have time to zip it up, I hear footsteps rushing up behind me. My breath catches in my throat. The footsteps are pounding rhythmically in my direction. *Shit, shit, shit.*

"Excuse me." It's a man's voice, and it sounds serious.

I clear my throat and turn around, my mind searching frantically for a credible excuse to offer the security guard. But instead of him I find a young doctor in a white uniform looking at me. "Are you here with Miriam Abelman?"

"Is she okay?" I blurt out.

"Yes, yes, don't worry, it happens with people in her condition. We'll be discharging her now. I suggested she stay for the night, but she refused."

Wait, what was that? "What condition?"

The question surprises the doctor.

"Oh, I thought that . . . ," he begins, not bothering to hide his blunder. "Well, in that case, it's better if she tells you herself. Just try to convince her to have the surgery as soon as possible.

The procedure itself has made great strides, and the chances of survival are constantly improving."

"Chances of survival?" I ask, on edge now. "What are you talking about?"

"Just . . . try to talk her into it, all right?"

And with that, the doctor turns and briskly walks away. Just as I'm about to run after him and press him for more details, I see Mia stepping out of an elevator at the end of the hallway, her backpack slung over her shoulder. I run toward her. She sees me but seems less than pleased. She walks in my direction, looking gloomy and weak. Once I'm at her side I take her backpack. There are dark circles under her eyes.

"Hey," I say, as gently as I can. "How are you feeling?"

She keeps walking as if I weren't there. She has a hard, cold, evasive look about her and at the same time seems a little ashamed.

I walk beside her, respecting her silence. With every step, my anguish grows; with every step, *chances of survival* drones in my head, like a spiteful echo taunting us both. I glance at her. She's broken. This time it's not about me, it's about Mia, and I refuse to let my problems upset her any more than they already have. She needs me, and I won't let her down.

MIA

The moment I saw Kyle talking to the doctor I knew it was all over. How can so much bliss vanish in the blink of an eye? But now it's too late; now he knows and he'll leave me, like they all do. Just a few hours ago everything was perfect, and now it's in ruins. I walk as fast as I'm able to—which is very slowly—down the long white hallway that leads to the exit. Kyle is at my side. He glances at me and at times seems on the verge of saying something, but he doesn't. Most likely he's looking for the best way to tell me he's leaving, that he has no desire to hang around a ticking time bomb like me. Well, he won't have to waste his breath. I've decided to spare him the effort.

Every step I take wears me out, causing more pain. I'm tired of hospitals, tired of being tired, sick of struggling all the time. My arms hurt from the needles, and I can still taste that horrible medication they made me swallow. I know it's for my own good, but what makes them think they know what's good for me? Why do they all think that the surgery and the suffering that goes with it is the best solution? And this time, I felt lonelier sitting in that hospital bed than I ever have. I missed Kyle, missed having him by my side, holding my hand while I was forced to lie to the nurses so they wouldn't discover who I am.

I'm an idiot. I shouldn't have let myself get so attached to Kyle. I promised myself I wouldn't get close to anyone ever, and the day I lose him, it's going to tear me up. I bite my lip—my best weapon against the tears threatening to burst. When we get to the exit, the doors open onto a circular parking lot with two roads at the center. And although the streetlights are on, it's so dark I can't see where our van is.

Kyle points to a sidewalk off to one side. "It's over there."

I don't look at him and don't reply. I can't risk having him talk more and tell me it's over. Not now, not yet. I see the van up on the curb, badly parked, tilting sideways slightly and with the emergency lights on. For a moment I'm touched. For Kyle to have left it like that he must have really been worried. But that glimmer of hope is snuffed out when I realize that at the time he didn't know what a disappointment I would turn out to be.

I lumber toward the van to the rhythm of my weary heart. Kyle walks beside me, uneasy, as if he doesn't know what to do or say. "Mia," he finally ventures in a soft, gentle tone. I don't flinch. "Mia, what was the doctor talking about? What's all this about surgery?"

I can't answer him. I can't tell him that there won't *be* any surgery, that I've given up, that I don't want to go on, so I open the door and quickly get into the passenger seat, sinking my teeth even farther into the flesh of my lip. Tasting the acrid metallic flavor of my own blood, I type the address of the airport into the GPS.

As Kyle climbs into the driver's seat, I prop the phone up on the dashboard.

"Where are we headed?" he asks. He waits for a moment, and when he sees that my only reply is to look straight ahead without batting an eyelash, he takes the cell phone and checks the address. "You should go in the back and lie down," he says.

The thought of it sends a chill through me. But I can't bring myself to tell him that I don't want to be alone, or be away from him, that I want to spend my remaining hours by his side.

"I don't think you're in any condition to visit any prospective mothers tomorrow, besides . . ." He pauses, appearing to have registered the GPS address, because his demeanor suddenly changes. "*The Madrid airport?* What the . . . ?"

All right, I have to get this over with, but I don't want him to see me cry and can't stand the thought of him pitying me, so I cast about inwardly for that cold, distant place devoid of emotion, that refuge that has enabled me to survive since I was a kid. Sadly, it doesn't take me long to find it again. "You have to go back," I say, stone-cold. "Tonight."

"Whoa, slow down," he says, turning to me. "Are you going to tell me what this is all about?"

"You wanna know what this is about? It's about me having a genetic defect in my heart that *boom*"—I gesture with my hands, mimicking an explosion—"can hit me at any time." I grab the cell phone from him and place it back on the dashboard. "Expiration date, remember?" I feel his eyes on me, and I can't bear it, so although it's past midnight, I throw my shades on and carry on with my bitchy rant. "So I'm releasing you from our agreement. I totally get it, don't worry; nobody wants to be around someone who's sick and could drop dead at any second." And as an afterthought I hear myself say, "Believe me, I'm used to it."

Kyle gapes at me. He's gone white, as if my words have drained his face of all color. I cross my arms and grind my teeth with a fury I don't recognize. Oh boy, am I angry: at life, at him, at my defective heart. Above all, at my *mother*.

"What are you talking about?" he says abruptly, as if everything were peachy. "I'm not about to up and leave you now. Besides, we made a deal, right? Come on, give me the next address."

I can't make sense of his words, and it leaves me paralyzed.

"Okay then," he says, leaning over and picking up my backpack. He places it between the seats and takes out the notebook in which I've listed the addresses. I turn away from him and curl up in my seat. I can't think straight. Is he being serious? Is he really going to stick around? No, I can't bring myself to believe it—I can't let my guard down and risk falling to pieces.

"Plaza de España, Seville," he says. "This isn't a specific address. Okay, so what is it? A place you want to see? I don't see any potential mothers here."

How do I tell him that Plaza de España is the reason Noah wanted to come to Spain in the first place? He used to joke that he didn't want to die without having photographed it. I wanted to do it for him. But of course I can't tell Kyle that; there are lots of things that I won't be able to tell him anymore. Besides, maybe he's just planning to leave me there, in Seville, or maybe he feels so guilty about Noah that he wants to help me find my mother as an act of charity, or something to cleanse his karma. I've read about people who do that kind of thing.

He glances over, and seeing that I don't intend to answer him, he types the address into the phone. "All right," he says, starting the engine. "Plaza de España it is."

I feel drowsy, so I put my seat back and lean against the window, curled up into a ball. And although I pretend to doze, I'm watching him through my dark shades. I've never realized how useful sunglasses can be. I silently study him, trying to decipher his true intentions.

There's a smile playing on his lips, and he looks calm, though his chest is quivering ever so slightly, as if he's crying to himself. He's swallowing hard and breathing deeply, like someone trying to send the tears back where they came from. And for an instant I think it might just be true, that he might really care about me and not leave me after all. But I refuse to get my hopes up. I can't afford to.

I'm overcome by exhaustion, by confusion. I want to sleep, to sleep forever and cherish this image of Kyle by my side: Kyle, who doesn't look at me as if I'm a nuisance, a burden to get rid of; Kyle, who does care about me and whom I care about far more than I should.

KYLE

When we finally reach Seville, dawn is just starting to break. Mia's been asleep almost the entire trip, apart from when we left the hospital and she just sat there silently for a while, observing me. Obviously, she didn't think I could see through her sunglasses, but to spare her the embarrassment I pretended not to notice. She made me smile inside, and a good thing, too, because I think I would have broken down otherwise. I spent the rest of the trip racking my brains over the missing person report and struggling to make some sense of the news about Mia's condition, trying to convince myself that a girl like her can't possibly die just like that, that no God would be so cruel as to take her away, that there must be a cure for her. The doctor spoke about an operation and that I need to persuade her to go through with it, so I've been rehearsing dozens of ways to bring up the subject when she wakes up.

The Plaza de España is located in a park and is for pedestrians only, so I look for a parking spot that's close by. If Mia wants to see the place, she won't have to walk far. She was so worn out when she left the hospital, I doubt she'll be in the mood for much sightseeing when she wakes up. After two laps of the park, I find a spot on a side road lined with a canopy of trees. I kill the engine and look at her. God, she's so still it scares me. I hold a finger under her nose to check her breathing. *Phew,* she's alive. And to my surprise, I catch myself thanking a God I still haven't made peace with.

I take the opportunity to study her as an artist would study his muse, a muse that inspires me more with each passing day. I was a moron for not seeing her for what she is from the very beginning—an absolute beauty. Everything about her is refined, ethereal, as if she were less earthbound than the average person. If it wasn't so corny I'd say she's like an angel, or as she would probably put it: a star-bound girl. And although my body is crying out for some sleep, the urge to draw her, to capture her on paper one more time—perhaps the last—is overpowering.

Trying not to make noise, I lean down to get my sketchpad out of my backpack, and doing so I hear a horse whinnying somewhere outside. Okay, this place may be out of this world, but that horse sounded all too real. I look up, thinking that my exhaustion is making me hallucinate, but no. There are two police officers up the road in front of us, on horseback, leisurely trotting our way. Shit. I look at Mia. Her sunglasses have slid off her face, and the way she's leaning up against the window will make it too easy for them to recognize her. I can't let them see her. And since drastic times call for drastic measures, I throw myself on top of her, and taking her face into my hands I pretend to kiss her, my lips just inches from hers.

Her eyes flick open. Disoriented, she starts to smile, still teetering between two worlds, then a frown takes over and she glares at me. "Wait, what are you *doing*?" she says, shoving me back.

"Shhh, it's the cops. Go with it."

She glances at the street, and spotting the police, she sinks down into her seat. "Oh boy, oh boy," she whispers, panting. "Cover me up. Please, don't let them see me."

I draw close to her again, stopping, to my regret, a millimeter from her mouth. Her whole body is shaking beneath mine. The horses are approaching quickly now. We're staring into each other's eyes, so near we're breathing the same air. Her gaze drops to my lips, then instantly back up to my eyes; my gaze follows suit. Our breathing is ragged. Am I misreading her, or does she want this as bad as I do? I've been fantasizing about this position for days, but none of those fantasies included cops, or missing persons, or anything remotely dangerous. God, everything's on fire—my lips, my chest, my hands, and other regions that shall remain nameless. There's no way I can resist this for much longer; that's asking too much. In my mind, which is light-years ahead of my body, I'm already kissing her with an all-consuming passion, holding her tightly against my body, kissing her neck, sliding my hand along the curve of her hip and back up again to other uncharted territory, and then, just as my body is about to catch up with my mind, we hear the clicking of horses' hooves receding. *Shit.* I back off slightly, but my yearning for her has me paralyzed, dumbstruck.

As if nothing had happened, she clasps her hands around my neck and raises herself a little, peeking into the side mirror.

Seeing the police trotting off, she drops back down with a gasp of relief. "Thanks for that," she says, averting her eyes as she lets go of my neck.

I'm tempted to say *the pleasure was all mine,* but I think better of it. Under that cool facade of hers she looks a little uncomfortable, maybe even embarrassed, but refuses to show it.

"The thing is," she says, clearing her throat, "I have this phobia of cops, you know? Nothing you need to worry about, of course. Just one of my quirks, I guess."

Wow, she can lie at the drop of a hat. I straighten up and play along, as if what just happened were a figment of my imagination, as if her body hadn't trembled under mine and her eyes hadn't zeroed in on my lips. "So you're okay?" I say, playing it just as cool. "That kind of fear must not be good for your . . . you know. Do you want us to go to a pharmacy or see a doctor?"

She shakes her head. My questions are making her uncomfortable. When she finally straightens up in her seat, her hair is bunched up on one side. I try my hardest not to laugh but can't help it. She's funny even when trying to look serious. She clears her throat again, and as she fixes her ponytail, I take the opportunity to get the missing person ad from my backpack.

"I don't get it, Kyle," she says, snapping her hair band in place. "What made you think I wanted to hide from the police?"

I hand her the report, and her pretty eyes open wide. "This time," I say, "you're going to tell me *everything.*"

She takes the document and reads it, her slender, pale fingers beginning to shake.

"Hey, hey, it's all right," I say, not wanting her heart to get worked up. "I just want you to tell me what's going on so that we can do something about it, okay?"

She nods several times before speaking. "All right, I'll tell you, but can you take me to the bus station first? I really need to get to Cuenca by this afternoon. I'll explain on the way, promise."

"The bus station? What are you talking about, Mia? No way I'm taking you to the goddamn bus station!"

Mia shrinks down into her seat like a startled puppy. I don't mean to scare her, so in the most comforting tone I can manage I say, "C'mon, it's just one day off. Don't have to be a doctor to know that you need to rest. We've still got time, right? We'll find your mother, together."

She nods, but her eyes tell me she's not convinced.

"I just need some air," she says, and points to the street. "Mind if we . . . ?"

"Sure, why not, but with those cops around I don't think it's a good idea."

She bites her lip, weighing her options. Then, as if she has cracked a code, she grabs the sunglasses off the floor and puts them on. "How's this?" she asks. "I don't even recognize *myself* with these on."

I wince slightly. "Not bad, could be better."

I take my cap out of my backpack, the one my mother packed for me, and put it on her. I hate caps, but to avoid getting the usual lecture from my mom on the dangers of ultraviolet rays, sunstroke, and the ozone layer, I took it without saying a word. If it prevents my mother from worrying more than she already does, so be it. On Mia, the cap slides right down over her eyes and stops at her nose. She doesn't move a muscle as I laugh my ass off and adjust the strap so that it fits her. "Much better," I say. "Unless they have X-ray vision, there's no way they're going to spot you."

She looks in the mirror and doesn't seem convinced. She angles the cap sideways a little. "Now we're talking," she says. "Let's go."

KYLE

Mia opens her door, and before getting out she stretches
her arms and legs like a cat after a hundred-year hibernation. She
doesn't let on, but her strained lips and bleary eyes make it clear
she's still in pain. I pick up my backpack and get out. I walk over
to her side, and like a perfect gentleman I offer her my arm. I wish
my mom could see this; she'd be tickled.

"Here," I say. "Take my arm."

She looks away. "That's okay," she murmurs, her tone haughty.
"I can manage, thanks."

Well, either she's lying through her teeth, or what happened
between us a few minutes ago was all in my head and I'm the
only one still feeling hot and heavy.

In an awkward silence, we slowly make our way along the perimeter of the enormous Renaissance-style palace made of pale bricks
till we reach the courtyard facing the main structure. The sheer majesty of the place stops us in our tracks at exactly the same time.
Her face lights up, and finally I see the Mia I know, the Mia who

has captivated me so thoroughly. The palace forms a semicircle and seems to envelop us both, to shelter us within its walls.

There are people gliding past in small rowboats on a canal that wends its way around the entire plaza. My dad would flip out if he saw this. He would be launching into a speech about the tiled alcoves that adorn the palace walls, and the balustrades of marble and painted ceramics that run along the canal. And to round it all out with a fairy-tale flair, there are tourists riding leisurely in horse-drawn carriages across the square.

I look at Mia. Taking it all in, she's about to say something, but sensing my eyes on her she seems to remember that we still have to have a talk. Her shoulders sag, her gaze drops, and she starts walking. "Okay, here it goes. I had to run away from my foster home," she begins, struggling visibly. "I didn't tell anyone where I was going."

If she's about to tell me they abused her or something, I swear I'll kill them. "Why?" I ask, concealing my irritation.

"They wanted to force me to have that operation, and, well, maybe what I said about being eighteen wasn't exactly—"

"Wait, hold on," I say, feeling my face darken. "*Force you?* The doctor said you need that surgery to happen *now*."

"Yeah, I know, and it's gonna happen." The flagstones seem to claim her attention as we walk. "Just . . . not yet."

A carriage is approaching us, and while we stand to one side to make way for it, I notice its big wooden wheels and its elegant interior, upholstered in leather. For a moment I picture Mia curled up in my arms in the carriage, and just as I'm about to propose we take a ride in one, she speaks up. "They should be ashamed. That's animal exploitation; there's no other word for it."

Oh Lord. In the words of my beloved grandma, *You look better with your lips buttoned.*

"Mia," I say, trying to reel her back in. "You still haven't told me—"

She pretends not to hear and instead points to an alcove as if she'd seen a magic tunnel to another world, and says, "Look. That's freaking awesome."

Nice try. But before I can protest she's already walked over to the alcove and taken a seat. The brick walls and benches are embellished with hand-painted tiles, like a puzzle from the distant past. I can't deny it, this place is astonishing, and just watching her enjoy it is a joy in itself, but I'd rather pick our conversation up where we left off.

"Check this one out," she says, slowly sitting down in another alcove nearby.

She raises her head, and with her eyes shut, she inhales as if she were drinking in the sky itself, as if it weren't even air but peace filling her lungs, and a happiness that's pure, untouched, unlike any other. A happiness only she can know. "Thank you," she murmurs to the sky in a whisper so soft it hurts.

A chill creeps up my back. God, I just don't get it. How can she be thanking the Almighty? She should be royally pissed off. And as if she'd overheard my thoughts, her eyes pop open and lock onto mine, sending my heart reeling. We stare at each other for a few seconds, in a silence bristling with things unsaid. I flinch first. When I manage to look at her again, I make sure she knows I'm annoyed and that she can't go on playing her cagey little games.

Mia takes another deep breath, and we resume our walk along the canal in a silence I wish she would break. But she doesn't.

After a minute-long wait, I say, "Mia . . . getting back to your surgery, the doctor—"

"Okay, getting back to my surgery, of course I'm going to do it, but only after I've met my mother." She turns to me, tilting her head. "Can you imagine the irony of waiting my whole life for this moment, just to end up dying on an operating table before meeting her?"

Damn, why does she have to be so blunt about it? Stifling a mounting urge to vent my frustration, I ask, "Is it really that dangerous?"

"Half of those who undergo this kind of surgery don't live to tell the tale."

As she says this, she fixes her frozen pupils on a fountain in the distance. A punch to the gut couldn't have hurt me more.

"That means half of them live, right?" My voice sounds hoarse, much more than I would like it to.

Her shoulders rise and fall with a sigh. Nothing else moves, not even her eyes, which are still riveted on the distant fountain.

"Why didn't you tell me?" I've given up trying to hide my irritation. "Didn't you think I had a right to know?"

Hanging her head, she nods several times, and I notice a light mist in her pupils, as if the ice were beginning to thaw. "It's just that . . . I didn't know if I could trust you," she whispers. There's a hint of sadness, of guilt, in her tone, but the way she's biting her lip tells me that even now she's not sure. This hurts me.

"All right," I say, with more conviction than I feel. "But the fact that you ran away from home doesn't explain how the hell that report ended up in a hospital in Spain."

"I have no idea. The surgery was scheduled for today, and I guess my foster family must have reported me missing but . . ." She pauses, thinking, then looks up. "What I can't figure out is how they found out I'm here in Spain. I made sure to cover my tracks."

"You must have left a clue without realizing it."

"No, really, I was careful. I didn't tell anyone where I was going and didn't leave anything lying around that would make them think I was coming here."

"Your computer maybe, or a pen drive, who knows."

"No way, I wiped everything from my hard drive before leaving, and I don't have a pen drive."

"Wow, you're good at this stuff," I say, trying to lighten things up.

"Nah, I had help." She starts walking again, studying the flagstones as if trying to decipher their mosaic patterns. "I don't know; maybe it was Noah's folks. They're the only ones who knew about this trip, but I doubt they'd talk to my foster family about it. They don't even know them . . . it doesn't make sense."

My stomach tightens at the mention of Noah, but I don't let on. "Well, whatever the case may be, now they know, and we can't risk them finding you here, so—"

"They won't find me." She says it without a flicker of doubt.

"How can you say that? We might have lucked out today, but riding around in that screaming van isn't exactly subtle. As soon as they run the plates on it—"

"Way ahead of you," she says with a roguish grin. "I put everything, the van, the campsites, the flight, in Miriam Abelman's name, which is the me that's on my forged passport. Totally untraceable."

I'm astounded. This girl will never cease to surprise me. And as it dawns on me that *never* and *always* are no longer words I can use with Mia, my jaws clench shut.

She laughs and, running her hand along a tiled balustrade, says, "I might as well get something out of being a Sherlock Holmes buff, right?"

"Yeah, but as far as I know, Sherlock Holmes wasn't known for forging IDs."

"Different times. But if he had needed to, he would have done it."

"So how did *you* do it?"

She gives me another sly smile, which makes her even sexier. "I know people. Remember Bailey's ex-boyfriend?"

Of course, what an idiot; how did I not think of him? "You mean the hacker turned forger?"

"Exactly. He gave me a special rate for being a regular customer."

She looks tired but doesn't complain, so I pretend to be tired myself and take a seat on the balustrade. Mia sits down beside me, and while she does I pick up my backpack and take out a pack of chocolate chip cookies I got from the hospital vending machine. I offer her one. "You must be starving. Here, take one."

She puts a hand on her belly and wrinkles her nose. "I'd love one, but my stomach is burning from all the crap they gave me at the hospital."

My stomach is rumbling, but if she's not going to eat then I won't either. We look at the water in silence. There are couples and families floating along the canal in colored wooden rowboats. Mia's eyes follow them with a kind of nostalgia, a longing. I want to hold her in my arms, to watch the boats together and tell her that everything will be okay, that we'll get through this, that her heart will get through this, but I can't. I can't tell her anything, because anything I do tell her may not turn out to be true.

MIA

I hated having to lie to him, but what else could I do? Tell him that I have no intention of going through with the operation? That in a few days, or weeks, or if the stars align, in a few months I might no longer be around? No, I just know that Kyle wouldn't understand, that very few people would. Besides, this place is too beautiful to spoil with arguments that lead nowhere.

Kyle is sitting next to me on the low wall of colored tiles. I look at his reflection in the water and wish with all my might that he'd hug me, that I could snuggle up to him, feel his warmth, his scent, his powerful arms around me. I would keep that memory with me forever, but I can't. What happened earlier in the van was embarrassing enough. My entire body was thrumming under his, as if a roaring fire had taken possession of all my senses, my lips, my hands, my breasts, and a few uncharted regions. If he hadn't managed to detach himself once the cops were gone, I don't know what would have happened. At the very least, I would have kissed him, and that's something I can never, ever, even in my wildest dreams, allow to happen.

"You using that trick you learned at the group home?"

My heart lurches as I'm caught red-handed recalling my most shameful memories. I turn to him before I have time to collect my thoughts, and apparently, I have that no-idea-what-you-just-said look, because he goes on, "Yeah, you know, that trick where you focus your attention on something real hard until you get it."

He points to a pair of ducks paddling at our feet, and at that very instant I realize that while I was mooning over our little episode in the van, I was staring at the ducks all along, almost forgetting to blink.

"Seriously," he says. "If you're hungry I'll take you to dinner somewhere, but can you stop eyeing the ducks like that? I know they're free-range and all, but it's a little creepy."

"Nooo." I laugh and give him a shove. "What are you talking about?"

"So does it work?"

"Does *what* work?"

"The trick."

"I guess," I say without much interest.

He wrinkles his brow suspiciously. "Hey, since when do you pass up the slightest chance to lecture me on a topic?"

He manages to coax a smile from me, though I don't find that topic particularly funny. He's waiting for an answer, but the words refuse to come out. I'm worn out, and not only physically, so I just hope that if I don't reply he'll drop the subject. He doesn't. Instead he narrows his eyes, takes my chin in his hand, and, lowering my jaw, peers into my mouth. "Phew," he says, "I thought the cat got your tongue."

I giggle.

"C'mon, spit it out," he says. "Does it work or doesn't it? Because if it does, we have to get a patent on it. No kidding. We could get rich and travel the world, and I wouldn't have to sell my sketches on a street corner."

I'm touched by his words, touched by the way he looks at me. I think everything about him moves me. But he's still waiting for an answer. "Yeah, I think it does work, but not for everything."

Kyle does a winding motion with his finger, prompting me to elaborate. I plunge inside myself, to that place where memories are as vivid as the day they happened, where my emotions lie dormant, and try to explain something I'm not sure I want to explain. I don't look at him as I speak; I couldn't, even if I wanted to. "Back at St. Jerome's, Sundays were the days they would take us into the Great Hall, a place we were strictly forbidden to enter on any other day. At noon, the couples who wanted to adopt would come to see us, usually after they'd finished Mass. It was the best day of the week, I guess. We would comb our hair, sometimes for hours; we'd put on the best clothes we had, and then, in the privacy of our solitude, we would each practice our most winning smiles. Anything to please those who might just become our future parents, anything to stand out and get noticed, to be given a chance to be loved. It was thrilling—agonizing—but thrilling. Many of us couldn't sleep the night before. When I discovered the trick, every Sunday I would focus on a visiting couple and wouldn't stop looking at them, drawing their gaze toward me with my desire to be the next chosen child, and . . . well, it worked on two occasions. So, to answer your question, I'd say yes, technically it works. Feel free to get that patent."

When I finally manage to look at him, his body seems to have been drained of every last drop of blood; he even seems to have forgotten to breathe. "And?" he sputters. "What happened then?"

"Well, I guess the trick doesn't work as well when you want your parents to love you, or at least love you enough not to send you back to the group home when they find out you have a defect."

"Bastards," he blurts out. "Shit, Mia, I'm sorry."

"There's always a silver lining, though. In this case it was that they never forced me back to the Great Hall on Sundays, plus I had a room full of toys to myself every visiting day."

He tries to look as if my words haven't burst his bubble, but his quivering chin gives him away. And although he notices that I've noticed, he tries to play it off by moving his jaw from side to side, as if it were sore.

"Mia . . . ," he begins.

"No, no, please, let's just change the subject. It's all in the past, and I don't want to waste a single second of what could be a very short life reliving moments I'd rather forget."

"Gotcha." He runs a finger across his lips, zipping his mouth closed. Then he picks up the package of cookies and takes one out, and just as I think he's going to pop it into his mouth, he crushes it between his fingers and flings a handful of crumbs to the carp in the water below. Good idea. I do the same.

Drawn to the crumbs, a mother duck hastily approaches,

followed by her brood of ducklings. We continue to throw crumbs, and while the ducklings peck at them, the mother duck waits and watches over her young ones. I can't help feeling a twinge of longing at the very heart of me. I try to convince myself that not all mothers are born with the same nurturing instinct. But a question begins to take shape in my mind: If my own mother couldn't stick around, why should Kyle be any different? Is it out of pity? Out of a desire to put his karma in order? Or could it be because he's beginning to feel something he shouldn't?

With as much stealth as I can muster, I look at him out of the corner of my eye, seeking a clear answer. But that's not what I find. Kyle, grinning, suddenly turns to me and asks, "What?"

Oops. I'll have to work on my stealthy glances. It takes me a moment to screw up the courage to pose my question. "Kyle, I need you to be totally honest with me. Seriously, whatever your answer is, I'll understand."

"You got it. Shoot."

"Did you . . ." For a moment the words are caught in my throat. "Did you really mean it when you said that you're not going to leave?"

His smile goes thin. "Of course, Mia. Why would I want to?"

"Even though I could go at any second?"

"And risk missing out on a single moment with the most outlandishly fun girl I've ever known?" He shakes his head and attempts a smile. "No chance."

Those sad, profound eyes tell me much more than his words do. I try to read into them, to seize what it is he's trying to tell me without saying it, but my racing thoughts and clamoring questions are making my head spin. *Enough.* He wants to be by my side, and I can't ask for more. Hiding my turmoil, I smile in an attempt to thank him. And just then, two swans, one black and one white, emerge from behind a boat, as if out of thin air. "Oh my God," I say. "Do you see them?"

As I turn to Kyle, his cell phone is pointed at me, about to take a snapshot.

"Wait, what are you doing?"

"It's for your photoblog."

"No, no, no," I say, covering up the lens. "Take one of the swans, just the swans."

He brushes my hand away and takes a flurry of pictures, of me. "Your viewers are going love seeing the face *behind* the camera."

And having delivered that lovely phrase, he lowers his cell phone and meets my gaze. He's intensely serious, so serious it makes me weak in the knees. "Are you scared?" he asks.

"No, course not. I just don't like having my picture taken."

"I mean of dying," he says.

"Oh, that . . ." I shake my head. "Death has never scared me."

"So, what *are* you afraid of, Mia Faith?"

Falling for you? My mother not wanting anything to do with me? Dying alone? And one thing above all, which I actually say aloud. "I guess what I'm most afraid of is dying invisible." He doesn't get it. His frown gives him away. "If you haven't made a difference in anybody's life, if you haven't contributed anything to this world, what's the point of having been born? Of living? There *is* no point."

He looks at me as if processing my words.

"Hence, your photoblog."

"I guess."

I take another cookie and meticulously break it up into little pieces.

"How many followers?"

I shrug.

"Seriously? You don't know how many likes you've got, or stats of any kind?"

"Noah's the one who helped me set it up, and he wasn't much more savvy than I am."

Actually, Noah used to say that technology stifles art.

Kyle shakes his head, implying I'm hopeless, and handing me his phone, he says, "Open the blog in admin mode."

I have no idea what he's talking about. My expression must speak for itself, because he laughs and says, "Your photoblog, open your photoblog with your username and password."

"Okay, well, can't you just say that instead of speaking in riddles?"

I open the site for *Expiration Date* and hand him back the phone. He types in a few things while I continue sharing our breakfast with the ducks, swans, and carp in the canal.

"Unbelievable. You hadn't even activated the 'comments' option," he says, still typing. *There's a comments option?* "Okay, done. From now on you'll have all the stats on how many people visit your blog, and you'll see if anyone leaves a comment."

"Seriously? Thanks! That means so much to me." I'm so delighted I want to kiss him, but obviously I don't.

He chuckles and says, "You're incredible, you know that?" Kyle takes a piece of the cookie and tosses it in the water. Abruptly, his face goes stern and he cocks his head toward me. "Why didn't you tell me?" he asks. "You know . . . about your heart."

Because if you had known from the beginning, you wouldn't have wanted to join me on this trip. Nah, I'd better think up a different answer.

"I suppose that, for once in my life, I wanted to feel what it was like to be a normal girl."

Kyle ponders this for a moment, then with a sly grin he stands up and says, "Wait here for a sec, okay?"

I nod, suddenly intrigued, and watch as he makes his way over to one of the canal bridges. I take a thousand pictures of him, in my head. I shouldn't have left my camera in the van; that was dumb. And although I hate taking snapshots with my cell phone, I won't have many more opportunities to photograph him, so I grab my phone. I take one of him from the back as he crosses the bridge, one as he comes to an ice cream stand, one as he speaks to the lady selling the ice cream, one as he points to the list of flavors. Geez, how many scoops is he getting? The poor boy must be starving. Another snapshot as she hands him the cones, and a final one as he pays.

He approaches with a broad smile that kindles my heart. *Click, click, click* goes my cell phone. In one hand he's holding a cone with one white scoop, and in the other a cone teetering with scoops of all colors, plus toppings.

"You said you were having heartburn," he says. "What better way to put out the fire? Besides, you wanted to feel like a regular girl, right?" I nod in surprise as he continues, "Yeah, well, we covered that, remember? You can try all you want; you'll never be normal." He hands me the multicolored cone. "Sorry."

I'm in stitches, and as I take the ice cream, I say, "That's the nicest thing anyone's ever said to me."

"Well, it shouldn't be—you should have heard tons of *nicest* things in your life. But we'll fix that, real quick. Where does your next mother live?"

His words are like a breath of fresh air, of love, of freedom. He's even brought my appetite back. I take a huge bite out of my colorful cone. There's an explosion of mingled flavors in my mouth, a riot of rainbows. It's wonderful to be able to savor one more day on this planet. I quietly give thanks to my heart, to my life, and not least, to Kyle.

MIA

In the end, as much as I tried to persuade him to get back on the road, it was Kyle who talked me into spending the night here, in this park at the heart of Seville, and although my guidebook says it's totally forbidden to leave your van in the area, there were so many sights to see that I couldn't refuse. It's all so thrilling. Toward evening, after we took the longest siesta in human history and Kyle rejected my hundredth request to leave for Cuenca, he invited me out to try the legendary tapas, or bite-size specialties, on one of the cozy streets of Seville's old quarter. Oh my word, I've never seen such color, such life, such joy, such music, not to mention such food, all in one place. It makes you want to live a thousand years just so you can try it all.

Now the sun is up, and as Kyle predicted, nobody's hassled us about our van being parked here. Actually, what Kyle said was that if the cops were to see a van as trashy and pathetic as ours, they'd pity us too much to say anything. But I prefer to take our good fortune as a sign, yes, a sign, that today's going to be a great day. After devouring a whole package of churros for breakfast,

we've set off to find our next candidate. And while Kyle drives—
a little faster than usual, I have to give him that—I take the opportunity to bring my mother up to speed.

April 1

Dear Mom, my heart forced us to delay our trip
by an entire day, but we're finally back on the road.
I don't know if I've mentioned it already, but today
we're heading to Cuenca. Judging from the pictures,
the place is spectacular and I'm dying to see it.
What I'm not so sure I want to see is you. Don't get
me wrong, it's not that I don't want to meet you,
but I'd rather spend the last three days of this trip
with Kyle. And although we both avoid talking
about what's going to happen once I do find you,
that doesn't mean we're not thinking about it; at
least I am.

I'd love for him to stick around, for you to meet
him and see that everything I've said about him is
true. But you and I have a lot to talk about, and he
might get uncomfortable or bored, or maybe you'd
prefer us to be alone. I don't know. I wouldn't be
surprised if he got an earlier flight back to Alabama.
But you know what? Just the thought of him leaving
chokes me up. And although I tell myself that sooner
or later he will leave, that he has to leave and get on
with his life, my heart doesn't seem to have gotten
the message, is refusing to get it, and is threatening

to shatter once and for all. But that doesn't matter anymore. Kyle has to go. I want him to be happy, and that can happen only once he gets away from me, the sooner the better.

And speaking of my heart . . . it's fading. I can feel it, as if beating itself is already an effort, as if carrying on is too much to ask.

Anyway, once we get to Cuenca I'll tell you more, maybe in person—who knows?

3:00 p.m.

We just had lunch on the terrace of a Spanish restaurant in Cuenca. The city is right out of a fairy tale, with its Hanging Houses overlooking the valley and the river, its cobblestone streets, its ancient churches, and the wood-and-iron bridge that runs right through the city (by the way, if you ever cross this bridge, don't look down, it's scary). In any case, as you will already know if you're reading this, we didn't find you in Cuenca.

Still, meeting this particular María Astilleros was lots of fun. As I was asking her the usual questions I ask all my potential mothers, her daughter appeared. She must have been around my age, dressed all in black, with a pierced nose, a dog collar around her neck, and purple lipstick so dark it looked black. She came out the front door and as she strode past us pretending we had the gift of invisibility, her mother asked us if we thought the law had anything against exchanging daughters. She seemed dead serious too. Imagine that! Kyle and I were in stitches. I think we both needed a good laugh. Anyway, tonight we'll be sleeping in Guadalest, a town in the province of Alicante. Do you know it? Have you been there? Wait, what am I saying? You might be <u>living</u> there.

9:00 p.m.

Turns out you don't live there. Well, at least it was worth seeing the stone village perched on a rock, with its castle towering over yet another valley and a river. I took loads of pictures. But tonight, I told Kyle that I wanted to get to bed early. It's true that I'm tired, but above all I wanted to write to you. I wanted to tell you how I feel. While I was speaking with María Astilleros number nine, I felt a whirlwind kick up inside me, and at first I didn't know why, but then a question dawned on me: Mom, why am <u>I</u> the one looking for <u>you</u>? Why aren't <u>you</u> looking for <u>me</u>?

Kyle cares about me; I can see that. He tries to show me he does every day. And come to think of it, there are many people besides Kyle who seem to like me and are friendly to me. I guess what I'm trying to say, Mom, is that now I <u>know</u> I'm not an unlovable person, and it hurts me a great deal that I could be unlovable to you.

I've prayed millions of times to every god, every star, every luminous being willing to listen that the day I meet you I'll hear you say that someone forced you to give me up for adoption, or that you were too ill to keep me, that you had postpartum depression, a mental illness, or a life-or-death situation. Because if it was none of these things, then I won't be able to see how you could have left me. God, I was a newborn! Didn't you have any feelings for me? Did I disgust you?

Why did you do it? I've asked myself this question so many times. And occasionally, not often, I'm so afraid to know the answer that I pray I'll never find you, or I pray that I will find you, but just to be able to look you in the eye and make you cringe in shame as you confess the real reason.

I get that when I was born you were young and maybe had no real choice in the matter, but what about after that? It would have been easy to find me. So why didn't you? Why didn't you write to me, or call me, or do something, anything to let me know there's someone on this planet who does love me? You didn't even bother to find out if I was okay, if I was happy, because if you had, you would have discovered how much I missed you every single day of my life. It makes me want to scream.

I have to sign off now. Kyle just asked me if I was okay, and I don't want him getting out of bed and seeing me cry. Good night, Mother. All I ask is that you don't disappoint me.

April 2

Okay, I'm so, so sorry, Mom, but yesterday was not a good day for me. Please know that that's not who I am. It's only when the pain and the doubts get so overwhelming that I'm lost and start thinking disturbing thoughts and end up writing things I don't mean. Seriously, Mom, I'm sure you had a good reason for doing what you did. Can you forgive me?

Kyle must have noticed I was having a moment because he took me out to have breakfast in a famous town along the Mediterranean, and he's doing his best to keep my spirits up. The town is called Jávea and is very close to Altea, where the next candidate lives. It just might be you. I'll write more later on, okay? Kyle went in to pay the breakfast bill, but I can see him coming back now. I hope you do live in Altea, and that in about half an hour you happen to be home. Oh, and please remember to ask Kyle to stay with us. It would mean the world to me.

4:00 p.m.

Well, you weren't in Altea either, the small town of whitewashed houses and churches with blue domes, where you can smell the sea air as you walk through the streets. Kyle insisted we rest a little before the next visit. He's being so sweet to me, making sure I don't get too tired, that I eat well. He never complains about his own problems. And to think that just a week ago he was on the edge of a cliff, ready to jump. Just the thought of it makes me queasy. This planet would have lost an amazing person. The fact that he's managed to put his own pain aside to focus all his energy on me touches me more than you can imagine. His eyes, flat and lifeless a week ago, shine now with an otherworldly intensity. We haven't spoken about Noah again, of course. I can imagine that traveling with a girl like me is hard enough in itself.

10:00 p.m.

Our afternoon in Benidorm was pretty exciting. It's a laid-back city, but frenetic at the same time. It has low houses and skyscrapers, a blend of the traditional and the modern, beautiful sights amid eyesores: a little bit of everything. After checking the eleventh candidate off our list, we took a stroll through the city streets, teeming with restaurants and their outdoor terraces, small shops, bars with blaring music, and street buskers.

At one point I fell behind Kyle while looking in a shop window and lost sight of him. And just like that—still don't know why—I felt left in the lurch, alone, defenseless in the middle of the street like a

two-year-old. The electrical tornado raging inside me
left me rooted to the spot, unable to move, to react.
And a second before it hurled me to the ground,
there was Kyle. He didn't have to say anything. He
just looked at me, as if his eyes could see beyond
my pupils, as if he could sense the fragments of my
broken heart. He grasped my hand firmly and got me
out of that place.

Neither of us brought up the episode; we didn't
need to. We decided to have a quiet dinner at the
campsite, so after buying some bread, ham, cheese,
and tomatoes, we found a comfortable spot in front
of our van and feasted at the folding table. Kyle
opened up to me, more than he ever has. Maybe
getting to know me more intimately has given him
the courage to let his guard down. He told me about
his parents, his grandparents, things he did as a kid,
his vacation. He said they often go to a place called
Sedona, in Arizona, which sounds wonderful. His
maternal grandparents live there. Anyway, it was . . .
perhaps the best moment of my life so far. It made
me feel a part of something greater and gave me a
glimpse of what it must be like to have a family, to be
surrounded by people who love you and would lay
down their lives for you. . . . For a moment, I imagined
what it would be like to have more time, not to have a
heart with a manufacturing defect, not to have to say
goodbye to him so soon. He even made me want to

study photography, travel the world with him, get to know his parents, and visit Arizona and all the other places he's told me about. But what he made me want more than anything else was to never leave his side. And then I remembered that street in Benidorm, the anguish I felt, and poof, just like that all my desires went up in smoke. Why stay? What's the point, if after a few years he no longer feels anything for me, or decides to leave me, or something happens to him? No, I simply couldn't live each day of my life in fear of losing him. In fact, I don't know how other people can stand it. You open your heart to someone, you surrender yourself, you let them see your most intimate side, and then, from one minute to the next, your heart's in pieces. Thanks, but no thanks. Mom, have you ever had your heart broken? I suspect you have.

I guess that's why I was born with this defect, or rather, with this shield, a protection against the despair of humankind. Yes, now I'm absolutely and totally sure that's what it is. But if I'm so sure, why is there an endless stream of tears running down my cheeks as I write this?

KYLE

This morning we left Alicante in search of the next-to-last mother on our list. I really hope this is the one so we can finally get back to Alabama. I can't stand seeing Mia so exhausted, weak, and vulnerable, risking her life to find a mother who doesn't deserve to be found. Lately she's been taking lots of those pills she always carries around. She says the doctor gave them to her so she could travel safely in her condition. But when I ask her about it, she claims she's totally fine. And as if life itself wanted to show her what a wild-goose chase this is, we've spent the last half hour following the GPS on her phone—mine decided to give up its signal for the fifth time in two days—and driving through a maze of secondary highways and dirt roads, only to end up in the middle of nowhere.

After miles of not seeing a single house, nor a single soul for that matter, we come upon an enormous gated residence teeming with olive and fruit trees and horses grazing freely. As I pull up in front of the iron gate, Mia takes a picture of the faded wooden sign that says *Cortijo las Tres Marías*. This place is very different from the ones we've seen up until now. These people must be rolling in it.

"Hey," I say. "You sure we have the right address?"

"You bet I'm sure. I checked each one at least five times."

I believe her. "All right, let's do this."

The gate is open, so I start the engine.

"Wait. What are you doing? We can't just barge in without ringing first."

"But there's no bell."

"Yeah, well, what if there's no bell because they don't want anybody ringing it? Or because they don't want to be disturbed? Or because it's clear to everyone except you that you can't just breeze in whenever you feel like it?"

"It's okay, take it easy, everything's cool."

But my words seem to have no effect because as we make our way up the sandy driveway that leads to the house, she sinks farther and farther into her seat. "I don't get how you can be so calm," she says.

"What's the worst that can happen?"

She looks at me as if wondering what planet I'm from. "Want me to make you a list?"

Before she has time to tell me all the things that could go wrong—in her own head—I start to see the country house. It's white, U-shaped, with dark and burnished wooden doors, and a tower on each end.

"Stop, stop," she shrieks as the house comes into view. "Please, just turn around."

I put the brakes on and can't help laughing. "Mia, what the heck is wrong?"

"What are you, blind? Can't you see the ginormous mansion? This is a classy place. We can't just show up driving the poor Moon Chaser. What if they think we're a pair of hoodlums, or squatters, or burglars, or members of a cult? And what if they're calling the cops as we speak, and they deport me and force me to have surgery? C'mon, what are you waiting for? Turn around and let's go."

Wow, there must be a two-for-one record in *Guinness World Records* with her name on it: the fastest talker with the most twisted mind. "You're something else, you know that? How do you get so hysterical so *quickly*? If they didn't want people entering, they wouldn't leave the gate open."

"Yeah right," she says. "You obviously don't have all the what-ifs that I have running through my head. If you did, you'd be a gibbering drama queen too right now."

The honey hue of her big eyes is almost eclipsed by her black dilating pupils. Without thinking, I grab her hand. "Mia, it's going to be okay, trust me."

She looks as surprised as I am, but I don't let go of her hand, and she doesn't take it away. She's shaking, just a little, so I give her hand a squeeze, because she needs to feel the affection she doesn't allow me to convey in words. I want her to feel calm, safe, at home.

"Shall we go on?" I ask.

She nods, her eyes glowing, fragile, vulnerable. Pressing the gas pedal, I hold her hand as we make our way up the driveway. Touching her is like riding a never-ending roller coaster. I could drive like this all the way to Alabama; instead we pull up in front of the house much sooner than I'd like.

We park under a centenary olive tree a few feet from the entrance. Mia's eyes are glued to the arched, ornate wooden door.

"Ready?" I ask.

She turns to me, her eyes bursting with question marks, with fear, with longing, and only after a lingering pause does she manage to nod. She opens the passenger door and gingerly removes her hand from mine. Instantly I feel an emptiness, a void, the need for something even more vital than air. I can't even imagine how it will feel when I have to be apart from her the day she gets her operation.

In the end, I'm the one who rings the doorbell. Mia prefers to wait a few steps behind me. A maid in uniform opens the door. Her warm smile seems to work miracles—Mia cracks a smile in response. The woman invites us in and leads us to an internal patio, where she asks us to wait a moment while she informs the lady of the house. She even brings us a tray, apparently of silver, with homemade cookies and lemonade. Mia doesn't so much as glance at the refreshments, a bad sign for her, so in order to keep her what-ifs at bay, I tell her everything I know about these old country houses, which amounts to the little my dad told me when he found out we were coming to Spain. Basically, they're enormous properties typical of southern Spain, where the workers live near the owners in one or more houses. On this particular property there are stables on one side of the patio, servants' quarters on the other, and the main house at the center.

Mia listens attentively without saying a word. Once I'm done with my speech, she gets up, makes her way over to one of the orange trees lining the patio as if sleepwalking, and inhales the scent of its blossoms. "Have you ever smelled anything so delicious?" she says, not waiting for a reply, speaking more to herself than to me. "I just hope there are these kinds of aromas on Venus. There must be."

I don't like this subject, not one bit, so I try to steer her away from it. "I hope this lady is your mother, truly." *So you can finally get your surgery and stop talking about Venus.* "Inheriting a place like this wouldn't be too shabby."

Mia turns to me, her raised eyebrows telling me I've completely missed the point. "It's not like you to be so materialistic, Kyle."

Before I have time to defend myself, an elegant woman appears, riding a gray horse with a braided mane. It takes us only a few questions to discover she's not the woman we're looking for. But at least she seems to have taken to us. After telling us all about the country house, the horses, and the olive trees, she sees us to the door. And, living up to Spanish hospitality, she offers us a gift bag with bottles of wine, olive oil, and a wheel of cheese from her own sheep's milk, with an odor so incredible it makes my mouth water. Long live Spain.

As the door shuts behind us, I can almost hear another door closing inside Mia. She looks different, absent, disappointed perhaps. She slowly walks to the van.

"Hey, c'mon," I say, going for chirpy. "The fact that this wasn't the right one means the next one will be. Isn't that great? Finally, you'll get to meet your real mother."

If looks could kill, I'd be six feet under. *What did I do now?* "Everything all right?" I venture.

"Peachy." From her tone of voice it sounds more like *I'm pissed off, and I don't intend to tell you why.*

"What's up? Did I do something wrong? Was it something I said? Was it the cookies? I didn't eat that many, did I?"

She ignores me. Still walking, she gets her cell phone out of her backpack and says, "I'll type in the next address. The sooner you leave me with my mother the better; that's all I can say."

Damn it, why is she acting like this? It hurts like a bowling ball to the gut. She primly takes a seat in the van while I put the gift bag in the van's kitchenette, trying to keep my emotions in check. As soon as I get out and slide the back door closed, I hear her yell, "This can't be happening!"

My heart quickens, and I rush around to the driver's seat, convinced that it's something serious. Instead, I see her waving her cell phone around, looking for a signal.

"What's the matter?" I say, a slight edge in my voice. "Is your cell phone not in a hurry for me to drop you off at your mother's?"

She squints at her phone, biting her lip. "They promised that two gigas was more than enough for ten days, and now they're telling me I've used it all up. It should be against the law to give tourists false information. *Now* what are we going to do?"

"It's not the end of the world," I say, a little more flippant than I intend. "We can use my phone. I don't think a few days of roaming fees will break the bank."

"Well, this place *looks* like the end of the world, and if your phone gives up on us again I don't know how we're going to make it out of here."

I rummage through my backpack and find my cell phone. What I see on the screen wipes the smile right off my face. "Shit, I don't have a signal."

"Well," she says, mimicking me, "it's not the end of the world."

"I swear, the moment I get home I'm leaving them a review that'll make their eyes water."

Her arms are crossed, and she's giving me the I-told-you-so look.

"Okay, well," I say, not giving her the satisfaction of seeing me annoyed. "No sweat. Back in the Boy Scouts they taught us to find our way using only the sun. So if you can tell me which *general* direction we're heading in, I can get us to a highway. North? South? Any idea?"

She sighs and rifles through her backpack.

"If you don't know the direction it's not a problem," I say. "I can ask the lady we just met to print out a map. I don't think she'll mind."

Mia, with her head literally buried inside her backpack, is practicing the art of the cold shoulder. "Where are you *hiding*?" And now she's talking to inanimate objects.

"I don't know what you're up to in there, but seriously, I'll go back and ask the lady if she—"

"Found it."

She pulls her head out of her backpack and holds up her American SIM card with a triumphant smile. "Be prepared. Isn't that what they teach you in the Boy Scouts?"

"You're the best. Seriously."

"Yeah, well," she says, shrugging her shoulders in resignation. "I'll just let the roaming fees eat up all my nonexistent savings."

"We'll get another SIM card once we're back in civilization," I say. Raising three fingers, I give her an impish grin. "Scout's honor."

I start the engine, and as we head down the driveway, Mia switches her SIM card. Once she's put the new address in the GPS, she places the phone on the dashboard and curls up in her seat, her back to me.

I try to put myself in her shoes, to understand, but it's not easy. Looking for a mother without even knowing whether she wants to see you must not be much fun. And the fact that she's the last one on the damn list is even worse. Not to mention the cops looking for her and all the rest of it. She must be worried sick.

"Mia," I say cautiously.

"Hmm?"

She doesn't turn around, and I get the feeling she's doesn't want me to see her face.

I continue. "I don't want you to worry about anything, okay?" No reaction. "I'll help you talk to the police. We'll explain what happened." Still nothing. "We'll get it all straightened out; you'll see. Once they know about your surgery, they'll let you return to Alabama without putting up a fuss."

She shakes her head ever so slightly, nothing more.

"You won't be alone, Mia." And with an ardor that surges through my chest, I whisper, "You'll never be alone again."

Her only response is to curl up even farther in her seat, with her face still averted. No matter how much I rack my brains trying to read her reaction, I can't. The only thing that's clear to me is that she doesn't want to talk about it. And that's how we spend the next four hours—Mia lost in her own world, which she still refuses to share with me, and me putting on the entire playlist of her "favorite singer in the entire world" in a poor attempt to lift her spirits.

MIA

The sky is bursting with the most delicious colors: pinks, greens, yellows, even a little indigo. I'm standing in front of a red wooden door. Next to it is one of those old-world wrought-iron birds with a bell underneath. I ring it. The door opens almost instantly, and a woman appears, looking like me, same hair color, same eyes, same lips, just twenty years older.

"Yes?" she says, drawing out the *s*.

I open my mouth, ready to unload a million things, but for some strange reason I can't make a sound.

She crosses her arms, slightly irritated. "I don't understand what you're doing here, *again*," she says.

I try with all my might to speak, but still nothing comes out.

She looks over my shoulder, and her lips curl into a disturbing, malicious smile. "Finally, they're here," she says. "I was beginning to think I'd never get rid of you."

I spin around, terrified, and see two doctors approaching me. They're wearing white coats, caps, and gloves, as if ready to operate. This can't be. I want to scream, I want Kyle to help me, but my voice is gone. My feet feel like extensions of the floor; I can't lift them. I start screaming at the top of my lungs, but I can't even hear myself. *This is not happening.* Where's Kyle? The doctors walk up to me, one of them holding a huge scalpel. *They're going to open me up. They're going to open up my heart. Kyle!*

"Mia?"

What? I open my eyes. Kyle is looking down at me. I'm panting and my armpits are drenched in sweat.

"Hey, you okay?" he says with a gentleness that soothes my lungs. "Sounds like you were having a nightmare."

I latch onto his arm and hoist myself upright, still not knowing where I am. What I do know is that I'm happy to see him, even though his eyes have lost some of their luster. He looks wistful.

"Yeah, I'm all right." I don't know why I say this when I'm far from it. "I . . ."

I look out the window. We're in a kind of plaza in a town of low houses. At one end is a building with three flags, at the other a stone church with storks' nests in the belfry. All right, we're on planet Earth, more specifically in Spain, that much is clear.

"We got here a while ago," he says. "But you looked so out of it I didn't want to wake you."

Gradually my memory resurfaces, and I recall why I feel choked with sadness. How can he be so happy about me meeting my mother? I don't get it. He promised me he *didn't* want to get rid of me. And that thing he said about the cops? I guess inside me there was still a glimmer of hope that at least he understood me, that he supported me in avoiding this nightmare of an operation, but no. Turns out he's just like the rest of them.

"It's right over there," he says, pointing to a modest-looking house through the window. "Plaza Mayor, number fifty-four."

It's a squat house, painted white, with tacky green tiles along the perimeter. Everything about it feels alien to me, out of place, screaming *You don't belong here; you don't belong anywhere.* Why isn't anything the way I imagined it would be? Why don't I feel the way I should be feeling? An entire life spent waiting for this moment, and now that it's here, I can't muster up the slightest bit of joy. I turn to Kyle and catch him studying me in silence, his eyes heavy with sympathy, with sadness.

"I tried to park in the plaza," he says. "No luck. In the half hour we've been here no one's budged."

I hadn't even realized the plaza was packed with cars and people on all sides. There must be some kind of festival because there are little flags hanging from the rooftops and lampposts, and the balconies are strung with garlands. Kyle looks uncomfortable, his eyes fixed on the steering wheel.

"If you prefer," he begins. "I can wait for you here. I imagine you want to do this thing alone. I get that, and . . ."

But his words are at odds with his tone of voice. His tone tells me what I want to hear; it tells me that he doesn't want to leave me either.

"Will you come with me?" I ask.

A huge smile eclipses his wistful eyes. He nods. "We can park in one of the side streets," he says, starting the engine. "I took a drive around earlier and saw a few spots."

As we make our way through the plaza, the silence between us swells with things we're not saying, so many things that it's almost deafening. As we turn into the first side street, we find a spot. A neon-green van, driven by a nun, is about to pull out. Kyle stops a few feet away, and as we wait for her to maneuver, the silence between us grows even thicker, tauter, fit to burst. As he pulls into the parking spot and heaves up the hand brake, I feel like I'm being torn up from the inside, as if that hand brake were signaling the end, as if he and I, what we had, was a pipe dream about to expire. He looks at me. I look at him too—how could I not? How will I stand not to look at him when he leaves? When *I* leave?

"Well . . . I guess our journey ends here," he says with a smile that just fails to hide his sorrow.

I try to find the right words, something that will make it clear how much he means to me, without revealing how much he *really* means to me. Too confusing, and I'm dazed by the pills I took, so all I manage is a nod.

"I guess you and your mother will have lots to talk about, and . . ." He strokes the steering wheel, and I feel that stroke gliding over my whole body. "In case I don't get another chance to tell you, I wanted to say thank you, Mia." His stare is so intense it shatters the ice inside me. "For this trip, for allowing me to share these days with you, for opening up to me, and—"

No, I don't want to hear this. I can't. "Stop, Kyle, please." I put my hand over his lips. If he doesn't stop I'm going to end up crying in his arms.

He takes my hand away with a warmth that weakens me. "No, Mia, I have to tell you. I need you to know that you saved my life." He looks at me even more intensely now, the Tennessee River welling up in his eyes. "And I'm not only talking about that day at the waterfall."

No, no, I'm starting to break down. I just can't listen to these things; they only make it harder, too hard. They make me *doubt*.

"Please stop talking." I bite my lip so hard it bleeds.

Without giving him time to respond, I lean on the door handle and with a superhuman effort shove the door open. It's the hardest thing I've ever done in my life. Climbing Everest would be child's play compared with what I've just done. My whole body is crying out for me to stay, to throw my arms around him, kiss him, stay by his side forever, but I can't do this to him. My forever is just too brief; my forever wounds like a hot knife. I love him too much to tell him how much I love him. Oh my God. Did I just think these words?

As soon as my feet touch the ground, the sun dazzles me and my mind is a blur. I wipe the tears from my eyes, trying to drive away a fury that is foreign to me. Kyle appears next to me, and with him the ground reappears beneath my feet. And so, we begin to walk side by side for a moment that lasts forever; for a moment that is over too soon. I look up at the sky and beg all the stars, concealed by daylight, to come to my aid, to bring about a miracle, to make this searing pain inside me stop. But it doesn't work.

And as we come up to the door, the door I've spent my whole life picturing, the door whose threshold I'm no longer sure I want to cross, we stop. I peer at the doorbell, but I can't bring myself to do it. I don't want to do it. I don't know what I want anymore.

"Should I?" Kyle asks, placing his finger on the bell.

I'm torn, but finally I nod. Kyle presses the white button very slowly, as if he didn't want this moment to end either. A shrill *ding-dong* makes my soul recoil. I look at Kyle, asking him a thousand unspoken questions. He nods as if he were able to read right past my gaze, telling me everything's okay. But it's not okay; nothing's okay. Footsteps approach quickly from behind the door, and my heart jumps with them. A key turns in the lock. Against my better judgment, I grab his hand. I need to feel his touch. He responds with a pressure that reassures me, that makes me feel at home. The door opens. It's her—it has to be her. Her face, her hair, and her height are all me, just older, though her checkered apron and wool slippers aren't exactly my style. Kyle looks over at me, his eyes laughing from excitement.

"¿Sí?" the woman asks, a little taken aback.

I open my mouth but don't know where to start. I'm drawing a blank.

"María Astilleros?" Kyle rescues me.

"La misma," she replies. "¿Quién me busca?"

"Sorry to bother you," Kyle continues. "Do you speak English?"

"A little rusty. I haven't really practiced since I was an exchange student in the US for a year."

"I . . . ," I manage to blurt. "I'm looking for someone and . . ." Again, my tongue is in knots.

Kyle jumps in. "You wouldn't happen to have been in Alabama in the spring of 2007?"

Too direct. I give his hand a tug.

"Alabama?" she says frowning. "No, it was a college in upstate New York."

I don't know why, but I'm suddenly flooded with relief and can even talk again. "I'm really sorry about this," I say, taking a step back.

Now it's Kyle's turn to tug at my hand, glancing at me as if to say *What's wrong with you?* "You sure?" he says to the woman. "You didn't by any chance give birth to a baby girl while you were there, did you?"

I dig my nails into his palm. The woman begins to laugh. Thank goodness for that. "No, I'm sorry; I can't have kids. Although I would love to. Why all the questions?" Something behind us catches her eye. "That's strange," she says. "What's happening out there?"

Kyle and I turn around at the same time. Four police officers are getting out of two cars. One of them has some kind of GPS device in his hand. They point in our direction. *Uh-oh.*

"Oh, shit," says Kyle. I couldn't agree with him more. He turns to me. "How did they find you?" He turns back to the woman. "Please, you have to help us. I'm begging you."

The poor woman wrinkles her brow, at a loss.

"We haven't done anything wrong, I swear," says Kyle. "We're just looking for her biological mother."

The cops are getting closer.

"It's true—I swear it, too. Please help us. If they find me they'll arrest me and send me back to Alabama, but I can't go back, not until I've found my mother. Please, *please*."

The woman stares at us as if trying to process everything we've said. Then she looks at the approaching officers and opens her door wider. "Come inside. Quick. There's a back door."

We rush inside and shut the door behind us.

KYLE

We run hand in hand to the end of a long dark hallway with doors on each side. Mia starts to lag behind. I turn around. She's pale, almost bluish, and is having trouble breathing.

"Mia!" I call out, with more panic in my voice than I would like.

There's terror in her eyes. I slip one arm under her knees, the other under her waist, and hoist her up into my arms. Without resisting, she latches onto my neck and presses herself to me, as if wanting to aid me in our escape.

"I'm sorry," she murmurs, her face against my shoulder.

"I'm getting you out of here, Mia," I say, my determination fueling my anger. "I swear."

The instant I cross the arched doorway that leads to the patio, the doorbell rings, making the hair on the back of my neck stand up. We glance at each other, our eyes pleading. The patio has a well at its center, and dozens of flowerpots and knickknacks lying around. What I don't see is the back door.

"It's a trap," Mia says in a whimper. "Kyle, this woman's turning us in."

"No, Mia. She wants to help us; I'm sure of it."

I wonder what kinds of things Mia's lived through to think that way. We hear the front door open at the other end of the hallway and words exchanged in Spanish. I'm frantically looking for the back door as we hear María talking nervously. Then footsteps come rushing down the hallway toward us.

"There!" Mia shouts. "Over there!"

She's pointing to a corner of the patio where there's an old fridge. I run over to it. Bingo. Behind it is a door choked with dust and spiderwebs. The key is in the lock. In one synchronized movement, as if we rehearsed it, I bend my knees slightly and Mia turns the key and slides it out of the lock. The hinges have obviously seized up over time because the door won't move.

"¡Denténganse!" someone shouts behind us.

I don't turn around. Mia does, her face aghast. Although my knee is killing me, I take a step back and give the door a resounding kick. It opens.

"Run, Kyle, run!" Mia's slender arms grip my neck so tightly I can hardly breathe.

I rush out, feeling the police panting at our heels. I shut the door and lean my back against it, Mia's body held tightly to mine. They try to force the door open. I do my best to keep it closed as Mia, stretching out her arm, slots the key in and locks the door. As she straightens up, our eyes meet for an instant, and we exchange a look that's so urgent it makes me dizzy. A vicious kick from the other side of the door shakes the hinges, sending a jolt of fear through Mia's delicate frame.

"It's okay," I say, in the most unruffled voice my throat can muster. "We'll get to the van and get the hell out of here."

She nods, but her face tells me she's not so sure.

I try to get my bearings. The van is parked on the street a few feet to our left, but if the police double back and come out the front door, we'll run right into them, so . . .

"Over there," Mia shouts, pointing to a parallel road at the end of the street.

Evidently her neurons are firing faster than mine. Practically without looking, I cross the street with Mia in my arms. Some idiot driving a flashy car he doesn't deserve starts honking at me in road rage. I ignore him and head right into the short, narrow, parallel road. We hear the crash of the door as the cops knock it down, then some yelling and running feet. Mia can't stop shaking.

"Those guys have watched too many cop movies."

"Kyle, look!"

As we reach the end of the parallel street, a police car emerges from the road running perpendicular. I freeze. The voices and footsteps behind us are approaching fast. I wheel around and weigh our options.

"Here, Kyle, here."

Again, Mia beats me to the punch. She points to an iron fence that leads to a small patio of a religious building. As I race onto the patio, I catch a glimpse of the sign out front that says *Convento de las Carmelitas Descalzas.* Mia's body tenses as she sees a statue of the Virgin Mary, darkened by years of damp air. I climb the three steps leading up to the building's entrance and push the door open with my shoulder.

We enter an old church. Slender shafts of light filter through the long stained-glass windows. It smells of wax, dust, and aged wood. I get chills as I hear the door squeak shut behind us. I set Mia down on a bench and scan the place. There are wooden pews, a pipe organ, a figure of Christ on the cross, and a dozen other statues peering down at us in an eerie silence. There's a door behind the altar, but that's not what I'm looking for, not now.

"Kyle, we can't waste any time; let's go. What are you doing?"

"Stalling," I say. "We have to slow them down."

And as if there were no need for words between us, she nods, grasping my plan as I put it into action. We look at the old, solid wooden table next to the entrance. Its thick, sculpted legs and massive surface betray its weight. My knee is close to giving out, but all the same I shove the table with everything I've got. It feels like I'm pushing a solid block of concrete. We hear voices yelling outside. I lean my weight against the table, but it doesn't budge an inch. A lancing pain courses through my knee.

"Kyle!"

Her terrified voice ignites a strange sensation in me, a feeling of power, of superhuman strength. And as if I were getting a hand from my friends at Marvel and DC, I give one last heave, with even more force than my muscles are capable of. *The door is starting to open!*

"Ahhh!" I yell, pushing furiously. The table begins to give.

"Kyle, hurry up!"

I slide the table over just a fraction of a second before they barge in.

"¡Policía!" they shout, with no trace of courtesy. "Open the door."

Mia gets to her feet and looks at me. Still out of breath, I ask her, "How on earth did they find you?"

She shakes her head, trying to think. Then she opens her eyes wide, as if suddenly realizing something slightly embarrassing. The police are pushing and hitting the door, but the table seems nailed to the floor.

"My SIM card," she says. "They must have tracked me down when I switched to my American one." She slaps her forehead. "How could I have been so stupid?"

"Don't beat yourself up about it," I say. "Sherlock didn't have much use for modern technology either."

Cracking a jittery smile, she takes her cell phone out as if it were a grenade with no pin and removes the card.

"Let's go." I take her hand and drag her toward the altar. "We have to find another way out of here."

As we walk up the aisle, Mia angrily tosses her SIM card in a box labeled *Donations* and says, "Try and find me now, tough guys!"

The frantic knocking and shouting outside the entrance wipe the smile off my face.

"¡Abrán la puerta!" they yell. "Están detenidos."

When we reach the door behind the altar, I bend down, ready to pick Mia up again, but she waves me away. "It's all right, really," she says. "I can walk."

Seeing her downcast eyes, I have my doubts, so I lift her up anyway. "You can walk as much as you want once we're out of this mess." She balks. I look at her right in the eye. "Another relapse and it would be the fucking end. Do you really want to be sent back to Alabama?"

That does the trick. Not only does she stop resisting, but she helps me push open the back door. The shouts from the police go up a notch. We pass into what looks like a sacristy—a narrow corridor with cloakrooms on both sides and priests' vestments. I run toward another exit at the far end, which leads to a long hallway with lots of doors, all alike. One of them is open. Mia taps my arm. I look inside—one narrow bed, a chest, and a single black wooden pew.

"Get in there," she says, panicking. "We have to hide."

Instead I pick up my pace and keep walking. "If those two cops just knocked down a door you can be damn sure they'll search every corner of this place."

She looks at me without a word, but her eyes are screaming *help*. Trying to prevent my eyes from following suit, I say, "We have to get to the van before these RoboCop-wannabes get to *us*."

The hallway, which veers to the right, leads to a double wooden door. Mia takes a deep breath, but the air seems to hitch in her lungs. Powerlessness and the fear of losing her rattle me like a depth charge as I come to a stop in front of the door. I set her down as gingerly as I can, and we hold hands.

As I push the door open, the wafting smell of recently baked cookies hits us right in the nose. It's a kitchen. There are nuns pulling trays of cookies out of an oven, others packaging them, kneading dough in a corner, scouring dishes in a big stone sink. They all freeze as we walk in, but their faces are so impassive it gives me the chills. Mia squeezes my hand. There are two more doors at the far end. One of them has to lead to the street.

"Hi," says Mia, in that angelic voice she does so well. "We're kind of lost. Is there another way out of here?"

We hear police sirens at the far end of the kitchen. Shit, they must have already driven around back. Mia's eyes are imploring me to do something, not to bail on her.

"Please, sisters, I'm begging you," I say, with the blameless look of someone who hasn't killed his best friend. "You have to help us. We haven't done anything wrong." *At least, she hasn't.* "And—"

"We love each other," Mia takes over, injecting some drama. "And we've eloped, because our parents were against it, and now they've called the police on us and . . ."

Mia goes quiet as their confused looks make it clear they haven't understood a word. We hear a door opening in another room. Men speaking Spanish. Mia starts to breathe hard, her hand going clammy in mine. We turn, ready to double back.

"No." It's the firm, unyielding voice of an old woman. "Se han equivocado de puerta, la tienda está al otro lado."

We turn around. An old nun with thick glasses is speaking to us from the far end of the kitchen. The other nuns turn to her as if she just turned off their favorite TV show.

"Vengan conmigo. Les acompañaré a la salida," she says. And then in loud, clear English, she adds, "Come this way, quickly."

MIA

A glimmer of hope eases my ailing heart. As we follow the nun through a door on the opposite side of the kitchen, Kyle takes my hand and squeezes it, as if he is afraid to lose me, as if I might suddenly vanish into thin air. We enter a pantry full of boxes of cookies arrayed on wooden shelves. Sheer heaven, if it weren't for my pain. With every step it gets more oppressive, like a fist trying to knock me out of this world before my time is up. I'm scared; I don't think I've ever been this frightened. I can't die here, not like this, not yet.

Kyle turns to me as if sensing my condition, his bright eyes shimmering with concern. He doesn't say anything; he doesn't need to. He simply lifts me into his arms, making me misty-eyed in spite of myself. The nun turns around and looks at us through her thick brown glasses. For an instant she observes me, attentive, moved, as if trying to piece together information that simply won't fit. The brusque voices and footsteps of the police approach the door we just passed through.

"Let's go, let's go," whispers the sister, indicating a door at the end of the hallway. "This way."

Kyle follows her through a door, which she shuts and locks behind her; then we walk down a narrow corridor and come out onto a patio surrounded by stone arches. Kyle's footsteps break the spooky silence of the place. Every stone, every column seems to reveal secrets I can't quite discern. Kyle's heart pounds against mine, agitated, quickening, but at the same time, wistful, or so it seems to me. I lean on his shoulder as he advances, and oddly, I feel at home, a home that knows no walls, no boundaries.

The nun passes through one of the arches. Kyle follows her into a small chapel without a door. Inside there are only eight pews, a simple altar, and a confessional. The mingled smell of dampness and incense gives me chills. I bury my nose in Kyle's neck. The woman strides over to the altar.

"What are we doing here?" Kyle asks her, a little wary. "They'll find us."

The woman replies without turning around, "Have faith in the steps that guide you, my son."

Kyle looks at me with a frown but follows her to the other side of the altar. On the floor, beneath a worn red rug, is a trapdoor. At this point everything happens in quick succession. Kyle sets me down, opens the trapdoor, and, following the nun, helps me down the steep steps that seem to never end. Luckily they do, and with me back in Kyle's arms we wind our way through a network of underground corridors. The nun walks beside us and lights the way using her cell phone. It strikes me as an ancient, secret place.

It smells of soil and dampness, a witness to the passage of years that appear to have stood still.

Kyle glances at me every so often as if wanting to make sure I'm okay, that I'm not on my way out. The nun does likewise and, from the sound of it, is praying under her breath. The pain in my chest is subsiding, but the nun looks exhausted, her flushed complexion glazed with perspiration. Finally, we see a door at the end of the passageway. As we near it we hear the stern voice of a man reciting words devoid of emotion. It sounds like the priest's sermons at St. Jerome's. The nun comes to a halt before the door.

"How are you, my dear?" she asks, breathing hard.

Kyle looks at me as if his life depended on my reply. I nod, wishing with all my might that I could make myself invisible.

"Will you be able to walk?" she asks. "You'll attract attention otherwise."

"Oh, of course," I say, gesturing to Kyle to put me down. But he doesn't seem to want to. "I was just getting my breath back," I insist. "I'm okay now."

They share an I-don't-believe-you look; then Kyle sets me down and grabs my hand so firmly it feels like he wants to defy death itself.

"I'll go out first," the nun says. "In case the police are out there."

I nod, and we watch her as she slowly opens the door, takes a deep breath, crosses herself, and walks out. Kyle gives a sigh, looking frazzled. I count one, two, three, up to seven, before she comes back.

"All clear," she says. "May God be with you."

"Thank you so much," Kyle says.

"We're indebted to you, forever," I add.

"No, my dear, thank *you* for allowing me to help." And turning her steady gaze on Kyle, she adds, "God dwells in all of your deeds, whatever mistakes you make or have made in the past."

Kyle's breath catches in his throat for an instant. The woman graces us with a final smile before vanishing behind the door. I'm about to walk out, but Kyle stops me.

"Sure you're all right?" he asks. "If you like we can rest here till it gets dark and—"

"I can't stay here for a second longer," I tell him, and I tug on his hand as we cross the threshold, which, hidden behind a confessional, takes us into a church full of people dressed in their Sunday best.

"Podéis ir en paz," says the priest in a tone both sad and solemn.

The service must be over because everyone is standing up and heading toward the entrance. We blend in with the crowd until we're through the double wooden door and out into the street. We're back in the plaza, right opposite the house belonging to the woman who I thought was going to be my mother. A police car is parked in front of the church door, with one officer leaning against the car door talking on a radio. He doesn't look in the best of moods.

"Oh my God, do you see him?"

In reply, Kyle drags me along until we're with a group of teen-age kids who are talking and laughing as they walk. We stick to the group on the far side of the police, our hands locked together.

I recite every prayer I know, any prayer I can think of, as we pass the officer. We're so close I can hear his every word. Our hands tighten their grip; we don't even breathe. One of the teenagers laughs loudly. The officer looks in our direction. *He's going to spot us!* Just then, a flock of pigeons takes flight, and he seems momentarily distracted. We keep walking, looking straight ahead. I hear the voices of other police officers over the radio. We gradually get farther and farther away, and it's only when we reach the street on which our van is parked that I dare to glance back.

"We've lost him," I whisper.

Kyle nods without stopping, alert to every movement. As we reach the van, he opens the side door while looking around in every direction. I get in and sit halfway between the front seats and the back so that I can watch everything without being seen. He gets into the driver's seat, starts the engine, and looks up into the rearview mirror, where our eyes meet. He's startled but doesn't flinch. I sense that he's plumbing my depths, seeking answers to questions unasked. I'm afraid he *will* ask them, and I pray he doesn't. There are no more mothers on my list, and no more reasons for us to stay together. Or perhaps there are *many* reasons, maybe *too* many. I should never have asked him to come on this trip with me.

KYLE

As soon as we get in the van, I start the engine. Me at the wheel, Mia hiding out in the back. I don't even bother with the GPS—the only thing we want is to get the hell out of this place. I start down one street, then another and another, till we get to the outskirts of the town. I brake at a stop sign. It's a wide road surrounded by countryside.

"Hey," I say, "you okay back there?"

"Course," she says, peeking her head through the seats. "Everything's fine."

I don't know why she insists on lying to me when I can tell a mile away that nothing's fine. She looks so weak it frightens me. The purple rings under her eyes and the bluish tint of her skin don't lie. She's also having trouble breathing, although she must be used to hiding it.

She leans her hand on my backrest, ready to get into the passenger seat, when I see a blue van coming up on my left. *Cops!*

"Mia, get down!"

She drops to the floor. I swallow hard as the van approaches, about to turn left. Everything slows way down like a scene moving frame by frame. They look over at me, and I look back nervously. Just as they come up next to us, they stop. Shit. I guess looking scared out of my wits wasn't the best move.

"Everything all right?" they ask me through my window.

I nod, attempting a casual smile. They give me a surly nod of their own and drive off. Not daring to breathe yet, I press the accelerator and slowly turn right. I drive in total silence for a few hundred feet.

"Clear?" whispers Mia impatiently.

After checking every mirror a dozen times and making 1,000 percent sure they're gone, I reply, "All clear."

Mia takes a seat, her eyes glued to me. For an instant we just look at each other with a gravity that's unlike us. Then Mia clears her throat and solemnly says, "Well, I guess now we'll have to add a clause to your contract that includes these types of . . . circumstances, don't you think?"

The tension in my face suddenly dissolves, and I burst into uncontrollable laughter. Mia smiles with one eyebrow raised, then starts to giggle herself. Soon we're in stitches. It's a laughter laced with nerves, but a laughter that liberates, a laughter full of bottled-up tears. I don't want to be apart from her, I don't want her to die, and I don't want to live with this constant, lurking fear that something bad is about to happen to her. As our laughter subsides, a sadness takes its place, one that weighs us down. Again the air between us seems to thicken. Mia looks out the window, concealing her face. "Take us far away," she says. "Far away from here."

I don't answer. What is there to say? I need to stop, take her into my arms, and tell her that everything will be all right. This sadness is one of those that drains you, that pounds you into the ground till you're beat, and I know it all too well. So, when I see a sign that says *Hotel Rural los Tejos* with an exit pointing left, I turn without thinking twice.

"Hey, what are you doing?" she says, a note of apprehension in her voice.

"I'm exhausted, Mia," I say, even huffing to look more convincing. "I'm not used to this kind of stuff." And I make sure *stuff* sounds like something truly awful.

Mia shakes her head and, still looking out the window, her voice turns dry. "Make sure you never enter a lying competition. You're pitiful at it."

At least she's not putting up a fuss. Following the sign, I turn onto a narrow unpaved road lined with trees. The fields are full of poppies, white and yellow flowers, and some goat herds. I could spend days sketching this place. But more than that, I could spend days drawing Mia's face just as it is now. It's the illumined visage of a girl whose most beautiful dreams are sliding before her very eyes.

As we drive, she shrinks farther into her seat, as if this place, this moment, even this life, were too big for her, as if somehow it was no longer hers to live. I don't know why, but I have a strange feeling she's hiding something from me, and it burns me up inside, it consumes me, and above all, it pisses me off.

It doesn't take us long to reach the hotel. The place is breathtaking, all stone and wood, looking like something out of the Middle Ages. The reception is in a lounge with a fireplace, so spacious it houses two benches for people to sit and warm themselves. My dad would go wild if he saw it. Mia looks fascinated, as if in a dream that won't end.

"Buenas tardes," says the receptionist, walking up to the desk.

"Hi," I say. "Do you have a room for the night?"

"We sure do," she says, punching a few keys on a computer. "Would you like a suite or a standard double room?"

A suite, I yell inwardly. But I look at Mia and wait for her to answer for us both. She doesn't. She's so spaced out she doesn't seem to hear.

"Actually . . . ," I say, in spite of myself. "We'll take two single rooms, please."

As I hand over my dad's credit card, the void I feel in the pit of my stomach begins to swell, and the worst part is, I don't know why. We've seen all the mothers on her list, and now we have no choice but to go home to Alabama. So why isn't she talking about it? Why isn't she talking about her surgery, or the trip, or what will happen tomorrow? If she weren't hiding something from me, she'd be talking about it nonstop.

MIA

It's the most beautiful room I've ever seen in my life, and it's all mine. But still, I can't help feeling a twinge in my stomach at the thought that I could be with Kyle right now, in a suite, no less. I feel a strange but thrilling warmth coursing through my body. I should have a talk with those nuns back at the convent; I'm pretty sure I deserve sainthood for having resisted temptation. Pretending not to hear him hasn't been easy, especially when my body was burning at the mere thought of spending a night with him. Okay, I'll have to search my mind for something more wholesome to focus on. Thinking about my mother is no longer an option, so I'll concentrate on this room.

The bed is huge, and there's a balcony overlooking a river. I check out the bathroom. *Oh my word,* it has one of those bathtubs with jets of gushing water. It takes me a while to figure out how to insert the bath plug, and once I do, I let the hot water run. I feel like Julia Roberts in *Pretty Woman*, minus the profession. My body is begging me to lie down, and I feel out of sorts, as if I were floating, as if I were not completely inside my body. I'm seized by a chill of fear—I don't want to die yet. I close the faucet a little so that the water runs more slowly. We'll be having dinner in an hour, and I want to get some rest before my bath.

Back in the room, I take out the bottle of pills from my backpack. *Only two left!* Okay, I need to calm down. I take the pills and throw myself onto the soft bed. It's hot in here, but my whole body is shivering. I cover myself with the silky bedspread. My fear looms so large, is so oppressive that I want to cry like a little girl. But I refuse. I grab my phone and scroll through my photo gallery looking for pictures of Kyle. In one, his gray eyes are looking my way as he smiles at me, holding up my colorful ice cream. Yes, it's *me* he's smiling at. *I'm* the one who's making him smile. But a wicked voice in me pipes up, saying, *Yeah, but not for long,* and just like that my bubble bursts. My body is too sluggish to get up from the bed, my soul too heavy to keep struggling. I should turn off the water, but my eyes are drooping, I can't keep them open, and I can't get up. *Help.*

KYLE

The room isn't bad. What most certainly *is* bad is that Mia isn't with me. I let my backpack drop to the floor and collapse onto the bed. We agreed to meet in an hour. How am I supposed to stand the wait? She didn't look good at all. If something happens to her . . . no, nothing can happen to her; it would be too *unjust*. The blue sky filters through the open window that opens onto the balcony. The tops of the poplars sway in the wind as if gesturing to me, as if wanting to tell me something. I'm still angry at God but find myself asking him, imploring him, *begging* him not to let her die.

I get my phone and open her photoblog, scroll through the pictures, lingering over the few she's actually in. Without expecting it, I come upon a selfie of her and Noah. My heart starts to ooze its scorching lava of guilt. Noah looks so happy. I haven't seen his face since that wretched day.

"I'm sorry, man." My voice is breaking.

He keeps smiling, as if saying yes, he does forgive me and understands.

"Miss you, dude. I miss . . . just talking, having fun like we used to." The rivers of lava almost block out my view of the screen. "Man, I don't know what to do about Mia. I don't want her to die. I love her, you know? Never felt this way before. I'd give my life just to save hers and bring you back."

A bird with blue wings lands on the railing of my balcony. I don't budge. It looks at me and trills a few beautiful notes before flying away. I follow its flight path and observe the sky. It seems brighter somehow. Well, I'm not usually one for signs, but I thank whatever it is that might be listening to me, then look back at Noah's picture.

"I don't know if you can do something from up there, but watch over her, will ya?"

MIA

My eyelids open slowly, one at a time, like heavy blinds struggling to lift. The moment I feel the soft touch of the bedspread, I give thanks that I'm still breathing. I feel better, more present, though still a little drowsy. I look out of the open window, and as I begin to admire the dark star-studded sky, it hits me—*Oh, shoot, I overslept!* I grab my phone and use the hotel Wi-Fi to check the time and see twelve missed Telegram calls and at least twenty messages, all from Kyle. I open the last one. It's a selfie of him in the restaurant, when it was still daytime. The caption reads, *Waiting for you downstairs, in the restaurant.* Oh boy.

I get to my feet as fast as I can, and as I'm walking out the door I remember the bathtub. Fearing the worst, I rush into the bathroom. The bathtub is full, but the faucet is off. *Phew,* it must have some kind of sensor.

I pick up my backpack and hurry downstairs.

KYLE

I've bitten all my nails down to the quick—on both hands—and that's something I've never done in my whole life. After knocking at her door, calling her on Telegram, and leaving her I don't know how many messages, I finally went into her room. She was sound asleep. Her breathing was so slight I had to touch her to make sure she was okay. I couldn't resist sitting next to her for a while, but not for long. If she'd woken up and found me staring at her like a weirdo, I don't know what she would have done.

But that was two hours ago, two hours in which I racked my brain with all the what-ifs I could think up. What if she isn't asleep but unconscious? What if she dies because I didn't take her to the doctor? What if she never wakes up again? What if she dies during surgery? What if she has no feelings for me? The what-if game is contagious; that's for sure.

For the last hour I've managed to do some sketching. That is, sketching *her,* since I can't think about anything else. The restaurant closed a while ago, but they told me I could hang around here as long as I wanted. It's nestled under some trees on the banks of a river. As I finish the sketch, I hear someone approaching. It's her—it has to be her. As she emerges from between the trees, with her short dress and yellow jacket on, I almost cry from relief. I'm turning into a weeper, for Chrissake. And although it annoys me to do so, I thank whatever might be up there for helping me out. I feel Noah's presence, as if he were looking down on us, gracing us with his smile. It gives me goose bumps.

"Sorry," she says as she walks over. "Really. I overslept and—"

"I know."

She stops, then continues walking but much slower, a questioning look on her face.

"I saw you," I say.

"Have you taken up astral traveling lately?"

"That would have been much easier; I'll keep it in mind for next time. But seriously, you didn't answer my calls, I got worried, so I asked the reception for a key and basically saved you from drowning."

Her eyes open wide. She even blushes. "Well . . . ," she says, sounding disappointed. "I would have expected something more from an artist. I don't know, something like climbing up the balcony, sending in a drone or something. But thank you anyway."

She coaxes a smile from me.

"You hungry?" I ask, uncovering the plate of fish and fries I saved for her.

"Thanks, but not really."

Shit, she isn't feeling well. But she sits down anyway and takes a french fry.

"Listen," I say finally. "About the trip tomorrow. I think before we head to the airport, we should stop at a police station and clear everything up."

"Airport?" she says, laying down the fry. "No way. I *can't* leave yet. I have to keep looking."

"For what? You've already found all the women on the list."

"Yeah, but maybe I screwed up the age range, or—"

Frustration overpowers every one of my neurons, making my words sound harsher than I want them to. "You can't be serious!"

"Just a few more days."

"No, Mia, you have to go back. You need that fucking operation. This isn't some game."

"I know . . . but I can't just give up now. We're so close. I can feel it."

I'm getting desperate. "You can't keep putting your life on the line to look for a woman who might not even want to be found. You've done your best, Mia." My words hurt her; I can see it in her quivering chin. "I'm sorry, but—"

"No, no . . . ," she says, cutting me off. "You're right, I guess. Actually . . ." She shakes her head, looking down. When she looks up, her eyes are alight with a strange mixture of anger and helplessness. "I just want her to look me in the eye and tell me why she didn't keep me, how she could bring herself to abandon me and forget I ever existed."

"Maybe she did it because it was best for you," I say, almost without thinking. "Maybe she thought you'd be better off with someone else. Who cares?"

"I care, Kyle!" Her gaze is racked with pain. "You don't understand."

"No, Mia, *you* don't understand! There are plenty of people out there who simply aren't cut out to be parents, okay? And your 'need to know' can't be worth dying for, worth wrecking our lives by going before your time, goddamn it."

She looks at me, visibly distraught, struggling to reply. "I just need . . . a few more days."

I get up, feeling powerless, pissed off, and so exasperated that I blurt, "Maybe if you stopped obsessing about finding a woman who did nothing except give birth to you, you'd actually start turning your attention to the people *around* you who actually love you." Shit, I didn't mean for it to come out like that. But at least she can't go on pretending she doesn't know. She goes quiet. "I need to cool off," I say, and walk off toward the river.

MIA

I'm still trying to process Kyle's words when he takes off his shirt and dives into the water. Those were thunderbolts of a reality I didn't want to hear, nor see, nor admit exists. Did he say he loved me? Is that what he wanted to tell me? *Dream on, Mia,* says that malicious voice in my head, spewing its poison once again.

I observe him for a moment, but he's still underwater. He comes up momentarily for air, then plunges back down. His backpack is on the chair, his sketchbook on the table. I turn to the river, then back to the sketchbook. I pick it up, opening it to a page bookmarked with a pencil.

The striking beauty of the drawing makes my eyes well up. It's a picture of that day on the roof of our van. He's holding me, the shooting stars and sky above the only witnesses to our . . . our *what*? What is this thing we have? There's a penciled caption. *If you cry because the sun has gone out of your life, your tears will prevent you from seeing the stars.* —*Tagore*

I read it three more times. Each word hits me, sears itself into my mind with the fire of its intention. I turn back to the river, looking for the only star in my entire sky. He's on the opposite bank, with his back to me, motionless. Everything in me, every atom, every particle, every sense, begs me to join him. I take my shoes off and make my way over to him, crossing the wooden bridge, not able to take my eyes off him even for an instant. He turns to look at our table, and when he doesn't spot me there he starts to look around nervously. As soon as he sees me, he seems to relax and waits for me, his gaze following steadily as I walk along his side of the river. As I reach him, I'm trembling. I want to speak to him, explain how I feel, tell him how much his drawing and his words moved me, but I can't. I sit down on the bank and dip my feet into the water.

"It's cold." That's all I manage to say.

Kyle stands up in front of me. His eyes, like a raging river, ask me countless questions.

"I might be wrong," I say. "But I need to see this through, Kyle. Please, I'm begging you, just give me three more days."

He just looks at me impassively. I pretend to scratch a spot between my shoulders, and crossing my fingers, I opt for a despicable lie. "If I don't find her, I'll go back home and have the surgery. I promise."

Lying to him makes me nauseated.

He nods, then says, "Three days, Mia, no more."

"Kyle . . ." My lips seem to have said his name without consulting me.

He looks at me expectantly, his enormous pupils mirroring the whole moon. I fight to hold myself back, to stop myself from doing what I'm about to do, from saying what I'm about to say. But I know it's a losing battle. "In your sky . . . ," I say, "are there a lot of stars?"

I've caught him off guard. The mixed emotions glowing in his eyes make it clear. "Well," he says, getting closer to me. "In my sky, there's one star that shines far brighter than the rest."

I look at him, and he returns my gaze; the entire firmament enfolds us in its blanket of night.

"If anything goes wrong . . . ," I begin.

He puts his finger to my lips, but I brush it away as gently as I can. I have to say this. I want him to know.

"If anything goes wrong, Kyle, I'll wait for you on Venus."

His eyes narrow, his chin struggling against the rising tremors. He wraps his arms around my waist. I wrap my legs around his. Looking directly into my eyes, he closes in. Like magnets, my lips draw closer to his. His lips thirst for mine. Our lips meet, and for an instant we don't move, just savor the soft, ardent touch. Our craving wells up like a tidal wave, surging and sweeping all before it. My body is shaking with a desire I've never felt before. He parts his lips and glides them along mine. I melt in the waters of the river. He kisses me, I kiss him back, and we fall into one long kiss that reaches forever.

MIA

April 3

    Very, very early, a.m.

    Can't sleep, Mom, so I've decided to dash off a few lines, although to be honest I'm not sure I want to. For a second, I was torn between writing to you and going down to the reception and flinging all my diaries into the fireplace. Still don't know what stopped me. Guess it's because today is one of those days when I need a mother to confide in, to turn to for advice, someone who can listen and understand and tell me everything is all right. And although you're probably just a figment of my imagination, I feel better believing you're more than that.

    I shouldn't have kissed him. Mom, it turns out that Pretty Woman was a saint compared with me. How could I have done this to the greatest guy alive?

After kissing for more than an hour, he saw that I was getting cold and insisted on walking me up to my room. He wanted to come in, that much was obvious. And I wanted him to, oh, Mother, how I wanted it. Never wanted something more, but it was out of the question. This whole situation is becoming way too dangerous. He makes me doubt; he makes me want things I shouldn't want, things that are not in the cards for me. I've even found myself feeling afraid—do you see what it's come to? I'm starting to <u>fear death.</u> Not dying itself, but being taken away from Kyle and him being taken away from me. But it's too late now. This decision was made a long time ago. I don't want to go on.

I'm an idiot, a real nitwit, but you know what? If you hadn't left, none of this would be happening. If you had come looking for me, if I had meant something to you, I might have been able to let someone else mean something to <u>me</u> too.

I slam my diary shut so hard it goes flying across the floor. Then I let my feeble body collapse onto the bed and can still feel Kyle's presence on me—his skin, his scent, his touch, his everything. And I spend the rest of the night longing for him, losing sleep, shedding tears that ran dry years ago.

KYLE

I spent the first half of the night tossing and turning in my bed, and the second stealing out into the starry night and sketching Mia nonstop. I missed her, a lot, too much. Before dawn, and after a few laps in the pool, I sent a message to my folks, on the verge of telling them all about Mia, about her illness and everything, but didn't. At times I feel that if I don't talk to someone and vent the turmoil inside me, I'm going to burst.

As soon as they opened the breakfast buffet, I got a table near the river. Mia came down a little while later, although I can't really tell if it's her or a clone that's replaced her. *This* Mia is avoiding me and behaving as if last night never happened, as if our kisses hadn't left the slightest trace in her memory. And here I was dying to kiss her again this morning. When she came down she just waved a greeting, as if I were a colleague, not deigning to even look at me. Since then she's just been sitting there, looking up new maternal candidates on her phone.

"So anyway," she says, oblivious to everything around her. "I've broadened the age bracket a little, which gives me five more possible candidates." If she were to look at me right now she'd realize how little I care about her wild-goose chase. "If we hurry, that is . . . ," she continues, immersed in Mialand.

"Some coffee?" asks a waitress, holding a pot.

Mia looks up, and in doing so our eyes meet, by mistake obviously, because she instantly looks away and turns her attention to the waitress. I continue to look at her steadily. This is getting on my nerves.

"Yes, please," she answers, and squints at the waitress's name tag. I'm guessing this is all part of the ignore-Kyle-at-all-costs strategy. As soon as the waitress finishes serving the coffee, Mia goes prim and proper, "Thank you very much, María."

"Victoria," the woman says, correcting her as she turns to pour me a cup.

Mia looks at her, one eyebrow slightly raised, her lip turned down at one corner, as she does when she doesn't understand something and is annoyed about it. I love it.

"My name is Victoria," the waitress says. "In Spain we have two names, but we normally only use one."

"Oh, I'm sorry. In that case, thanks a lot, Victoria."

Victoria. Of course, how did I not think of that before? I get lost in a train of thought as the woman walks away, and I hear Mia's words as if spoken from afar. "As I was saying, I think we can get to all of them before Wednesday."

My brain, oblivious to her Mother Mission Impossible, finally finishes processing the new piece of information. "And what if the what-ifs did serve a purpose after all?" I ask her, speaking half to myself.

Mia finally looks at me, albeit with the irked expression of someone listening to gibberish. *Fine.* I take out a pen from my backpack and write the waitress's name on a paper napkin: *María Victoria Ruiz Suárez.* I show it to her. Mia looks at the napkin, but apparently her neurons have lost some of their bounce this morning.

"How about . . . ," she says, a little edgy, "you talk in plain English for once."

"All right, so now we know that some people in Spain have double-barreled names, right?"

Mia nods.

"And from what I read, they also have two last names . . . so how do you figure her name would be written on an official American document?"

Mia shrugs, but her widening eyes tell me I've piqued her interest.

"Check it out," I say, and crossing out *Victoria* and *Ruiz,* I read, "*María Suárez.* Mia, what if you've been looking for the wrong person this whole time?"

Finally, Mia is back, *my* Mia, the one who actually looks at me, her eyes full of pure, childlike hope. She says, "You think so?"

"Let me see your birth certificate."

She hastily takes it out of her bag, unfolds it on the table, and crosses her arms over her backpack as if wanting to protect it from the outside world. The certificate reads *María A. Astilleros.*

"*A,*" I say, my head nodding on its own.

"But there are hundreds of names that start with *A.* It could take years."

"What if?" I say, and write out, *María Amelia_____ Astilleros*.

She goes silent, seized by an emotion which seems to frighten her, and shrinks down in her seat. "Do you really think . . . ?" she asks, her voice small.

I nod. Maybe her mother did want her after all; maybe she gave the hospital her name and they named Mia after her mother. Who knows? She bites her lip, the tears threatening to surface, and turns back to her phone. I can't help watching her. She's a beauty, an absolute beauty. The rings under her eyes have faded a little, and her complexion has recovered some of that shine that reminds me of stardust. And even like this, doing her best not to cry, she's looking in better shape already.

"Okay," she says, her words quickening. "I've found eight Amelias with Astilleros as a second last name in Spain. But three days is going to be really tight. I have to plan our itinerary down to a T, and fast. We have to get going. C'mon, we've got to have breakfast. No, wait, *you* eat, and I'll look for the nearest of the eight women."

Not wanting her to choke on her words, I get up and head toward the buffet. "Want anything?"

"Nah," she says, her eyes glued to her cell phone. "Well, okay, whatever they have."

The buffet is made up of three tables with white tablecloths. I stride directly over to the one with the bread rolls and muffins. While waiting for a man and a woman—a real couple from the looks of it—to get a few slices of bread, I notice one of those stands with tourist brochures. One of them catches my eye. It's a brochure advertising an excursion to a cave with a statue of the

Virgin Mary. *No way.* It's the Virgin on Mia's pendant. I grab one and three bread rolls and rush back to our table.

"Look, it's identical to the one on your necklace."

Mia takes the brochure and studies it with much less interest than expected.

"Where did you get that pendant?" I ask, pointing to her slender neck.

My question seems to burst her bubble. She takes it between her fingers and with a wistful air says, "I was wearing it when I arrived at St. Jerome's. Guess my mother put it on me. I spent years trying to figure out what it meant, trying to understand why she wanted me to wear it, why she left it to me in the first place. I made up stories, believing it was some sort of clue, a sign she had left so that I could find her, but . . ." She lets the necklace fall like someone letting a dream slip between their fingers, then shrugs. "I guess I've grown up since then, at least a little."

"Our Lady of Covadonga," I say, reading the brochure.

"Yes, I've read everything possible about it online. It's in the north of Spain, a region called Asturias. As you can imagine, it was the first place I checked out, but there weren't any women with her name there." Suddenly her face lights up. "Although now . . . maybe . . . oh, Kyle, you're the best!"

Mia conducts a quick search on her phone. Her smile warms my heart. "Oh my God, Kyle. Look, here's one, *María Amelia Nieto Astilleros.* It has to be her." She springs to her feet so fast the table rattles. "Let's go."

I laugh and gesture for her to please sit down. "Hey, your driver needs some carbohydrates. Give me a sec, okay?"

She does sit back down but doesn't stop looking at me. Suddenly, the thought of wolfing down a bread roll in front of Mia, who can't even bring herself to blink, doesn't seem like much fun. "You win," I say, putting the roll down. "I'll eat this on the road."

What's a lost breakfast compared with a found smile?

KYLE

She didn't eat anything after all—her bread roll is resting intact on her lap. As soon as we got into the van, she reclined her seat. After writing in her diary for a while, she started looking out the window, her gaze reaching far beyond what my naked eye can see. She didn't say a word, didn't even take pictures. I'd give a fortune to know what goes on in her head, to have her share even a fraction of her harrowing world with me.

Mia takes a deep breath and, stretching in her seat, reaches over to get something from the back. It's a red blanket. According to the van's thermometer it's twenty-seven degrees Celsius, which must be about eighty degrees for us, and yet still she's bundling her whole body up. It's no use asking her how she's feeling or what's wrong, since the answer will be a lie anyway.

"Hey . . . ," I say, without yet knowing what I want to say.

When she turns to me and I see her sluggish look, under eyelids that seem to weigh a ton, my words come out all by themselves. "We still have five more hours to go until we reach Asturias. Why don't you get some sleep?" Her only reply is a slight side-to-side movement of her head. "If I see anything really interesting, I'll wake you up. Promise."

She gives me a steady look, without a word and without the slightest movement, not even a blink. I can't tell if she's thinking, studying me, or off in her own world.

"Sure you don't want to crash out in the back?"

She doesn't answer, just looks down at my right hand, puts hers over it, looks back up, leans back, and closes her eyes. The mere touch of her skin puts me at ease, like a balm healing a million wounds at once. I very carefully slide my fingers between hers. She lets me, even squeezes my hand a little, as if saying yes, she's still here, that she'll be back, that maybe I just have to wait a while. And although driving with just one hand on the wheel frightens me more than I can say, there is no way I'm letting go of her hand, even if I were staring into the jaws of the underworld itself. So I drive like that for hours, sheltering her frailty in my hand, sensing that she's entrusting me with that part of her that could shatter at the slightest touch. I can almost hear her say, *Don't fail me, don't let me fall.* Never, Mia.

What does seem to be falling is the temperature. We've just passed through a long tunnel, and emerging from it a green sign welcomes us into the province of Asturias. The landscape here couldn't be more ravishing—high mountains covered with vegetation and tufts of snow, lakes, and a sky alive with thick clouds in every shade of gray. Mia needs to see this; it's going to blow her away. Besides, I promised her. I ease off the gas pedal and turn to her. She's still asleep, in the same position she was in at nine o'clock this morning, so about four hours ago.

"Mia . . . ," I whisper.

She doesn't seem to hear.

"Hey," I say, giving her hand a gentle squeeze.

Not the slightest response. Shit. I give her a tug. Nothing. A little harder. Zero.

"Mia," I say, my voice rising. "Mia, what's wrong?!"

I slam on the brakes and stop the car on the side of the road. Then I pounce on her.

"Mia," I beg, panic-stricken. "Mia, talk to me!"

But she doesn't. I take her face into my hands, I shake her, talk to her, but there isn't the slightest reaction. She's still, very still, far too still.

God, no. I floor the gas pedal, and praying aloud, I take her somewhere they can take care of her.

KYLE

I should have forced her to see a doctor. I should have told my folks everything. I should have . . . I don't even know what the fuck I should have done, just something different, better, *good*. Shit, shit, shit. That's been my fucking mantra in the three hours I've been in this waiting room without walls. I picked up my phone like two dozen times, ready to call my parents, but I couldn't bring myself to do it. I promised her I wouldn't. And in this place, all I've been hearing is "We have no news yet," "I don't speak English," or "The doctor will contact you as soon as we know more."

The tension is eating away at me, consuming me, making me tear my hair out. Doesn't anybody see this? Is no one going to help me put an end to this shit? It doesn't look like it, so I go on the offensive and stride up to the nurses' station.

"What the fuck are you doing to her?" I hiss.

"Por favor señor, siéntese," says one of the nurses for the umpteenth time this afternoon.

God, somebody must be able to tell me something. I turn to

a man in his fifties, wearing a white coat and a smug air as he saunters down the hallway.

"Excuse me, do you speak English?"

He shakes his head without stopping, even appears to pick up his pace a little. Why the hell is he wearing a white coat if he couldn't care less about helping people? Asshole. I return to my seat, and as I do Mia's backpack gets snagged on the backrest and falls to the floor. I almost burst into tears, as if by dropping her backpack I were dropping her, as if I were failing her. This waiting game is more than I can bear. I pick up the backpack, and through the half-open zipper I see a medium-sized envelope. I take it out and look inside purely out of restlessness: just to do something, to focus my attention on something other than my fear that she may be suffering, lonely, and that I might lose her. Inside I find her passport and the plane tickets. I look at it just to read her name written on it, even if it's the false one. But what I see wounds me like a double-edged knife. Mine's a round-trip ticket. Hers isn't. It's a single. What on earth is this supposed to mean?

"Kyle?"

I look up, startled. It's a doctor, wearing a white coat and a stethoscope around her neck. "Your friend Miriam asked me to come and talk to you."

I jump to my feet, my heart in a frenzy. "Is she okay?" I sputter.

"She's stable for now. She's been taken out of the ICU." That may be, but the doctor's expression doesn't bode well. "However . . . ," she says finally, and I dread what may come next. "Her heart is very weak. I understand that her religion prevents her from undergoing heart surgery. She's already explained that the Amish see the heart as the 'soul of the body,' but it's vital. If she doesn't . . . she will die."

"I know . . ." *I know it all too well.* "How long do you think she can hold out?"

She shakes her head and gives me a long, hard look before answering, as if she knows her reply could tear me up. "A month, a week, a few hours . . ." Desperation is howling in me. "We just don't know."

"Can I see her? Please, I have to see her. I have to try to convince her."

"Yes, of course." She checks the watch on her wrist. "Visiting hours start in two minutes. I'll take you up to her room."

I walk next to the woman as she leads me through a series of long hallways that seem never to end, my mind raging like a beehive. Everything is out of joint, jagged, brutal, like a Cubist painting by a madman.

MIA

I know I don't have much time left. My heart lets me know that with every beat, with every stifled, arduous breath I take. This morning, without my pills, I couldn't even hold up my end of the conversation with Kyle. I felt myself drifting away, disintegrating, barely able to understand what was coming from his lips. I thought that after getting some sleep I might be able to make it to my mother's house, but I was wrong. Feeling his hand on mine gave me strength to keep going, but not enough to keep me from another cold hospital bed, my only company the machines whose constant beeping I've come to hate so much.

I feel strange, as if I were walking between two walls that are closing in, and no matter how hard I try, I can't find my way out. The thought of dying and never seeing Kyle again is unbearable, but so is the idea of carrying on. Every last part of me is gripped by anguish. One thing is for certain: I have to get out of this room at all costs. *Where is Kyle?* I asked the doctor a while ago if she could talk to him. Maybe she didn't find him; maybe he got tired of waiting or just got tired of my problems, period. And just when the most evil part of my mind is about to send me hurtling into the land of despair, the door gently opens. It's Kyle. His smile, though a little forced, lights up the whole room.

"Hey . . . ," he says, and after shutting the door, he drops down next to me like someone shouldering an unbearable weight. "How you feeling?"

"You have to help me, Kyle," I plead in a whisper. "You have to get me out of here."

"Easy now," he says, taking my hand. "Everything's okay."

"No, it's not." *Can't he see that?* "If I stay here they're going to find me, they'll find out who I am, and—"

He cuts me off as if he hasn't understood or refuses to understand what I'm saying.

"It's all right, Mia. These people know what they're doing. I know things aren't going according to plan, but you can't keep putting it off. They said they can operate first thing tomorrow morning. And as far as your mother is concerned—"

"No!" I scream without meaning to. "Please, Kyle, you can't do this to me; you promised." Desperation is speaking through my lips. "I promise I'll come back and have the surgery tomorrow. I swear."

"Bullshit, Mia!" he says, suddenly getting to his feet, his jaw quivering in a rage that catches me off guard. Then he backs up a couple of steps as if he finds me repulsive. This is more than I can bear. He shakes his head. "How many times have you lied to me already?"

Everything is swimming before my eyes. He takes something out of his pocket, takes two steps toward me, and tosses it onto my bed. It's my plane ticket. I curl up, wishing the sheets could swallow me whole.

"You never intended to *have* the operation, did you? After finding your real mother, you just planned to let yourself waste away like a . . ."

He holds the final words back, then shakes his head and looks away. God, let him look at me, please, let him look at me. Then he does, but only to say, "And I admired you for not being afraid of death, when the truth is you're nothing but a coward."

"No, Kyle."

"No? Tell me it's not true. Tell me you were going to have the surgery."

I go quiet.

"Damn it, Mia. Would you rather die than take the risk of staying alive? Do you really prefer to leave the people who love you high and dry, rather than risk . . . what exactly? Having someone love you? Or loving someone *yourself*?"

"Please, Kyle."

"You don't give a shit, about me or anyone else. All you care about is yourself."

"Stop it!"

"You don't even care about this mother of yours for whom you've pulled out all the stops. You're just looking for her because . . ." His eyes cast a defiant look at me. "Why *are* you looking for her, Mia?"

"You don't understand!" I shout.

"Well explain it to me, then," he yells back, his voice outdoing mine out of sheer desperation. A thousand incoherent replies vie for attention inside me. I can't think straight. "I . . . I don't want them to open my heart."

"Why *not*, Mia?" He glares at me with a crushing contempt. "Are you afraid there's nothing *inside*?"

His words detonate in my very depths as he walks toward the door. *No, he can't leave now.* He stops and looks back over his shoulder. His glassy eyes betray an obliterating pain. My soul aches. I'm past comprehending. He seems about to say something, and I pray that he does, that he erases this moment and writes a new one, but he doesn't. He just lets his head hang to one side, walks out, and shuts the door behind him.

No, no, no, no. I can't stop looking at the door, as if I could magically make him reappear.

"Kyle . . . ," I say, knowing he won't hear me. "Kyle, that's not how it is. I do care about you, a lot. You shook up my whole world. It's just that I need time; I need to know that you won't leave me. Kyle, come back. Kyle, Kyle . . ."

KYLE

I rush out of the room with only one thing on my mind—to get out of this goddamn hospital as fast as possible. Instead, I end up walking a few laps around the building. Although the anger is eating me up, Mia is my North Star, and as long as she's alive I won't be able to leave her side. Shit. I kick a can of soda and find its sticky orange liquid dribbling all over my sneakers. Great.

Looking around, I see a kids' playground, with swings and rides, and make my way over to sit down on an empty bench. I glare up at the overcast sky with a fury that could unleash a storm. Why, God? Why? Why? Why? Oddly, with each pleading word I find my anger subsiding, giving way to a sadness, then to a nauseating sense of guilt. Was that me who just yelled at the girl I love, the girl who just made it out of the ICU and could still go at any moment? What an *asshole*.

The sound of my cell phone pulls me back from the brink. I let it ring three times before getting it out of my backpack. It's Josh. His picture appears on the screen, one taken before the accident. A bolt of lightning, followed by its fearsome friend—the roll of thunder—splits the sky in two and rattles me as if the bolt had passed right through every cell in my body. And just like that, without knowing quite how or why, I feel myself starting to unravel. Physically I'm still sitting on the bench, but the rest of me is hurled back to that night, to that car, to that ordeal.

I'm driving. Josh is next to me. It's cold out and the road is wet. We're approaching that fucking curve. I'm trying to force the Kyle of that day to brake, but I'm not in control of his body; all I can do is watch things unfold from his point of view.

Josh, totally wasted, sticks his cell phone in front of my face. He laughs.

"Don't, man," I say. "I'm driving."

I try to push his hand away, but he insists. The curve is a few yards away.

"No, you've got to see this," Josh says, and shoves the phone closer to force me to see what he wants to show me. *But I can't see the road.*

"Move!" I yell, pushing him away with everything I've got. He laughs again. I finally manage to get him off me but see an old man crossing the street. *We're going to hit him.* I jerk the steering wheel to the left. My gaze shifts and I find myself staring into Noah's eyes. His car is coming around the curve from the opposite direction.

"Nooo!" I shout as I slam on the brakes.

But the road is too wet and the brakes don't work. *We're going to fucking crash.* Noah looks at me, his face contorted in confusion, in fear. I reach out my right arm to protect Josh, but I can't avoid the head-on collision with Noah, and I can't prevent his eyes, now bleeding terror, from closing for good as the twisting metal lodges itself in his flesh. I can't prevent the life from leaving his body. *It's out of my fucking control.* I scream but can't even hear myself. Then everything goes black. There are noises, sirens, yelling, crying, people calling out, pain, emptiness; an enormous void that smothers me until the moment I reemerge in that hospital bed, the bed they literally tied me to "for my own good."

As if falling from a great height, I reenter my body and find myself sitting on the bench. My cheeks are wet, and it's not only from the rain that has started to fall. I look down at my cell phone and, as if someone else were moving my fingers, dial Josh's number. While I wait for him to pick up, I breathe in the scent of damp soil, of fresh air; I look up at the sky and everything seems a shade brighter, cleaner, less cruel, though maybe not.

"Hey, dude." It's Josh.

I can't get a single word out.

"Kyle? You there?"

Slowly, my lips loosen up. "Yeah, I'm here, Josh. . . ." Again, the silence is looking to overpower me, but I don't let it, and I continue, "It's all coming back. . . ."

Now the silence does win out, and my mind goes still, for the first time in ages. On the other end I hear a voice in despair. "I'm sorry," Josh whimpers. "I'm sorry. I couldn't bring myself to tell you, man." His sobs are crushing me. "It was me; it was my fucking fault. I was fucking wasted. I showed you that damn message. . . . It was a stupid message, Kyle. A fucking joke from my brother. Can you believe it? Noah's dead because of a goddamn joke." Acrid tears are clouding my vision. "I'll never forgive myself," Josh says with a hatred that resembles my own. "I just wanna disappear and put an end to this fucking nightmare. I deserve to be in a fucking wheelchair. I'm a piece of shit, Kyle."

I take a deep breath, trying to regain speech. "You know what?" My voice is breaking. "Noah wouldn't want this for you, and . . ." I find Mia's words on my lips. Mia, always Mia. "God wouldn't want you to beat yourself up about it either. I know that now. I'm sure of it."

"Kyle," he whispers. "My mom's coming. I have to hang up."

"Call me, okay?"

"I will."

He hangs up. I put the phone away, and as I inhale the crisp air, I see a little girl staring at me. She has a tube in her tiny nose and no hair. She can't be more than three years old. Her bright eyes seem to be laughing. She kneels, plucks a flower, and gives it to me. I smile through my tears, and in her small eyes I see Mia. The girl waves and runs off to play with the other kids. A young woman looks over at me from another bench. Must be her mother. We exchange wistful smiles. Mia's image appears before me, in her hospital bed, pleading with me to get her out of there, and I realize she's no less vulnerable than this little girl.

Over the last month I've learned the meaning of suffering, of desperation, of pain, and yet I still can't imagine what Mia's been through. What if she's too fragile, too delicate, too *good* for this world? What if all her talk of Venus is true, and she would be happy there, finally; who am I to stand in her way? Although it would kill me, who am I to demand that she stay? Shit, if only I'd inherited a more selfish gene.

Now I want to see her, to ease her pain, to let her know she's not alone. And if it's what she really wants, I'll support her and make her final days so unforgettable that not even death will be able to wipe them from her memory. I get up, and although my decision feels right, my whole body's shaking as I walk, my face still bathed in the silent rivers of my eyes.

MIA

Why isn't he coming back? Why won't he call my room? Is there anything more cruel than having to wait around like this? Lying here in bed, hoping he returns, without my phone and unable to contact him, is worse than my worst nightmare. So I've made up my mind; I'm busting out of here to go look for him. As the nurses finish up their usual drill of draw-blood-pop-pills-rinse-and-repeat and I'm finally alone, I start to peel off the bandage that holds my IV tube in place. Before I can get it off, there are three loud knocks at the door. *Kyle!* It has to be him.

"Come in," I call out, my eyes on the door as it opens.

The curly red hair of the doctor who took care of me in the ICU is the first thing I see; the second is the chart in her hand. My disappointment struggles to conceal itself.

"Is there a problem with your IV?" She points at my failed escape attempt. "If it's bothering you I can call a nurse and—"

"No, thanks," I say, a little more curtly than I mean to. "It was itching; that's all."

"My shift is up in a few minutes and . . . well, I just wanted to make sure you're okay."

"I'm fine, thanks," I reply without looking at her, my tone clearly implying *I'd like you to leave now.*

But she doesn't seem to catch my drift. "Where are your parents, Miriam? Here in Oviedo with you?"

"No." *Do you really care?* "They're back home, in . . . Virginia."

"I'm sorry, but you'll have to help me get this straight." Indignation is written all over her face. "Your parents don't want you to have surgery for religious reasons, and yet they allow you to *travel* in your condition?"

"I begged them," I say, trying to come up with something credible. "I didn't want to die before fulfilling my dream."

"Which is . . . ?"

"To see the world."

"I understand." But it's clear she doesn't, at all. She looks down at my chart and says, "There's some information missing in your file, like your passport number, your address . . ."

"Yeah, uh, I actually don't have my stuff with me. But I can bring it in tomorrow."

"No, Miriam," she says, frustration wrinkling her brow. "You don't seem to grasp how serious your condition is. We need to keep you here tonight."

"You can't force me." She's managing to get a rise out of me.

"No, please, calm down; getting riled up isn't good for you. Of course no one's forcing you to do anything, and I fully understand that your religion doesn't allow you to have the operation.

However . . ." She shakes her head, the lines on her forehead standing out. "You're still a kid, Miriam. You have your whole life ahead of you. What kind of God would want you to die without at least trying to heal yourself?"

Why is she meddling in things that don't concern her? My rising anger is making me nauseated, drawing contempt from my lips. "And what kind of God would want me to stick around in a world where everyone, without exception, ends up suffering?"

She looks at me for a moment, her compassion visible. Her big green eyes radiate something good, something I can't define, something that, despite my anger, I find myself warming to.

"My . . . ," she says finally. "Those are harsh words for a girl your age. But I know where you're coming from. I used to think that way, too, years ago." *Really? I don't believe you.* "That is, until I met one particular patient, an elderly man, who changed my entire outlook on life, and . . ." She points to the edge of the bed. "May I?"

My mind is screaming for her not to, but my head nods. Something in me needs to keep hearing her soothing voice. She takes a seat next to me. There's a sweet blend of jasmine and violets in her smell that delights me. My former foster mother used to cultivate them in her garden.

"The man was brought into our hospital after suffering a heart attack," she resumes. "It was his third in a year, and there was nothing we could do to keep him alive. At least that's what we thought. After a few minutes his heart started beating again. Once he recovered, he told me that he had seen his whole life pass before him like a movie, and it had dawned on him that all the suffering he had caused, and endured, had been senseless and unnecessary. He had realized that *lack of love* is the cause of all suffering. 'He who loves never suffers,' he said. 'Only he suffers who waits for others to give him the love he cannot feel.'"

Her words recall truths I already know but have long forgotten, truths that have languished in a corner of my soul and, for some reason, are a balm to me now. The kind doctor puts the bandage back on my arm, and in doing so, she notices the gitano's words still scrawled on my arm.

"Exactly," she says. "Countless years spent studying medicine only to realize that no surgery can mend a broken heart. Only love can do that, only the love we give, not the one we expect to receive."

I observe her in silence. Until a minute ago, I would have given anything to have this conversation with my mother, to cry in her arms, seek her advice, have her comfort me, tell me what I should do; but that's not going to happen, and I'm starting to care less if it does. This doctor, whom I don't even know, is offering me her affection, just like that, because she wants to, and this makes me want to cry, though not out of sadness. Holding back the tears I ask her, "Do you have kids?"

My question makes her uncomfortable, but she tries to hide it and shakes her head.

"Well, let's just say you did," I continue, "and it was your daughter who needed the operation. What would you say to her? Would you encourage her to go through with it?"

"Of course. I'd tell her to keep fighting, always."

"Even if opening her heart might be for nothing, and the recovery could be long and painful?"

"This life has so much beauty to offer, if we could just learn to see it . . . a few days of pain are nothing compared to the chance to be happy."

Her voice resounds within me like a sweet echo rippling endlessly. I still have a hard time believing her, but who cares? It sounds like milk and honey to me. It makes me think of Kyle and these past days spent by his side.

"If I decide to do it . . ." I hear my words as if someone else were speaking them. "Do you promise to perform the operation yourself?"

A quiet satisfaction passes over her slender lips. "Of course."

She pushes a lock of my hair up behind my ear, and her warm touch gives me a slight chill and a pleasurable tickle at the same time, something new to me. If I had met her any other day I would have asked her to stay, to talk to me about things, but I can't, not today.

"Try to get some rest, Miriam," she says, getting up. "I'll come and check on you at eight, when my shift begins, and we'll start getting things ready."

As she walks to the door, it hits me—did I just say yes? Did I really agree to the operation? Oh boy. I've never been so scared in my life. I start shaking, and that darn machine starts beeping like the dickens. Enough. I refuse to give in to the panic. The doctor turns around and gives me a questioning look. I take a deep breath, and the beeping eases off. She nods and jots something down on my chart. As she does so, I look through the window at the sky. Night is falling on what could be my last day, and all I want to do is spend it with Kyle. The search for my "mother" crumbles like a castle made of sand, like a figment of my imagination that never even existed. Now I feel how absurd it's all been—everything, my whole life, has been utterly meaningless. Frustrated over a sun that never wanted to shine for me, I neglected all the beautiful stars right under my nose.

The doctor is on her way out again but turns around once more with a melancholy air. "Good night, my dear. Get some sleep."

She leaves, releasing me without knowing it from my lifelong misery, my confusion, my sheer insanity, and suddenly, all I can think about is the brightest star of all—Kyle. Where *is* he?

I take off the bandage, the IV, and the electrodes connecting me to the machine and very slowly try to get up. Unless I'm mistaken, my clothes are still in the closet.

KYLE

Having prepared a little surprise for Mia, I walk into the hospital and run into four police officers at the entrance, speaking to a man in a white coat. I overhear Mia's name mentioned. Without having the slightest idea of how I'm going to get her out of this place, I walk into the elevator and press the button to the sixth floor. The only thing I know is that I have to get to her before they do. Just as the door shuts completely, I glimpse the man in the white coat pointing at the elevator. Shit.

On the way up, I try to think up a plan. Mia's room is at the end of the hallway, the part farthest from the elevators, which means we won't have time to reach them without being seen. I'll have to hide her, but how? Where? Damn it, I should have watched more movies about rescue attempts and all that crap. As the elevator comes to a halt, I slide through the doors. What I see sends me reeling. Mia's right there, alone and exhausted, hobbling her way down the long corridor. She smiles at me, her lips quivering.

"Hey, hey, hey," I say as I rush to her side. "What are you doing out here?"

"Looking for you." Her voice, so weak I can barely hear it, is killing me. "Kyle, I . . ."

"Shh." I slip my arm around her waist to steady her and point to the elevators. "They're on their way up."

Her startled eyes turn to look; the hum of the elevator's engine signals its arrival. We look in all directions, searching for a place to hide, but the entire hallway is lined with rooms, surely with patients in them. The elevator comes to a stop. Mia gives me a pleading glance. All right, then, we have no other option: I open the first door on our right, enter, and close it behind us while scanning the room. There's an elderly woman in one bed, hooked up to various machines. She seems to be sleeping. The other bed is empty. There's a fixed window on one side and a bathroom door and a wheelchair on the other. Mia looks at me as if imploring me to tell her what I've got planned.

"I ran into four cops downstairs," I whisper. "They mentioned you. We don't have much time, okay? As soon as they reach your room we'll have to make a dash to the elevators."

Mia nods with a smile of half-hearted mischief. "Yeah, dashing is my strong suit, as you know."

Okay, I wasn't thinking straight. Footsteps and voices are approaching in the hallway. We stare at each other in silence, her eyes begging for a rest, mine pleading for the chance to see her for the rest of my days. The elderly lady in the bed murmurs a few words in her sleep. The footsteps pass us by and recede down the hallway. When they subside, I open the door and look out. It's deserted. I pick Mia up and run toward the elevator. We make it in without being seen, as far as I can tell. Mia punches the ground-floor button. I take a deep breath and quickly exhale. Mia, looking frazzled but still smiling, leans her head on my shoulder. She strikes me as different somehow, more at ease.

"Thanks for not leaving me in the lurch."

"I'd never do that. Do you hear me?"

I'm not sure she does, because she shuts her eyes instead of answering. The only thing I hear as we make our way down is her frail and fitful breathing.

As the elevator touches down on the ground floor, I look around to make sure there are no police officers, and without quite knowing what to do next, I stride over to the exit. People are watching us, but there's more sympathy than suspicion in their eyes. I don't slow down and don't look back for a second. I cross the threshold, and once we're out I walk along the sidewalk in the direction of our van. My heart is hammering in my chest. I'm leading my girl toward a certain death, a consensual suicide, and I hate myself for it. But that's what she wants, and I love her too much to refuse. A sense of powerlessness runs riot in me. I set Mia down in the passenger seat, get behind the wheel, and speed away from the hospital, leaving behind my last flicker of hope.

KYLE

The dark sky bristling with stars is the only witness to our escape, or at least I hope it is. We left the hospital half an hour ago, and for the moment it looks like no one's following us. Mia has spent the entire time lying on her side, her luminous, honey-colored eyes fixed on me, a serene smile on her lips. I've never seen her this way before, so at peace, so . . . happy? Unlike the vortex wreaking havoc inside me, she *does* seem content with her decision.

"Kyle," she begins, her voice still too sickly. "I . . ."

"Shh," I say. "Try to get some rest; we still have more than an hour to go."

"Where are you taking me?"

She can't be serious. I glance over to make sure she's not delirious, but her quizzical face looks genuine enough. "To your mother's house, of course."

"No, please, don't."

What is up with her? I slow down a little and face her.

Taking my hand, she says, "I've lost too much time waiting to see the sun." She rests her lips against my knuckles before continuing. "I just want to spend tonight with the brightest star in my sky." And before my brain can finish processing her marvelous words, she adds, "I have to be at the hospital at eight tomorrow morning. I'm going to have the surgery, but right now, take me somewhere nice, will ya?"

Her words light up my entire night, fill my void, breathe new life into me, brighten the darkness itself, even the farthest reaches of space. I bring her hand up to my lips and kiss her with all the affection that envelops this universe, and maybe more.

MIA

With every minute that goes by I feel better, somehow calmer, more at peace. I don't even know where he's taking me, but it doesn't matter—I'm with him, and that's enough for me. I think it's the first time in my entire life that I've felt this way. Up until now I've always had the lurking sensation that there was something I wasn't doing right, that I was making mistakes, to the point of feeling guilty. And now . . . I don't know if it's the surgery, or being with Kyle, or having met that doctor, but that feeling of dread has vanished completely, nada, gone, and I couldn't be more thrilled.

We've been driving up a winding road for a few minutes, and yet, defying the dizziness and nausea, I continue to lie on my side, looking only at him. He seems happy, even though his wan face and trembling hands can't conceal the fact that he, too, is scared to death. I certainly am, but only in those fleeting moments in which my mind strays toward the only two subjects I've forbidden it to go near: parting with Kyle tomorrow, and the operation. I look out the window. Venus is perched alongside a waning moon, shimmering in a sky already bursting with stars. The lush trees raise impregnable walls on a forest floor so green not even the night can keep its luster hidden. At times I can't tell if I'm dreaming, or awake, or if the dream is dreaming me.

Kyle turns to me and, as our eyes meet, gives me a smile, *that* smile, the reason I want to remain on this forsaken planet adrift in the darkness.

"Hey, do you see that?" he says, pointing to my right.

I turn and notice one of those brown signs that displays tourist attractions. Its letters unveil an unexpected surprise: *Santuario de la Virgen de Covadonga*. My fingers instinctively reach for my pendant as I turn back to Kyle, my eyes alive with gratitude.

"In case things with your mother didn't work out like you hoped," he says with a light blush. "This was my plan B, bringing you up here."

"Oh, Kyle," I burst out. "Thank you. I've always wanted to see this place."

"Thank *you*, Mia. If I hadn't met you, I wouldn't have seen it either. And, jokes aside, this place is out of this world." His words warm my heart. "Check that out," he says, gesturing toward the top of the mountain.

High up, hovering like a cloud, the majestic basilica of the Virgin awaits us, its matching towers reaching up as if to tickle the belly of the sky. It looked gorgeous in the photos, but in the flesh it looks unreal, as if it had passed through dimensions and emerged from a better world. I roll down the window and drink in the crisp night air, the scent of forest, of water, of all things flush with life. Kyle parks the van beside the entrance of the cave I visited countless times in my dreams.

"We made it," he says as he pulls the hand brake. "I just need you to wait here for a few minutes. Can you do that?"

"Who do you think you're talking to?" I reply with a wink.

"Good," he says in a tone that verges on an order, and hastily gets out.

I take in the vibrant silence of the night. The trees, the open space, even the asphalt, seem more alive without the daytime bustle. I hear Kyle behind me; it sounds like he's moving things in or out of the side door.

"No peeking," he calls out from somewhere.

I giggle under my breath, because he's right. At any other time, curiosity would have won out, but not tonight; tonight all I need is the beauty I'm surrounded by. I wish everyone could see such splendor. *My camera.* I almost forgot about it. I take it out of my backpack and start snapping pictures of everything that catches my eye. And just as I'm about to ask Kyle to publish them tomorrow in *Expiration Date*, I find him standing at my door with the roguish grin of someone up to something; he then opens the passenger door like a perfect gentleman.

"Here, hold these." He hands me two one-euro coins. "We're going to need them later."

It's clear that he's read all about this place. I wrap my arms around his neck as he lifts me once again into those arms, two pillars of the only home I care to dwell in.

"Make the most of it," he quips. "This is the last night I'm going to let you be this lazy, got it? Next time you'll have to walk by my side. Or better yet . . ." He frowns comically, pretending to ponder. "Maybe next time I'll be draped in *your* arms."

I'd give anything for that to come true, at least the walking part. I look at him, and although our lips are smiling, our eyes share the same fear we dare not mention. I lean my head against his shoulder and observe without uttering a word. He goes quiet too. The silence of this place is just too imposing for us to break. We make our way down a stone path that penetrates to the very heart of the mountain. The rock walls that surround us tell of battles, of love, of sorrow, but above all of human insanity. The path leads to a cave. On one side, against the rock, is the statue of the Virgin who, nestled against my neck, has kept me company throughout my life. On the other side a cleft in the rock, bordered by a railing, seems to open up onto the sky itself. Kyle carries me along the rail, and with an elegance that makes me feel like a princess, he gently sets me down on a wooden bench. Then he steps back and inspects the scene with the fascination of an artist.

"I don't know what this place has to do with your birth and all that," he says, "but there's something about it that is so *you*, so . . . you know, elvish."

I'm not exactly sure what he means by that, but if he gives me one more stunning compliment tonight I might just die of acute flattery. My desire to see every last bit of this place quells the exhaustion looking to crush me, so I grab the railing with both hands and hoist myself up.

"Hey, hey, what are you doing?" he says, sliding his arm around me. "You sure you're okay?"

I don't answer; I don't even look at him, just squeeze him and hold him close to me. He gives me a single kiss, reviving every cell in my body, and together we lean over the iron railing. Beneath our feet a jet of water gushes forth from the rock, forming a slender cascade into the natural pond far below.

"The wishing fountain," I whisper. "I've always dreamed about this place."

"It wouldn't surprise me if this place had dreamed about *you*."

I glance over at him, still surprised that anybody's lips could utter such glorious words. I don't say anything; I can't. I simply hand him one of the coins, noticing the face of a king on one side.

"Ready?" he says, stretching his arm out over the railing.

How could I not be? There's only one wish for someone who, like me, already has it all: *May this happiness last forever.*

Our gazes intertwine. Then Kyle peers up at the sky with the grandeur of one who speaks with the stars; he looks back at me, his eyes bathed in hope, and together we set our coins free, watching them fall to their watery resting place.

Kyle holds me tight, and with one of those smiles that makes my knees buckle, he says, "Don't think my plan B ends here."

KYLE

I just hope her wish was the same as mine: that she makes it out of that surgery alive. As I carry her back to the van, I can barely think of anything else; it pounds in my head like a drum heralding an imminent war. I ask her to shut her eyes. I don't want her to see what I've prepared, but mostly I just want to watch her for a while without her knowing it. The moonlight brings out that otherworldly, ethereal halo her skin always exudes. God, I'd stop and draw her right now if I could. Come to think of it, there are lots of things I'd do with her right now if she weren't feeling so weak.

It wasn't easy getting everything ready without her finding out, especially the pastries. I had to go to three shops to find seventeen cupcakes, each one a different color. A special girl deserves a special surprise. I can't wait to see her reaction when she sees them.

"Careful," I say as we reach the van. "I'm going to sit you down in a chair, okay? But remember, don't peek."

She keeps her eyes closed tight, as if she's afraid they might open by themselves. I put her in the chair I set out earlier, a few feet from the table with the cupcakes.

"What are you up to?" she asks.

"Shh . . ."

In a flash I place one candle on each cupcake.

"Can I open them now?"

"Shush," I say as I start to light them. "Good things come to those who wait."

Mia sniffs the air and frowns. "Something's burning."

"Quiet . . ."

One last candle. Then I take her by the hand, gently lift her to her feet, and lead her over to the table. "Okay, you can open them."

She does, and instantly her face darkens. She stares at the cupcakes, somewhere between startled and confused. "What . . . what *is* all this?"

I take her hands, my gaze intent on putting her at ease. "Mia, what this *is,* is me asking you to blow out a candle for every birthday you've ever had, in the company of someone who is happy you were born, who is grateful you exist."

My words are arrows of love that strike at the very heart of her pain. Silent tears are budding in her eyes. It hurts me to see her cry; her tears are drawing out mine, but I don't let them show.

"Thank you," she says. "It's the sweetest thing anyone has ever done for anyone."

"No, Mia, the sweetest thing anyone has ever done is bring you into this world, giving me the chance to spend these days with the most incredible person who has ever walked the earth. And unless you want some wax on your icing, I think you'd better blow out your candles."

She giggles between tears and nods, her head lowered. As she looks up again, something in her expression is screaming *help*. "Kyle . . . this is . . . you are . . . I . . ." The words can't find their way out for the tears.

I put my arms around her shoulders, and with my chin resting on the side of her neck, I whisper, "C'mon, Mia, you can do this; together we can do anything we set our minds to."

That includes defying death, I hope. She takes a deep breath, her lungs struggling to take in air, and exhaling feebly, she still manages to blow out every candle.

"Nice." I stand in front of her, my pupils yearning to penetrate hers, and in a tone that springs from the most luminous part of what is most worthy in me, I say, "Happy birthday, Mia; thank you for existing."

"Silly," she says with a playful punch to my chest. "You're making me cry over here."

"They say it's great for cleansing the lacrimal glands," I joke. "At least that's what they taught us in biology class."

Her tears don't stop her from laughing. God, if someone had told me from the start that I could come to love someone this much, I would have sent them to a shrink.

All right, I think phase two of my plan, *An unforgettable night for Mia*, has been a success. And to officially kick off the third phase, I grab my phone and call up the song she tortured me with during the first days of our trip, the one she referred to as "my favorite song in the whole wide world."

"My dancing skills haven't been tested yet," I say, offering her my hand. "But if you dare to give me this dance, I'd be delighted to step on your toes."

She chuckles and accepts my hand. I put her arm on my shoulder and wrap my arms around her waist, trying to make her feel loved, to hold her in the way everyone longs to be held, in a way that makes life worth living. As her hands glide along my back, we move to the rhythm of the song that will be seared into my memory forever. We're so close, so united that I can't tell where her body ends or mine begins. We're two beings sharing a single body, two bodies sharing a single gaze. I lean back slightly; I need to see her face. Her eyes search mine; my lips seek hers. We kiss, and suddenly I feel her shake, her whole body jolted by a tremor of her own fragility.

"You're shivering . . . you cold?"

She shakes her head with an expression that looks a lot like anger. Okay, I must have missed something. She punches me in the chest again, harder this time.

"I'm not cold, Kyle; I'm scared. All of this is because of you! You've turned my life inside out." Her stifled yell verges on desperation. "For the first time in my life I don't want to die, Kyle. I don't want to *miss* this."

Her eyes, wide open now, plead for me to soothe them. Inside, I'm a river of bittersweet tears; outwardly I take her face into my hands and say what I've never said before. "I love you, Mia."

Now she lets the tears flow, tears she's bottled up for years on end, and then utters the words that only a dream could summon, "Oh, Kyle, I love you too."

We kiss, over and over again, basking in a lake of rapture and warmth.

MIA

If there were a contest of unforgettable nights, this one would take it hands down. After delivering the most delicious words I've ever heard coming from Kyle's lips, he led me over to a makeshift bed beneath the starlit sky. He had it all laid out: the mattress, the blankets, even a couple of pillows. Now we're lying here, he on his back, me on my side, nestled in the warm crook of his arm. Holding me close, he keeps his eyes fixed on the stars above, as if he were carrying on a profound conversation with them. Oh God, he's so, so . . . that I can't resist running my hand over his chest.

"Hey," he says, a mellow smile budding on his lips. "You're still awake? You have to get some rest."

Okay. I force my eyes shut and ask my mind to let me sleep, but it's rush hour in my head. A few hours from now, when they wheel me into the operating room, I'll have to part with him, perhaps forever, and just the thought of squandering the time sleeping is more than I can bear. I need to kiss him again, to feel the warmth and softness of his lips, his *all* looking at my *all*. And what if this is the last chance? What if I never see him again? If I were to die, I think I'd die a thousand more deaths just to cross paths with him in another, gentler world. My mind starts to torment me, but this time I won't let it, not tonight. Leaning on his chest, I straighten up a little and—

"Ow!" My lips contort in acute pain.

"Mia!" His lips respond in sudden panic. "What's wrong? Talk to me."

I've never felt anything like this; the pain is splitting my flesh, paralyzing me. Everything around me is spinning. I try to breathe, but the air refuses to enter. *Help!*

"Mia!"

His cry unlocks my aching lungs, and as I manage to get a thread of air into me, I call out, "Kyle . . ."

His lips are moving, but there's no sound reaching me. I try to keep my eyes open, but they're forcing themselves shut. No, this cannot be happening. *Kyle. Kyle. Kyle.*

The next thing I know we're in the van and Kyle's flooring it. He looks at me, his eyes spewing a fear even more intense than my pain. I must have blacked out. He's gripping my hand. I try to talk, but my lips won't part. I squeeze his hand instead.

"Mia . . . ," he pleads. "Please, please, hang on."

I let myself slump against his shoulder. My gaze doesn't waver, but the whole sky seems to be crumbling before it. Venus, shining brighter than ever, draws me to her like a magnet. *No!* I don't want to look at her, but my eyes can't tear themselves away. She looms larger, closer, as if she were waiting for me. Oh Lord, all the times I prayed that I could go to her, shed this mortal coil; now it just might be too late.

My eyelids weigh me down like hunks of steel. They want to close, and I sense it's forever. *No!* I don't want to go. I clutch Kyle's hand and make a titanic effort to stay awake.

"Mia, stay with me, please." His voice implores me. "I love you."

KYLE

Two nurses swiftly wheel her down a hallway. I run after them. I want to say goodbye, to tell her it will all be okay, that I'll wait for her whatever happens, but they won't let me near her. She looks at me from the stretcher, her startled eyes pleading with me not to leave. I yell with all my might but can't even hear myself. I'm surrounded by a mass of voices, beeps, and a silence that dulls my senses.

They're about to push her through a pair of swinging doors. No, not yet. I pick up my pace, but one of the nurses blocks the way. "Please, sir." His voice is distorted, as if speaking from the underworld. "I already told you that you can't come in here."

Bastard! Blinded by anguish, I raise my hand, ready to hit him, when a soothing voice stops me in midswing.

"Kyle?"

It's the doctor I saw yesterday but she's in street clothes. She rushes over and brings my arm down. There's a forlorn look in her eye.

"It's okay, my dear. Take it easy," she says, walking toward the same door Mia was just taken through. "I'll come and find you as soon as we're done."

I stand there, dumbstruck, powerless, useless, for a long, long time. Everything shuts down; the world goes silent. *This cannot be happening.*

MIA

It hurts . . . it hurts a lot. My entire body is quaking, so much so that I'm afraid my teeth are going to shatter. What's happening? Where's Kyle? Why didn't they let him through? The nurses were talking about me. They mentioned my name, my real one, and the missing person report. I hear footsteps. The two men turn toward the door and exchange words with someone. It's that woman, the doctor from yesterday. Where is Kyle? She comes up to me, takes my hand, and strokes my forehead, and her misty eyes fill with an affection that washes over me.

"Amelia," she murmurs. "We'll get through this together. You have to keep fighting, do you hear me? I won't leave your side until you open your eyes."

She sounds so sweet. Then her face vanishes, everything vanishes, and I see nothing but a black void.

"Hurry, we're losing her!" That's the last thing my ears manage to hear.

I stop shaking and suddenly, everything is at peace. I don't hear machines, or voices, or anything. Everything goes quiet and still. Nothing hurts. I don't even feel my body anymore. I start to rise, I don't know how, and begin to take flight.

KYLE

My legs are about to buckle as I reach the van in the parking lot, and leaning my back against the door, I let myself slide to the ground. The stars are still out and shining, as if to spite me. And there's Venus.

"You can't take her!" I roar. "I won't let you!"

My lungs and every other fucking part of me swell with a rage that stings, and I yell my desperation at these heavens that want to take her. As exhaustion sets in, I'm left wondering what to do. And I have to do *something.* The operation could last for hours, and waiting around is unthinkable, so I take out my phone and dial.

"Mom . . ." My despair unleashes my tears. "Dad . . ."

I proceed to tell them everything, down to the last detail, and they listen and support me, and little by little I regain my senses. Then I call Josh, and we talk for a while, like the buddies we used to be. And when my cell phone battery finally gives out, the sun is up. I look up at it and silently greet Noah, asking him, begging him, that if anything should happen to Mia, he'll take care of her and accompany her to wherever the heck it is that we all end up.

Some people change your life forever.

Some people make you strive to be a better person.

Some people aren't invisible.

—Kyle Freeman

KYLE

It's been ninety-seven days since Mia entered that operating room, and every day, every damn day I miss her more. Summer is here, and although the heat outside is inviting, I spend most of my time at home, rereading her diaries. Her third and last diary was left unfinished, so I've taken the liberty of filling its pages on her behalf. Whereas she wrote them for a mother she didn't know, I write them for her now.

April 25

It's been twenty-one days, and I miss you so much I can't get a wink of sleep. This morning I went to the cemetery really early. My folks were still sleeping when I left the house. Yeah, it's not my favorite place, but I still hadn't gone to visit Noah since the accident. I know, you'd tell me that Noah isn't around anymore and it's silly of me to talk to a tomb, and you're right, but I owed it to him and his parents. I told him everything, about you, about our trip, everything. And I know that he's listening, that he understands me.

This evening, as I looked up at the stars, I wondered where you might be, how you might be spending your days. Do you like your new home?

May 5

I was up the whole night, not only because I was missing you loads but because today is the day I've been putting off for such a long time. You'll think I'm an idiot, or worse, an asshole, for not having paid a visit to Noah's parents since the crash. But I couldn't. At noon I picked up Josh. We took his car. Mine isn't equipped for wheelchairs. At the last moment he got scared and didn't want to get out, but I managed to calm him down. It wasn't easy. Noah's folks were still devastated, but in the end they said they couldn't hold it against us. It will take them time, but I think they'll be able to forgive us. We used to get along before. And I'm starting to think we'll be able to forgive ourselves too.

A huge burden has been lifted from my shoulders. And you know something? You were right. They said exactly what you said that day in the restaurant, that Noah loved us very much and would not have wanted us to feel bad.

Don't know if I told you, but in case I didn't . . . what I feel for you is like a snowball that grows bigger each day.

May 28

Today I went to pick up Becca, as I do every Sunday since returning from Spain. Sometimes we spend the day with my folks; other times I'll take her out for a while. She's rarely been out of our town. My parents adore her, and so do I. She's told me so many things about you that make me smile. God, if someone had told me I could love someone like you . . .

This afternoon, dropping Becca off at home, I ran into your former foster mother Mrs. Rothwell. She asked me about you, and for some reason I told her everything: what happened, why you did it. And although emotions don't seem to be her strong suit, she seemed to understand. She even got a little misty-eyed. By the way, Becca says she misses you to the moon and back. I miss you to Titan (a moon of Saturn and home to the Eternals, which is light-years away) and back.

June 10

I woke up wanting you so much I felt like my chest was going to explode, so I looked for you but didn't find you, of course. I went searching for you at the waterfall, where we met. Took the same bus I did that day, and you know what? It was the same bus driver. He didn't recognize me, though. Doesn't surprise me; sometimes I don't even recognize myself.

I sat in the same spot, on that rock where I almost lost you before even getting to know you, and thought of _that_ Kyle, the one so blind to the majesty of life that he was ready to throw it all away. He almost seems a stranger to me now, like someone from another life. _That_ Kyle didn't know that there are stars capable of eclipsing any sun, stars whose light can't be extinguished, stars that go on shining forever, wherever they may be. I stayed there till the sun went into hiding and the stars came out to light up the dark. And there she was, brilliant, ravishing, waiting for us; there was Venus.

June 25

You're not going to believe it. Today, Josh got some feeling back in his legs, just a little, but the doctor said it was a very good sign. They think he might walk again! I would have loved for you to be here with me. <u>Mia. Mia. Mia.</u>

July 1

I've been doing what you asked and posting on your photoblog daily. With all the pictures you took of our trip I've got enough to last me the next couple of years at least. And guess what? <u>Expiration Date</u> has had loads of views. Just yesterday there were more than a hundred comments.

You've never been invisible, Mia, and you never will be, not to me, not to anybody.

July 3

Finally, my folks decided to go on vacation for a few days, just the two of them. I've been trying to talk them into it for weeks. Tomorrow I'll take them with me to the airport; yeah, they insisted. Becca has never been in an airport, so I'll take her along for the ride too.

July 4

I've put the address into my GPS like twenty times already. I want to be sure we get there on time. We don't have to be there for another four hours, but that's okay; there are a few things I need to organize at the airport.

MIA

I'm flying and flying in a boundless sky. The clouds are soft and fluffy, and Venus is right there, as always, by my side.

"What can I get you, miss, meat or fish?"

"Neither, thanks, I'm a vegetarian."

"I'm very sorry, but special meals have to be ordered at least—"

"Twenty-four hours in advance, I know. I'll have the fish, then. At least *they* were able to swim in the open before . . ."

Ana, my Spanish doctor (and savior), is sitting next to me and bursts out laughing. "Well said."

In the end, the flight attendant didn't serve me anything, but that's okay, Ana brought loads of healthy food with her. She's never been to the US, so she decided to accompany me and spend a few days in Alabama.

I did end up meeting my biological mother. She came to see me in the final days of my recovery at Ana's house and . . . I don't know; I guess I've come to realize that affection doesn't always run in the family. We just didn't connect. With Ana, though, we hit it off immediately, like love at first sight. She hasn't left my side for an instant since my operation.

Having an adult caring for me so much isn't exactly what I imagined. It has its good sides, lots of good sides, but some bad ones too—she's a little bossy, I have to say. She didn't let me fly or see visitors for almost three months. Three endless months without seeing Kyle. In fact, she didn't even let me speak with Kyle on the phone, with the silly excuse that I was too emotional and my heart had to heal up properly first. But I love her anyway, and I think that not being able to see Kyle has made me even more mature. Each day that goes by without him I remember something, a detail, something he's done or said, the way he talks, sleeps, the way he does everything, and it's made me love him all the more. I know we're young and maybe it's early to talk of a happily ever after, but I believe that we've lived through enough things together to make our *I love you*s the kind that do last forever.

"Look," Ana says, pointing out the window. "We're about to land."

Oh boy, my heart is already jumping for joy.

KYLE

As it turns out, they all decided to accompany me, and when I say all, I mean *all:* my folks, Josh, Judith, Becca, Noah's parents, even my grandparents who came over from Arizona to spend a few days with us. I guess I'm to blame; I've told them so much about Mia they're all dying to meet her. They've even organized a huge party to welcome her home tonight, with streamers and everything. Today it'll be ninety-one days since I last saw her (ninety-one days, three hours, and twenty-five minutes, to be exact). At least I've persuaded them to wait for me in the coffee shop, which is something.

MIA

Once at the airport, my heart goes at full tilt, and this time it's not because of any defect; this time it's because of Kyle, and only Kyle. Ana is waiting to collect our luggage, but I couldn't wait any longer. I'm heading down the hall that leads to the terminal. I don't think I've ever walked so fast. I'm passing everyone. Before exiting, I look through the revolving door to see if I can catch sight of him. Nothing. I walk through the door, and as I come out I stop in my tracks. It's crawling with people, all waiting for someone, but no one waiting for me.

Maybe he hasn't arrived yet, or is at the wrong gate, or is in the bathroom. Or just plain forgot. Whatever the reason, I can't help but feel super disappointed. I let myself drift with the crowd of people leaving the airport, and just as I'm about to turn around and look for Ana, a sign on the wall in front of me restores my smile. It's a drawing and reads *Follow Venus*. I look in all directions and see other drawings hanging from different places: a flowerpot, a chair, even a door. They're all drawings of stars, and their arrows point the way. They're Kyle's drawings; I'd recognize them anywhere. I follow them: one, then another, and another, the final one leading to a large window that looks out onto the parking lot. I peer through it and see a parked van, just like Moon Chaser, but even more colorful and extravagant.

"I was wondering if you'd join me this summer, for a road trip through Alabama."

I spin around. It's Kyle, looking more insanely gorgeous than ever.

"Whaddya say?" he asks, as if we just saw each other five minutes ago. "We could live on whatever I make from my drawings."

I can't resist—I scream for joy and jump into his arms. He kisses me, and I kiss him back, and suddenly everything in my world is absolutely perfect.

MIA

August 15

    I don't know why I keep writing in this diary
now that nobody is going to read it. I guess it makes
me feel safe, protected somehow. And although it
sounds absurd, and probably is, I feel that the stars
themselves come down at night to read it, then beam
what I've written to the whole world, projecting the
hope that there is someone, somewhere, who is happy
we've been born.

    I'll have to continue my diary entry later on
because Kyle is walking over to me, and from the
playful look in his eye, I don't think he has the
slightest intention of staying quiet while I write this.
And you know what? I don't want him to. Yesterday
we got back from our road trip around Alabama, and
now we're in the woods having a picnic with his folks,

Ana, and Becca. We've just finished eating. The road trip was too awesome for words. Anyway, signing off for now. Kyle is here.

Hey, I had to steal Mia's pen for a second because she forgot to mention that the best part of the trip was the company. Oh, and she had me sketching every day so that we could support ourselves.

Oh, Kyle, lying through your teeth doesn't suit you. Your folks ended up paying for the whole trip.

Okay, well, let's talk about the things that matter. I see you haven't written about everything that's happened since your last entry.

And how do you know that?

Have you forgotten who your most faithful reader is?

Okay, so, in a nutshell (I don't tell him, but even now he still makes me blush), as I was saying, they prepared a picnic for us to welcome us home, and Ana, who had intended to stay only a few days, announced that she will be buying a house and settling down in Alabama for good. Plus, she's growing very fond of Becca, so much so that she's thinking of adopting her. I'm over the moon. Suddenly, I have something that resembles a family.

And a boyfriend, don't forget.

Yeah, a boyfriend I've just kissed.

All right, you keep kissing me and I'll finish telling the story. About a week ago Ana was offered a post at Jack Hughston Memorial.

She's delighted!

Anyway . . . Our sincerest apologies, but I'm afraid I will have to whisk this lady off to a more secluded spot where I can kiss her without having three pairs of parental eyes gawking at us.

KYLE

These past few months have been the toughest, and the most incredible, of my entire life. There are times when I think the universe set the whole thing up so that Mia and I could meet. Now I don't just think so; I know it. Noah—my brother, my buddy—is in a good place. Mia told me so. The moment she entered that operating room, everything went wrong and they thought she was dead. One minute later her heart started up again. I guess there are things that surpass our understanding, but at least now I know there *are* things, beings, whatever we wish to call them, that never leave our side, even when our own misery blinds us to them so much that we reject their aid completely.

Mia told me that when she died she went to a beautiful place, a mountain full of shimmering trees, and that there she met Noah. There were other people, too, though she didn't know any of them. Noah said he was fine, that death doesn't exist, that it's only a continuation of our journey. At first, my mind refused to believe it, but then my heart knew it to be true. Noah said that for a time he will stay there, and then he'll decide where to go next. It gives me goose bumps just thinking about it. As strange as it sounds, now I know that a hand from beyond this world arranged all the pieces so that things would happen as they have, so that Mia and I could find each other.

"A penny for your thoughts," Mia says.

For a moment, we look up into space, me leaning up against the trunk of a majestic oak, Mia lying with her head in my lap.

"Well, if everything goes as planned," I say, glancing at my watch, "you'll know soon enough."

"What are you talking about?"

It's exactly three o'clock in the afternoon, the appointed hour, and already we hear barking in the distance. I had to rehearse this scene with Becca about twenty times before she had it down. The fox terrier puppy I adopted comes running and jumps on us, licking us all over. Mia laughs. She's overjoyed.

"Oh my God, she's so cute," Mia says, tickling her behind the ears.

"All right, then, let's make the official introductions," I say, turning to the puppy. "Venus, this is Mia. Mia, Venus."

"Venus?" she asks, with that innocence that could light up the heavens.

"If Mia can't go to Venus," I say, shrugging, "I guess Venus has to come to Mia."

While Venus frolics around us, Mia sits up on my lap, facing me, her arms around my neck. "Have I told you I love you?"

I pretend to think hard.

"Okay, listen well, Kyle Freeman, to what I'm about tell you, and don't you ever forget it." Her voice goes low and soft. "I love you to Venus and beyond."

"And now *you* listen up, Mia Faith, and never forget." I kiss her. "I *love* you." Another kiss. "And love *you*." More kisses. "And will continue to love you till eons become eternity."

The light pulsing in her eyes mingles with mine, and we kiss as if there were no tomorrow, no past, as if this instant were the only thing we had and will ever have, this *now*, with my lips pressed against hers. And in this now, I know that I will never, ever stop loving her.

Remember: There's always someone, somewhere,
who is glad that you were born.

Acknowledgments

The day I began writing my first book, I was all of four years old. The frustration I felt at not knowing how to finish it was such that I left my dream on the shelf for a long, long time. I guess I had some growing up to do.

Many years have passed since that first attempt, years during which I met wonderful people whose words, gestures, inspiration, affection, and friendship have allowed me to place the words "writer" and "screenwriter" beside my name on my calling card, and have above all helped me make this book a reality.

Where do I start? With my daughter, who might get jealous otherwise? With my marvelous literary agent? With my beloved friends? On second thought, gratitude should have no particular order or degree, so I dedicate my first words to all those I may have forgotten, by saying that ultimately, I can never forget you.

Thank you to my agent, Mandy Hubbard, and her team at Emerald City, for placing their trust in my manuscript from the very beginning, even if its themes didn't necessarily reflect the latest trend. Mandy, thank you for your generosity, your sensitivity, and your implicit faith that *See You on Venus* would ultimately find its publisher.

To my editor at Delacorte Press, Kelsey Horton, whose

discerning eye, passion, and amazing insight strengthened this novel.

To Christian Villano, my translator, editor, and companion on this creative journey. For his abiding patience and understanding on receiving the hundreds of comments, questions, and notes I sent him. For his love of language and the way he has of phrasing his sentences, making them so much more than the sum of their parts.

To my daughter, Sarah, my most avid fan (and critic), whose antics remind me of the roller coaster that is adolescence, which some of us never completely grow out of. Thank you for your very personal way of telling me things—straight, with no filter.

To my son, Jason, for teaching me that in love there are no rules or conditions, that forgiveness overcomes all, and that sometimes, just sometimes, the only thing we can do is wait patiently, with a full and open heart.

To my parents, whose mistakes were a source of much pain but also of growth and inspiration. They allowed me to feel the pain of others and give shape to stories that are profound, mature, and full of hope. Thank you.

To my kindred spirits, Ana María and Marie Pierre, for their unconditional support, ever and always.

To Brian Pitt, for his desire to bring the tenderness of Mia and Kyle to the silver screen, and for having fought tooth and nail to make the movie version of this story a reality.

I will be forever grateful to all those who anonymously shared with me the indescribable suffering of knowing they were responsible for the death of another, and their often arduous paths to forgiveness. As someone taught me long ago: guilt is the opposite of love.

Thank you also to those wonderful and inspiring books whose characters show us that love does exist, and that life is beautiful for those who choose to see it. Without you, I would not even be here.

To Mia and Kyle, for the hardships, longings, fears, and joys they whispered in my ear.

To Anne, the brightest star in my universe. Thank you for showing me that the most colorful ice creams are often the most interesting. Without your love and your unwavering support, neither this nor any other story would have been possible. Thank you for helping me shine my light and that of my characters upon the world.

Thank you for existing.

ABOUT THE AUTHOR

Victoria Vinuesa is a multilingual screenwriter, novelist, and globetrotter from Spain with one passion: writing stories that touch people's hearts. *See You on Venus* is her debut novel.